ALICE ISN'T DEAD

ALSO BY JOSEPH FINK
(COAUTHOR WITH JEFFREY CRANOR)

It Devours!: A Welcome to Night Vale Novel

Welcome to Night Vale: A Novel

Mostly Void, Partially Stars: Welcome to Night Vale Episodes, Volume 1

The Great Glowing Coils of the Universe: Welcome to Night Vale Episodes, Volume 2

ALICE ISN'T DEAD

A NOVEL

JOSEPH FINK

HARPER ● PERENNIAL

NEW YORK ● LONDON ● TORONTO ● SYDNEY ● NEW DELHI ● AUCKLAND

HARPER PERENNIAL

HarperCollins books may be purchased for educational, business, or sales promotional use. For information, please email the Special Markets Department at SPsales@harpercollins.com.

FIRST EDITION

Designed by Joy O'Meara

Library of Congress Cataloging-in-Publication Data has been applied for.

ISBN 978-0-06-284413-2   33614080784464

18 19 20 21 22   LSC   10 9 8 7 6 5 4 3 2 1

To Meg, who took this road trip with me.
And to Jasika and Jon, who made it possible for me to share it.

This isn't a story. It's a road trip.

PART I

THISTLE

WHY DID THE CHICKEN CROSS THE ROAD?

Because the dead return, because light reverses,
because the sky is a gap, because it's a shout, because light reverses,
because the dead return, because footsteps in the basement,
because footsteps on the roof, because the sky is a shout,
because it's a gap, because the grass doesn't grow, or grows
too much, or grows wrong, because the dead return,
because the dead return.

1

Keisha Taylor settled back into the booth and tried to enjoy her turkey club. The turkey club did not make this easy.

A diner attached to a gas station, a couple hours outside of Bismarck. A grassy place between towns. Keisha's main criteria for choosing the diner had been ample parking for her truck. Once upon a time people chose food based on the season, or the migration patterns of animals. She selected her meals based on the parking situation.

Her difficult relationship with what the menu called "The Chef's Special Club" was made more complicated by a patron in the booth adjacent to hers. The man was eating an omelet, scooping big chunks of egg with long, grease-stained fingers, and shoving them into his mouth, each bite followed by a low grunt. He was a large man, with a face that sagged on one side, a lump on the top of his shoulder, and a long fold of extra skin hanging from one arm. His clothes were filthy and she could smell him from where she sat. He smelled like rot. Not bad, exactly, but earthy, like fruit disintegrating into soil. His dirty yellow polo shirt had the word *Thistle* on it. He was staring at Keisha with eyes that went yellow at the edges. He chewed with his mouth open, and his teeth and food were both a dull yellow.

Keisha did her best to look anywhere else. At the crowd of bystanders behind the on-location reporter on the muted televisions, a crowd she reflexively scanned for a familiar face. Or the bathroom door as the cook took his third visit since she had arrived. At a van driving by on the highway with a cartoon logo of chickens and the name PRAXIS! in bubble font. But the man's grunts were insistent and soon she couldn't look anywhere else. And then, to her horror, he got up, omelet hanging from his lips, and limped toward her like his legs had no muscle, mere sacks of meat attached loosely to his torso.

"Doesn't look much like rain," he said, plopping himself across the table from her and licking the egg off his lips with long wet passes of his pale tongue. The smell of damp earth got stronger. Her heart was pounding, as it often did when she felt trapped, which she often did. Her life, at the best of times, was a minefield of possible triggers for her anxiety, and this was not the best of times. "Hope you don't mind if I join you," he said. Not a question or a request, but a joke. He laughed, and his jaw sank crookedly into his neck.

"I was hoping to eat alone," she said down at her sandwich.

"Good people deserve good things." She didn't know what to say to that. He scratched his cheek, and some of the skin peeled away. "It's dangerous out here."

She didn't want to engage with him at all, felt even responding negatively might encourage him, so she started to slide off the duct tape patchwork that had once been a booth, grabbing her backpack and making a determined look toward the door against the pulsing of her panicked heart. He held a hand up, and she froze, wanting to leave but not able to find a way to do so.

"Want to see something funny?" he said, in a voice with no humor in it.

It is often said that bad experiences are like nightmares. But what Keisha noticed most in this moment was how real it was, how she couldn't escape its reality, how she would never be able to convince herself she had remembered any part of that evening incorrectly.

He got up, wiping the egg from his hands onto the word *Thistle* on his chest. His face was slack and not arranged right. He walked over to a table where a man sat. A truck driver probably. *The man looked like a truck driver*, she thought. What does a truck driver look like?

"Hey, Earl," the Thistle Man said.

"Huh?" said Earl, frowning. The Thistle Man grabbed him by the back of his neck and Earl's face went blank.

The Thistle Man guided Earl gently out of his seat, like a parent shepherding a sleepy child. Earl's eyes were empty pools of water. Neither Earl nor the Thistle Man paid their checks. No one made a move to help. No one looked.

Keisha didn't know what to do. She walked toward the door, wanting to help, having no idea how.

"You planning on paying for that?" said her waitress.

"What? Yeah. I was just. Yeah."

Keisha handed over what she thought was the right amount, left some sort of tip, and then was outside in a night unusually hot for early midwestern spring.

The lights on one side of the gas station were out. And in the shadows, the man in the Thistle shirt was cradling Earl. Earl was fully awake again, but the man's arms clung like ropes around Earl, and he couldn't move. She could see the pulsing of his muscles as he tried, the strain in his face. Behind them, in a different world, people sat eating waffles and sausages.

"Shh," the man in the Thistle shirt said to Earl, who tried to scream in response, but the scream was lost in the baggy flesh of his captor. The loose-skinned man didn't seem human. He was like a boogeyman from a vaguely recalled nightmare. The Thistle Man. He bent down and took a bite out of Earl, at the artery in his armpit. Earl made a noise like a balloon letting out air, and blood poured down his torso. He was crying, but still couldn't move. The Thistle Man reached his long fingers into the wound and tore off fragments of flesh, lifting them to his mouth. The movement was the same mechanical movement he had made with the omelet.

Keisha had only a moment to decide how to respond and didn't need even that. She ran, of course. Ran for her truck with her breath and heartbeat deafening in her ears. The Thistle Man chuckled as she went, slurping another fragment of Earl's body into his mouth.

As Keisha started the engine, she looked at Earl, who looked back at her. A man who had expected to go to sleep tonight, who had ideas about what the next few days would be like for him, had some sort of plan for the future. Who was, instead, watching the one person who could help him driving herself to safety, leaving him with only a monster to accompany him in his dissipation.

Although Earl and his murderer didn't know it, there was another witness. A small figure in a hoodie, standing behind one of the fuel pumps, the hood drawn over the face. The figure in the hoodie wasn't running away but was no more able to help than Keisha. Some moments can't be changed.

2

Alice's funeral had been a strange occasion. Not because she wasn't well liked. Almost everyone liked Alice the moment they met her. She had an ease and a casual intimacy that transformed the people she met instantly into friends. In this way she balanced out Keisha, who was withdrawn and anxious. At a party on her own, Keisha would feel lost, but with Alice she was able to step into conversations, letting her wife lead the way whenever her own line of thought faltered.

The funeral was strange because Alice's death had been strange. No cause of death. No body. No certainty. There was a disappearance, and after a long and increasingly hopeless search, the presumption of death. And so Alice's friends and her family mourned while holding the thought that maybe, after all, Alice was alive somewhere, although none of them, least of all Keisha, believed it.

Meanwhile the funeral presented Keisha with what was, in a practical way, a party to navigate, and she did not have Alice to help her. Instead Keisha carried her grief through the crowd, and her friends reached out and softly touched her and murmured, and she kept moving room to room, as though in one of those rooms, somehow, Alice would be waiting.

Two years after the funeral, knowing Alice wasn't dead, there were times Keisha hated her, of course. But through all of that she loved her. Loved her more than she had ever loved anyone. And so she would continue to look for the wife she loved and hated.

Keisha tucked up her legs on the small berth in the back of her truck's cab. On the pillow next to her, unread because she couldn't find the concentration, was one of the books from the library she had collected under the passenger seat. Outside the cab, she heard, as she swore she had heard every night since that night at the gas station diner, the whisper-scratch of fingernails. A sound so quiet it was easily mistaken for silence. But she was sure it was the boogeyman, the Thistle Man, waiting for her to get curious or afraid enough to investigate.

"This better be worth it, Alice," she whispered. Nothing ever could be.

She saw the Thistle Man again and again in the weeks following the murder. Behind the bathrooms at rest stops, in the snack aisle at gas stations, sitting alone at the biggest booths of the smallest roadside bars, places with one kind of beer on the menu and video poker in the bathrooms. Clumsy and brutal movements, like he didn't understand how his body worked. Sharp, yellow teeth. Yellow fingernails, not cigarette yellow, but translucent yellow below the surface.

In Horse Cave, Kentucky, she saw him in the buffet line at the Love's Travel Stop. He was leering at her, and eating pizza with snatches of his spindly fingers, and she, no longer hungry, put the jerky she had been about to buy back on the shelf.

In Haugan, Montana, she saw him perusing the bargain knife selection at the 50,000 Silver Dollar Bar and Gift Shop, the biggest gift shop in the state. Animatronic statues of angels flapping their wings. Ceramic wolves in ceramic landscapes. Signs with cutesy sayings like "A Closed Mouth Gathers No Foot." He held up a knife and winked at her and then laughed at something the salesman said. Later he would eat the salesman alive.

In Davis City, Iowa, the Thistle Man crossed the street in front of her. The town was small, almost all of it visible from its main intersection. Her breath caught when she realized what was gazing back at her from the crosswalk, smiling into the hanging folds of his skin, and winking, and then the light was green and she tested out the limits of her truck's acceleration.

In each instance, no one else reacted as though there were anything off about the Thistle Man. It wasn't that they didn't see him. She noticed many of them look at him, but then their gazes slid off him. He wasn't invisible. People saw him and then decided they didn't want to.

The night of the Iowa encounter, still shaken by what she had seen, she stopped to treat herself to a hot dinner rather than a protein bar eaten while driving. "So what do you do, honey?" said the man at the counter next to her. She had gone through some version of this conversation almost daily for the year she had been on the job. *Please don't. Please, no*, she thought. *I just want to eat this food and get back on the road, where the miles turn to cents turn to dollars turn to a paycheck.*

She nodded to the trucks parked outside. It was a truck stop. There was no one in this restaurant who had any other job except the people cooking the food and the people serving it. *What else?* her nod said.

He looked at the trucks, then looked at her, and grinned to show he had a new and exciting thought, a thought that would really change things for her.

"Honey, you don't look like the trucker type."

She wasn't big, she wasn't white, she wasn't male. Her hands shook as a rule, and her voice was soft when she spoke at all. But she drove a truck. She did it for a living. What does a truck driver look like?

Your days are numbered, motherfucker, she wanted to say. *There's a new world coming. Get out of the way or get on board, I don't care which.*

She took her food and moved to an empty table across the room. He made more of a meal of innocently throwing up his hands than he did of the lukewarm meat loaf on his plate.

"I was just saying, honey. Jeez."

She thought about dinners she and Alice had back home, before Alice's disappearance, before Keisha's long search. Nights where they made pizza. Dough from scratch. Sauce from scratch. Cheese from the store.

Keisha had loved making the dough for the crust. Flour and water in her hands, first separate then merging into a silky whole, the yeast and gluten giving it life and breath. Her hands and her shirt covered in flour because she had never gotten in the habit of wearing an apron. They would open a bottle of wine and eat the pizza they made and watch whatever on TV and fall asleep in a wine-and-bread coma.

Love is cooking together. It's creating together. That's what Keisha thought. She didn't know what Alice thought. It turns out she had never known what Alice was thinking at all.

Flour on their hands. Sauce on their hands. Their hands on their hands. Something forgettable on the television. Leg upon leg. *That was a life*, she thought.

She could go to the police. She could tell them, what? She had witnessed a monster eat a man, in a murder no media had reported on? And this same monster was now following her, although she couldn't prove it?

No, for now she would have to take this on herself, as scared as she was. Later that night, dinner over, man ignored as he tried to engage her again on her way out, and a good fifty billable miles of road driven, she switched on her CB radio, held the mic up to her mouth for a long time on the open channel.

"We talk about freedom the same way we talk about art," she said, to whoever was listening. "Like it is a statement of quality rather than a description. Art doesn't mean good or bad. Art only means art. It can be terrible and still be art. Freedom can be good or bad too. There can be terrible freedom."

She stopped to think but kept the send button held. She didn't want a response. She had heard enough from other people that night.

"You freed me, and I didn't ask you to. I didn't want you to. I am more free now than I have ever been, and I am spiraling across this country. Maybe you are too. I want our lines to cross. Even one more time."

She put the mic back. Switched the radio off.

Hand upon hand, she thought, *upon leg upon heart upon couch upon a day where we made pizza together. That's love, Alice. That's what it's made of. And so what is this?*

3

Grass and barns and metal windmills. Kansas scenery had delivered on Keisha's expectations.

Her anxiety was a low, manageable buzz. She had a song she liked on her phone. She hadn't bothered to figure out how to connect the phone to the truck's stereo, and so let it play tinny and soft from the phone's speakers, bopping along to a melody she couldn't quite hear but knew well enough to sing anyway. Sitting next to her was the second volume of a comic series that she was looking forward to starting over dinner. The air through the window was dry and cool. Not that she was ever calm, but if she were to be calm, it would look like this.

She had stopped to pee at a McDonald's with a plaque indicating it once was a historical school of some sort, but now it wasn't a school, it was a McDonald's, and she peed at it. Given how often people stop at those places to use the toilet without spending any money, she wondered, were they more restaurant or public bathroom on a sheer numbers level? It was an interesting question, and she had nothing but flat road hours to think it over. No plans to stop again until dinner, and dinner would be as late as she could make it. There would be miles done today. She could use the pay, and even more so the sense of movement. The feeling that she was getting somewhere even if she would have to turn right around and head back.

Thump. She felt the vibration through her seat before she heard the noise. *Thump thump. THUMP.* At first she thought it was her tires going funny, but then realized the sound was coming from the trailer. To be heard all the way up in the cab, above the whoosh of the air and the growling cough of the engine, it must have been seriously loud. (And there it was again, *THUMP*.) A beast the size of a grizzly bear, running back and forth, slamming into the walls.

There her fear was, right where she always left it, deep in her throat. Metal and acid washed over her tongue and perspired out onto her palms. Her chest was a closing door. A monster in her trailer. Ridiculous. Absurd. A fairy tale. But hadn't she seen monsters on these roads?

No way from the trailer to the cab, and so she just wouldn't stop. She would drive and drive forever. She wouldn't eat, her truck wouldn't take fuel, she would be saved by the miracle of sheer movement. Because she couldn't bear to think what would happen when her body or her truck forced her to stop.

THUMP, and her heart echoed the sound with a beat so hard she felt the skin of her chest pulse outward. Thanks to her anxiety, fear was a constant pulse in her life. And now this terrible racket. And she was alone in Kansas. Grassland out to the end of it.

When it gets dark over the grass, it really gets dark. Like being on an ocean, the distant lights of towns like ships. Only her on the road and a fuel tank that was down to a quarter. She would need to stop soon. There was no avoiding this conflict, but she could control how it was confronted. She had to find a way to do it that would be least likely to get her killed. Good luck to her. In the darkness of the fields there was a single billboard, well lit and maintained. It had a picture of a smiling family, and against a soft pink background it said a company name. PRAXIS.

She settled on pulling off in the parking lot of a Target. At least the crowds. Or if not crowds, then at least other people. And if not other people, then at least the lights, bright and sterile across the vast lot. The lights would keep her calm after the long empty of the grassland.

Keisha clutched her heavy flashlight, and she crept around the trailer. There was no noise, not a hint of movement. She had parked as close to the entrance of the store as possible, a bank of automatic doors blaring a welcoming fluorescence out into the cool evening, but still there were only a few cars around. Her hand shuddered as she reached for the latch. A metallic clink. The groan of the handle upward. The rattling complaint of the door opening.

She squinted into the darkness. Her cargo had been pallets of paper towels, and the boxes were torn open by swipes of what seemed to be giant claws. The towels were shredded and tossed about. And there was no need to search for the cause. A yellow baseball hat. Yellow fingernails. Skin in loose folds in places and in other places stretched over angular protrusions. Sharp teeth. Eyes, yellow and pink. Polo shirt, yellow and dirty. The word *Thistle* on the right breast.

"It seems we keep running into each other," he said, in his hollow, rattling voice. "How crazy is that?"

4

Keisha backed away, holding the heavy flashlight in front of her as a club. The man smelled like a compost pile that is almost soil.

"Where do you think you're going? I mean, where would you even go that I couldn't follow? Don't you know who I work for?" He indicated the *Thistle* on his pit-stained shirt. He was sweating thick mildew.

"There are people all over this parking lot," she said. This was self-evidently not true. It was a Target parking lot, but it was also late, and in the middle of nowhere. There were a few cars, yes, some people, but she didn't expect help from the world, and generally the world met her expectations.

He coughed up laughter, continuing to hobble toward her. "People?" he said. "People!" He shook his head and grabbed her arm. She didn't know how he got that close, but he was there, and he took her arm like a dance partner, gentle but insistent, and then with a tremendous strength, well beyond what even his large frame would seem capable of, he twirled her up against the truck. His skin writhed, like there were insects crawling back and forth under it. The smell was overpowering. His tongue was swollen and covered in a white film.

It was over. His arm was on her throat and he was pushing enough to let her know he could do it, but not enough to cut off air. She drew shallow, frightened breaths against the weight of him. She kicked for the crotch, of course, but it was like he felt nothing. And then she flailed at him with the flashlight. His body dented with the blows, whatever was under his loose skin sinking with the force, but he didn't stop smiling. Didn't even grunt. Pushed a little harder on her throat. The flashlight dropped and rolled away.

"I could take a bite of you right now and it would be over. I could devour you. And then what would become of Alice?"

Alice's name in the monster's mouth made Keisha slump, made her give up. If he knew about Alice, then he knew about everything, and then what was left? She had been searching for her wife for a long and terrible year. All those miles upon her, and now a monster. She adjusted to accepting her own death. As she did, a feeling sparked. It wasn't a feeling she recognized, but it spread like her anxiety, tingling at her skin, zipping up her spine, and exploding in her brain.

Fuck the Thistle Man, the feeling said.

She kicked and screamed with all the energy she had left. Perhaps she would go down, but it would not be quietly. Other people in the parking lot were finally turning, finally seeing. Even if she couldn't beat him, she could get them to look. A family, a father and two kids, and the kids were pointing, and the father was on his phone. He was talking urgently and gesturing toward her. She fought until the Thistle Man's arm on her throat lowered her into a quiet darkness she had apparently always carried somewhere in her mind, and then there was a siren, and the arm was off her throat, and the world returned to her, and a police car pulled up.

The police officer got out. A white man. No partner. Big. Not big as in muscular or big as in fat, just big.

She stumbled a few paces away from the Thistle Man, out of his reach. The policeman sauntered over. He was a man used to the world waiting for him. He must have seen the Thistle Man attacking her, but he didn't seem worried about that. He examined Keisha with heavy-lidded eyes.

"What seems to be the problem here?" he said.

She did her best to tell him. The noises, the stopping, the Thistle Man, the air, the lack of air, the struggle. He frowned. Made no notes. He turned to the Thistle Man, who hadn't moved, hadn't interrupted, had leaned with crossed arms on her truck.

"That true?" the policeman asked him.

The Thistle Man giggled, a high, childish sound.

"Doesn't sound like it's true," said the policeman.

She didn't know what to do. On one side, the police. On the other side, a literal monster. The policeman nodded to the Thistle Man. "If he has to come talk to you," he said, "then you've been asking the wrong questions." He lumbered back to his squad car, opened the door. "My advice," he said to Keisha, "is to stop asking the wrong questions." He tipped his hat at the Thistle Man. "You have a nice night now."

The Thistle Man did a lazy wave in return, as the policeman folded his towering frame into the car.

"I will, Officer," the Thistle Man said. "You know I will."

The police car drove away, but the Thistle Man made no move toward her.

"You see now. You see how it stands. Go home." He made a face of concern, worry even. "You can still go home."

He turned and stalked away into the night. To the lit edges of the parking lot, and into the sparse landscaping, and the vacant grassland beyond. Keisha stood frozen until she found it in herself to get back in her truck and drive away. No one in the lot talked to her or checked to see if she was alright. They looked at her and then looked away.

Police cars followed her for a few days after. No siren, no lights, but staying close on her tail. She had well and truly gotten their attention now.

But the Thistle Man was wrong. She couldn't go home. Because home wasn't a place. Home was a person. And she hadn't found that person yet. After five days the police stopped following her. They had let her off with a warning. It was a warning she was going to ignore.

5

It's a long and desolate way from Florida to Atlanta. The land-scape is constructed of billboards. There are no natural features, only a constant chatter along the side of the road. A one-sided conversation. Lots of anti-evolution stuff. Advertisements for truck stops with names like the Jade Palace or the Chinese Fan, written in racist faux-Chinese fonts, and wink-wink language about the massages available. Keisha winced. Lord, get her to Atlanta. At least there was cruise control, and a road so straight all she had to do was make sure she didn't go crashing off into a billboard telling her the Confederacy still could win, which was an actual billboard she had passed. The subtext of America wasn't just text here, it was in letters five feet tall.

Business wasn't booming. Many of the ads on the billboards were ancient. Announcements of local fairs from 2005. Fire sales for stores long since buried under pitch and concrete. A lot of vacancies, phone numbers to call for renting the space.

She wondered how much an ad on a stretch like this would cost. Even on her wage she might be able to buy herself one, maybe this bare one between an ad for dog grooming whose tagline was DECADENT DOGS and yet another thinly veiled ad for sex work. She could reach out to Alice that way, even if Alice could never respond. Shout at the passing cars long enough and maybe someone somewhere would hear it. Or, hell, she could pick up her radio again and tell her entire story to every bored trucker in range. But instead she would keep driving, keep moving, and hope eventually she would arrive somewhere. A conclusion, a great transformation, or, failing that, Atlanta by the afternoon.

She was weighing the merits of stopping for a coffee when she spotted a billboard that didn't fit. For one, it was spotless, installed maybe in the last week. It was a black billboard that said in tall white letters, HUNGRY? Was it advertising the concept of food? The idea of eating? If so, it wasn't effective, because when she looked at it her gut twisted. The billboard pointed her somewhere bleak and horrible, even as her conscious mind hadn't picked out why.

Another billboard, a few miles later. Same design; black background, white text, plain capitalized letters. BERNARD HAMILTON, it said. Then another that said SYLVIA PARKER. With each one she felt sicker and sicker. Someone was sending a message to someone, and the message felt to her monstrous and wild.

After Alice's funeral, Keisha had mourned privately for weeks, refusing to see friends, missing work. She had sat at home and allowed the grief to weigh on her, a physical pressing on her chest that strained the muscles if she tried to get up or even turn her head. If she had had someone else to look after, a child, an elderly relative, even a pet, then maybe she would have forced herself into something resembling the person she had been before. But even then, inside she would be a vessel of fluids and mourning. She wasn't the person she had been before and she never would be again. Sure, she had always been anxious and shy, but it had never been what defined her. She was able to relax when with friends and family. She had her hobbies and dreams. For some time she had been thinking about quitting her job to start a bakery, because the idea of arriving to work at four in the morning to make bread sounded like the best possible job in the world, but it had never been quite the right time for her to do that. All those parts of her were gone. It wasn't only Alice who had died. Each death leads to smaller, invisible deaths inside the hearts of those left behind.

Alice never called Keisha by her name. This is true for many couples. Chipmunk, Alice would call Keisha. Chanterelle. Often Chanterelle. Walnut Jones. Alice found that last one especially funny. Now everyone called Keisha by her name. "Keisha," they would say, in soft and worried voices, and Keisha just wanted someone with a laugh in her voice to call her Chanterelle, to call her Walnut Jones.

It wasn't an intervention from her friends that broke her out of her stasis, although to their credit they tried. Showing up with food and with concerned frowns and busy hands tidying a house she couldn't care less about. But none of them were able to reach her. Because they were trying to reach the Keisha they had known, and that Keisha was gone. No, it was not her friends who changed her, but that after two months she grew bored with her absolute grief, and so she pulled herself up against the weight of it and started going to grief counseling groups.

She sat in circles and described the shape of the monster that was devouring her. Because that's what, as a civilization, we do.

We try to talk our way through the ineffable in the hope that, like a talisman, our description will provide some shelter against it. But the monster continued to devour her, no matter how specific her description of it, no matter how honest the shell-shocked sympathy of her fellow mourners.

And when she wasn't describing Alice, over and over talking about Alice, as though her wife could be resurrected with stories, Keisha watched the news. The news was good, full of tragedy and loss that had nothing to do with her. So many people in pain, she couldn't possibly be alone, even though she felt as alone as could be. And then, six months after the funeral, somewhere in the third hour of Keisha's daily news binge: a murder, brutal, somewhere in the Midwest. Bystanders gawking, standing in a circle and trying to describe with only their faces the shape of the monster they had seen. Behind the witnesses being interviewed, unmistakable, staring at the camera as person after person babbled their way through the horrible story—Alice. Keisha laughed, and then sobbed, and then threw up, and then looked again and there was Alice still, looking back at her, not dead at all.

The names on the billboards kept coming. One every three miles. TRACY DRUMMOND. LEO SULLIVAN. CYNTHIA O'BRIEN. They felt more like a memorial than an advertisement.

At the next stop she pulled off the road and searched the names, one after the other. It didn't take long, because one name was connected to the next, and most of the articles were the same articles. Anxiety bubbled in her blood.

Found near major highways all over the country. Lives torn short under overpasses, on frontage roads, in broad wooded shoulders. Lost even in the age of GPS and Siri. Gashes on the torsos. Defensive wounds on the hands. Victims of an unsolved serial killings from a murderer who reporters had nicknamed the Hungry Man. The nickname came from the single common thread between all the murders. A human bite on the neck or shoulder or armpit. Not elegant pinpricks, the romance of a vampire, but ragged and clumsy. Every name was a human being who had died alone on the sides of highways. Or, worse, not alone.

6

Bernard Hamilton left for San Francisco immediately after graduating from college. He had no job set up there, no friends or acquaintances waiting for him. He had never even been to San Francisco. But youth is the time for great leaps of faith, and so he packed everything he owned into his Corolla and started the drive from Connecticut because he believed that to experience America is to experience its distance.

He called his mother every night, because she was worried he would be murdered, and he was willing to humor her silly fears. He was driving on major highways, staying in budget chain hotels with free coffee in the lobby. This was transit, not hedonism, and lots of people do it every year. He was no different from lots of people. Of course, lots of people get murdered every year, but he thought he was different from those people, for reasons he could not have articulated because the idea that nothing horrible could ever happen to us personally exists not in our thoughts but in the base of our necks.

Bernard told his mother about the Great Lakes, how Lake Michigan looked like the ocean, how he couldn't see the far shore even from the high floor of an office building in Chicago that he snuck into because he couldn't afford any of the viewing platforms or skyscraper restaurants. He told her about the flats of the Midwest, how there were no physical landmarks to divide anything from anything else. And then he got to Utah and he stopped calling. His mother contacted the police the first night she didn't hear from him, but the police told her that they weren't going to look for an adult man because he hadn't called his mother. But she was right, because he was dead and shoved into a bush in the parking lot of a budget chain hotel with free coffee in the lobby and his body wouldn't be found for four days. There is some version of the world where he made it to San Francisco, grew lifelong friendships there, found a career, found a partner, grew old. But that never happened in our world, which is a sadder, emptier place.

Each name on each billboard was a story with a promising start and an unhappy ending. Tracy Drummond was a church volunteer leading a trip to Mexico to build houses when she vanished during a dinner break in Waco, a day short of the border. Leo Sullivan was a trucker, who had last been seen eating dinner with a man in a yellow hat and was found a day later by a group of prison laborers clearing garbage from the side of a highway.

Keisha read the stories, scrolling down and down, and feeling sick with what she knew, and scared with what she didn't know.

The Hungry Man, who she thought of as that nightmare creature, the Thistle Man, had been active for almost two decades. He only struck occasionally, only sometimes left behind a life torn open and bleeding out. And now he was following Keisha. How long had he followed the others before he killed them? How long before those brutally strong fingers reached out of parking lot darkness?

Perhaps soon, because she knew that this was him taunting her. He had discovered her upcoming routes and had arranged for these billboards to be erected as a message to her. *This is who I am*, the message said. *This is what is coming for you.*

She pulled out of the truck stop, back onto the highway. Because what else was there? She had no hope that surrender would save her. No, if she were to be murdered, then it would be while moving. Alice wasn't dead, and neither, yet, was Keisha.

Another billboard. NED FLYNN. A body somewhere with a big bite out of him. All of these names were dots on a map. Last known whereabouts. Keisha was a dot on a map, too, but she hadn't settled into a final location yet. Her last known whereabouts were somewhere behind her and her body kept driving.

A few miles later she saw the final billboard. In design it was similar to the others, but there were more words on it, and the text was smaller to fit the space. She squinted as she tried to read it with eyes that she hadn't admitted to herself were approaching middle age. The words came into focus. She gasped and almost swerved off the road, almost did the Thistle Man's job for him. Her eyes were stinging and blinking with tears, but she managed to put on her emergency blinkers and pull slowly to the side of the road under the sign. She got out on the door not against the highway and leaned on the truck to support herself. Once she felt somewhat steady, she looked up again at the billboard.

CHANTERELLE, MISS YOU. GO HOME.

A nickname that no one knew except her and one other person. This was the final piece of the message. She had misunderstood. The billboards weren't a threat, but a warning.

Alice had had the same idea as Keisha when she had seen all these vacant billboards. Shout at passing cars long enough, and maybe the person the message was for would hear. She had put them up to show Keisha what was after her. Keisha dropped into a squat because she couldn't find it in herself to stay standing. She shook with new grief and with rage.

Go home, why? Because she wasn't safe? Because Alice thought she could keep Keisha safe? Because Alice thought safety was an option that had ever been available to Keisha? She hadn't been safe since she was born into this country, this angry, seething, stupid, could-be-so-much-more-than-it-is country. And Alice wanted her to turn and run?

Through the tears, she saw movement a hundred feet down the shoulder. A pile of clothes under the billboard stirred and rose into a human shape. Keisha sprang up, not sure if she was happy or furious. Alice had waited for her by the sign. Finally Keisha would meet her wife in person, would touch her. But the shape didn't move like Alice. If it wasn't Alice, then it was the Thistle Man, come to take her after weeks of promises and threats.

She reached for the handle of the door. Would she have time to get the truck back on the road before he reached her? Like hell she would. She tried to comfort herself that even the Thistle Man wouldn't be so brazen as to take her from the side of a busy highway, but she had trouble believing her own reassurance.

The figure moved toward her. She needed to go. She needed to run. But she didn't. Because what if she was wrong, and it was Alice after all? She couldn't let that possibility pass her by. The figure was close now. It was slight, and short, more like a child than a grown man. Keisha saw the scared, thin face of a teen-age girl. What was a girl doing by the side of a highway like this? There were far worse things than men circling these roads.

The figure reached out her hand.

"I know what you've seen," the girl said, "and I need your help."

7

Keisha's first impression was frailty, and so she mistook the girl for maybe fourteen. But there was a hard and adult aspect about the girl's face, and on reconsideration Keisha decided she was probably sixteen or even seventeen.

The girl considered back, giving Keisha a hard up and down, and then, apparently satisfied with what she saw, brushed by her and hopped up into the passenger seat.

"Excuse me?" said Keisha, unsure of what was happening. The girl was already tossing a backpack behind the seat and feeling around for controls to move it into a more comfortable position.

"What do you know?" the girl asked.

Keisha put her hands on her hips. "I know you're a kid and you shouldn't be on the side of the road like that, so I guess if we're making a list we could start there."

"You stopped and looked at one of those billboards. The new ones. You were looking at one of them and crying. Do you know who put them up?"

Keisha felt the weak and tired part of herself falter, but she wasn't about to let the kid see it, so instead she hopped up into the truck, too, and pushed past the kid's legs.

"Am I driving you somewhere?" Keisha said. The girl shut the truck door, which Keisha took as a yes and so she pulled back into traffic. Neither of them spoke. A few miles of silence. The girl smelled overpowering. Not like she needed a shower. Instead as though she had taken too many showers, over and over, until any natural human smell was replaced by perfumed soap. She smelled like a walk through a park condensed into a single, over-powering whiff. In small doses maybe the smell would have been pleasant, but Keisha found her stomach turning again and rolled open the window.

"Ok, maybe you don't know anything," the girl said. "Fine, I don't know anything either."

She kicked Keisha's book pile out of the way to make room for her feet. *Brat.*

"What's your name?"

"Sylvia. Sylvia Parker."

Keisha glanced at her. "I've heard that name somewhere."

"Common name, I guess."

"Where are you going?" said Keisha.

"Swansea, South Carolina."

"Bad luck. I'm on the way to Atlanta to exchange shipments and then I'm heading west. Where can I drop you off?"

Sylvia didn't look at her, instead watched the blur of billboards. "Swansea," she said again.

Keisha sighed. Fine. She was almost to Atlanta anyway. She'd get the girl to leave there, and until then maybe it was nice to have friendly, or at least nonhostile, company for the first time in months, even if the smell was a lot to handle. Sylvia's face softened and she turned her body back to face Keisha.

"No offense, I have to know if I can trust you," Sylvia said.

"I have no idea if you can," Keisha said. Sylvia nodded as though that were the right answer.

"You've seen it too," the girl said. "Visions out on the highway. The road takes weird turns for you, same as it does for me."

"What have you seen?"

"What have *you* seen?" Sylvia said, and smiled.

That was a good question. A lot that was impossible and terrifying. Keisha couldn't find the shape of the tongue needed to name them. She shrugged.

"Exactly," said Sylvia. Another half hour of silence, and then, as they entered the traffic that marked Atlanta long before the skyline was visible, she spoke again.

"Don't you wish sometimes that you could forget? That you could have your memory wiped, and then you wouldn't be a person wandering but a person who was almost somewhere, a person about to arrive, and when you arrived you could just stay?"

"Yes," said Keisha.

"Yeah. God, yeah, me too."

When they got to the distribution center, Sylvia clicked off her belt and hid in the back. Keisha didn't know if that was necessary, but also didn't know how to explain to her supervisors why she had a runaway child in her truck and so decided that it was probably for the best. Pallets of cereal were unloaded from the truck and replaced with pallets of travel-sized deodorant. When packaged, the two looked much the same. Brown boxes covered in plastic wrap. Only the logos were different. As Keisha waited for them to finish loading, a hand came out of the curtained back with a book. Sylvia was holding up *The Girl from H.O.P.P.E.R.S.*, the second volume from that comic series, which Keisha had just finished reading.

"Is this any good?" she asked.

"Hell yeah, it is."

"Ok," she said, considering the cover for a moment before tossing it back by her feet.

Once the new cargo was in place and all the paperwork had been signed off, they were back on the highway and heading west. Sylvia had made no move to leave, and Keisha hadn't found a way to ask her to. Sylvia hopped back up to the front.

"My mom and I, we used to travel a lot for work," she said, as though it were part of a conversation they had been having for a while. "And on breaks from school I would come with her. Lot of time spent in cars. We started to see what other people were missing. Between the rest stops and the Taco Bells. There's danger out there. There's a crack somewhere, and a terrible force is seeping through."

Keisha nodded slowly, not sure how to respond.

"Do you know what that terrible force is?" she asked.

"Mm," Sylvia said. "I need to get to Swansea, South Carolina, and I can't tell you why. Can you take me there?"

"South Carolina's the complete opposite direction from where I'm going. I have to get to a supermarket in—"

"You're the first person I've talked to, like really talked to, in, I don't know, weeks? Months? I need you to take me to Swansea. It has to do with, you know." Her hand spiraled out to indicate all the things neither of them was willing or able to specify.

Keisha snorted.

"Sylvia, I'm an adult. I'm an adult woman with a job. And that job says I have to deliver deodorant to a supermarket, not drive a teenager hundreds of miles to a town I've never heard of for reasons that kid won't tell me. I'm a responsible goddamn adult."

8

Swansea was not a bustling town. Nice, but also empty. Life had left this town. There was less of it than there once was. Sylvia directed them to an E-Z Stop on the highway, across from a farm stand that was closed, and two different car washes, both closed.

Keisha shut off the engine. "So what now?" she asked.

"We wait," Sylvia said. She picked up *The Girl from H.O.P.P.E.R.S.* and started reading.

"Alright then, I'm getting some jerky. You want anything?" Sylvia didn't look up. "Suit yourself."

As Keisha walked toward the E-Z Stop she kept asking herself what she was doing. A runaway child and a delivery that would be at least a day late. She probably wouldn't have a job soon, and then how would she look for Alice? And all because someone had spoken to her as a fellow human being for the first time in a long time and she had responded like a stray dog finally fed. She had risked it all so that she could keep this little bit of company going, as fucked up and weird as the company was. Or maybe, though she wanted to deny this, she felt that the kid could lead her to some new revelation or piece of evidence. Maybe she was using this runaway teenager to help her search. Maybe that's the kind of person she was. Or maybe she had found a teenage runaway and didn't want to abandon her. Maybe there was some instinct of protection in her that made her want to keep Sylvia close. Most likely some mixed-up combination of them all.

The drive to Swansea was only a few hours, but it had been late and so they had spent the night at a stop east of Atlanta. Keisha had tried to insist on giving Sylvia the cot, but Sylvia curled up in the passenger seat and either fell right asleep or feigned sleep well enough that Keisha gave up and slept in the back, feeling guilty right until she nodded off.

The guy at the E-Z Stop counter was withdrawn. Didn't comment on the truck, or the jerky. Didn't comment on anything. Laid-back. Or shell-shocked. Probably surprised to see a customer in a town this dead.

By the time Keisha got back to the truck, she had rediscovered some semblance of adult composure. Sylvia didn't acknowledge her, and so Keisha ate her jerky and waited. The sky changed shade, and then color. Sylvia fidgeted in her seat.

"He was supposed to be here already," she said.

"Who was?"

Sylvia rocked back and forth, and she seemed the youngest she had been since Keisha first saw her, slight and childlike, rising from the shoulder of the highway. Sylvia ran her hands through her hair, shook her head, and then reluctantly said, "You know about the Hungry Man?"

This violated their tacit agreement of not specifying their fears and experiences, and Keisha wasn't sure what to do with it. Finally, she nodded.

"The Hungry Man killed my mother," said Sylvia. "At a gas station a couple hours north of New York."

Sylvia and her mom saw the Thistle Man. Or, as she knew him, the Hungry Man. They saw him commit a horrible act. Sylvia wouldn't elaborate what it was, but Keisha could guess. And her mother did what Keisha could not. She tried to intervene.

After that, Sylvia didn't have a mother. She went back to Georgia, was moved from home to home. No one would believe her story. Or no one would admit that they believed her.

There was one policeman, Officer Campbell, who took a special interest in her. Something close to kindness. He warned her that she needed to stop describing what had really happened, needed to stop trying to get people to believe her. That it would be easier if she let that go.

But letting go wasn't an option for her. Keisha could understand that. If Keisha knew how to let go, she would have been thousands of miles away, living her life, pretending that she had never seen her dead wife on the television.

Sylvia ran away from the last of those foster homes, two days after moving in, and went looking for what scared her most.

"You want to find the Thistle . . . the Hungry Man?" Keisha could feel the arm against her throat, the must of his breath. "He's dangerous."

"Oh, is he? I must not know that. I must be stupid."

"Not what I meant."

"Yeah, it was."

Arm against throat. The policeman's glance of comradeship at the monster. The smirk on peeling, sagging lips.

"It's not what I meant," Keisha said with finality.

Sylvia snorted.

A few months before, Sylvia was sleeping in a city library. There was a window that didn't lock in one of the reading rooms, and she would slip in after closing, and, thanks to her inability to reach deep sleep since the death of her mother, slip out as the front doors were being unlocked. She checked her in-box on one of the public computers to find an email from Officer Campbell. He said that since she clearly was never going to let this go, he wanted to help her. But it had to be secret. No one could ever know. He told her to meet him, at this date and time, in the parking lot of the E-Z Stop in Swansea. And he would give her the information he had been able to find, all of it.

"I think he hoped that somehow I could put a stop to it, or at least tell the world. I don't think he knew what he had signed up for when he signed up for it."

"Ok," Keisha said. "Maybe the guy inside saw him."

They went in and asked the guy behind the counter if he had seen a cop car in his parking lot recently. A cop car from Georgia. The guy's eyes widened, but he shook his head. Keisha revised her impression of him. He wasn't laid-back. He had seen something. Something of the terror that she and Sylvia had seen. And he wanted desperately to forget.

She leaned in, gentled her voice.

"Man, hey, now look at me, I'm gonna need you to look me in the eyes. I know what you've seen tonight. I've seen terrible things too; so has this girl, and as long as we're all quiet, nothing's going to change. Those terrible things are going to keep on happening."

The guy didn't meet her eyes, tapped his hand on the counter.

"Do you want to live in a world where what you saw is possible, or do you want to let us try to change that?"

"I'm sorry," he said. Sylvia pulled at Keisha's arm, wanting to leave. Keisha's anxiety was a vibration in her limbs and chest.

"Ok, how about this," Keisha said, leaning forward and letting him see on her face every mile she had driven in search of the person she loved. "Whatever scared you, my man, know that I can be so, so much scarier than that."

His mouth twitched downward and his fingers fidgeted. "I'm sorry. I'd like to help but I don't know what you're talking about." He pointed, past the back wall of the store, to the thick trees behind it.

"There we go," she whispered, and she patted his hand. "There we go, man." Sylvia and Keisha went out back, where he had pointed. They looked down into the embankment lined with trees and Keisha spotted a side mirror sticking out of the leaves.

There was no blood, no body. But the windows of Officer Campbell's cruiser had been broken, all of them, systematically, and every seat had been slashed over and over. Not a trace of Officer Campbell. Keisha suspected that there would never again be a trace of Officer Campbell.

Sylvia groaned, an animal sound of despair, and she collapsed onto the hood of the car, a car that had belonged to the man who she thought would save her, a man who, as is often the case, couldn't even save himself.

9

The cruiser had nothing useful left. No notes or documents. The computer destroyed. No sign of what he had been planning to tell or show Sylvia. Keisha searched quickly because she felt that it wouldn't be safe for them to be in this town much longer. She finished up, slammed the door, wiping with her shirt any surface she might have touched.

"Ok," Sylvia said, her face hard, already on to the next plan. "He was based out of a precinct in Savannah. We'll go there, see if he left anything that could tell me what he wanted me to know."

"I'm not helping you break into a police station, Sylvia. You've dragged me far out of my way, but you're not landing me in jail. I have my own search to get back to."

"Alright, take me to Savannah, drop me off. I'll be fine on my own. Been fine on my own for a while."

"I can't just—" Keisha started but Sylvia waved it off.

"Of course you can. You already want to. I'm giving you per-mission. Take me to Savannah, leave me near that police station, drive away. You don't ever have to hear about this again."

"Ok. Yeah. Ok. I'll take you to Savannah."

"Thank you."

Sylvia didn't sound annoyed or angry at the possibility of being alone again. She sounded relieved. As they drove out of town, she asked: "What is it you're looking for anyway? What did you lose to end up circling these roads like me?"

"Ha." Keisha did not laugh, but said the word to indicate the possibility of laughter. And then she did her best to tell the story, as far as she understood it.

A year and a half before, Keisha had seen her dead wife on the news. After that first sighting, Keisha decided she couldn't afford to miss a minute. Multiple channels of twenty-four-hour news, and she did her best to cover them all, fast-forwarding, rewind-ing, searching for proof that she had seen what she had seen.

A fire outside of Tacoma. A landslide in Thousand Oaks. A hostage situation in St. Joseph. Earnest folks speaking earnestly, describing only the bad parts of the world. And among the con-cerned faces that the news cameras used as a backdrop, Alice. A fleeting face, sometimes, other times a long, head-on stare. Alice over and over. Keisha scrawled down in a notebook in which the first fifteen pages had been grocery lists, a list of every place Alice appeared, and that list became a map of America.

Keisha stopped going to groups. She stopped sitting in circles, stopped describing the shape of the monster that was devour-ing her, because now she knew that she didn't understand even the most basic shape of it. The counselors from the groups and some fellow grievers who weren't quite friends but weren't quite not friends called her for a few weeks, checking in, but after she assured them over and over that she was fine, they gave up and let her be, and then it was her alone in the house with the question that her life had become.

She quit her job, such as it had been. Ever since what she had believed to be a death, she had been taking a leave, anyway. She went through Alice's things. Her work stuff, her laptop, letters hidden under piles of clothes. Was that an invasion of privacy? Keisha wasn't sure. It's not an invasion of privacy to go through a dead wife's records. That's being organized. But Alice wasn't dead. So did she deserve privacy?

Keisha didn't care. Alice had made herself a mystery, and now everything she left was a clue. She was a missing persons case and everything she had ever touched was evidence, right down to Keisha's hands, her skin. The abandoned wife, exhibit A.

Again and again, in the papers and computer files. Phrases Keisha didn't understand. Praxis. Vector H. References to a war, to "missions." And more than any other, to Bay and Creek Shipping. Over and over Alice had written about Bay and Creek Shipping.

Keisha had called about a job with Bay and Creek the next day.

"Shit," said Sylvia.

"Yeah," said Keisha. Neither of them said anything else for a while.

On the way through Georgia, they passed a house by the highway with a pile of trash burning on its front lawn, big orange flames, thick plume of smoke. A man standing there watching it burn. Sylvia only saw it for a moment, and only in the corner of her eye, and that slice of time was stuck in her head that way forever. The man never moving. The fire never consuming. Keisha never saw him. That moment of time didn't exist for her at all.

Even after a couple days, Sylvia smelled as strong as ever. Something natural, but not. Organic, but aggressively so.

"What's that smell?" Keisha asked.

"I was wondering how long you'd be polite. It's heather oil."

"Why are you drenched in heather oil?"

"Yeah, I dunno," Sylvia said. "I've heard the Hungry Man, he doesn't like it. Wards him off. Probably bullshit but . . ." She shrugged.

"You heard that? Where did you hear it from?"

"You think we're the only lives he's touched? You think you're the only one he's talked to? Word gets around. I've been wandering this country for almost a year now. Others have seen him. I've met them. Most were too scared to be as helpful as you."

Sylvia smiled at her and Keisha managed back a grimace that was a distant cousin of a smile.

"Bad news. I'm real scared too. Kind of all the time. Used to go to therapy and shit."

"Ain't important if you're scared," Sylvia said. "You're helping anyway. Can't control feeling fear. Can control what you do while feeling it. Learned that too."

"A hard-won lesson of life on the road?"

"Nah, I used to go to therapy too. Anxiety bros?" She held up a fist and Keisha bumped it. Sylvia did a big exploding movement with her fingers, adding sound effects. They both laughed.

"Sure. Anxiety bros," Keisha said. "I'm still only taking you as far as Savannah, though. Then I have to get back to my thing."

"I know. Man, I hope you find her."

"Yeah."

"Hope she wants to be found."

"Yeah," Keisha said. "Yeah."

Another silence. Keisha didn't want to say what she was about to say but was unable to stop the words.

"Shit," she said. "Let's break into a police station."

"Thank god," said Sylvia. "I kept thinking, 'She's gonna offer to help me, right?' And then you didn't and I was, like, 'Man, I thought she was a good person.'"

"So I'm a good person now?"

"Good? Remains to be seen. You're cool, though. Let's do this."

10

Savannah looked like a city half remembered from a visit years before. Hazy and dreamlike. Brick buildings sagged into themselves. The trees were more moss than tree. The park at the center of town was full of gutter punks. Kids who had run away out of choice, not out of fear. Two of them catcalled passersby, the same line over and over. They'd removed themselves from the system enough to stop showering but not enough to stop harassing women.

Keisha and Sylvia walked the few blocks to the station and scoped it out. The front of the station was a big glass window, fine, but the rest was cinder-block blank, barred windows, a back door hazardously blocked by a dumpster, nothing that could be crawled through or into. It was a box with one available opening, and that opening was right on the street. Even trying to case the place was hard. There were cops everywhere, hanging out, chatting, and staring at Keisha and Sylvia as they tried to casually walk by.

"Nothing casual about the two of us, I guess," Keisha said.

"Could we just run in and run out?"

"There's one usable door. You run in, it'd be tricky to run out."

They took their fourth walk down the block. An officer across the street watched them with open suspicion. Keisha felt her heart pound seeing the uniform, remembering a dark parking lot in Kansas.

"Not the front then," she said. "I'm going to walk down that alley, meet me on the other side."

At the end of the alley was another dumpster. *Well, fuck it then.* She climbed up on it and from there got on the roof. Body prone so there would be no footsteps, she crawled along the top of the building. There were skylights at regular intervals. She peered over the edge of one, down at a desk that needed decluttering and a floor that needed mopping. She inched her way back, hopped from roof to dumpster to ground, and continued through the alley to where Sylvia was waiting.

"So here's what, Sylvia. I'm going to need you to make a distraction."

"What kind of distraction?"

"That I don't know, but I need to do something very stupid and very loud, so I need you to do something stupider and louder than me."

She grinned.

"I know just the thing."

"Oh, man, don't tell me. I'd have to try to stop you. Just do it."

Keisha clambered back on the roof and waited. She couldn't see anything from her crouched position, but then, if she couldn't tell when Sylvia's distraction started, the distraction hadn't been big enough. As she waited, she wondered how stupid she was, letting a teenager lead her to sitting on a roof waiting to do some silly stunt that would land her with a felony charge. But all that became moot as time passed with no sign of Sylvia, and Keisha knew that it had gone wrong and that Sylvia had been caught, with Keisha aiding and abetting her in this nonsense.

Then the distraction came, and it was big enough.

Sylvia had strolled a few blocks away, broken into a car, and hot-wired it. A few years on the road had made her good at that, for the days when hitchhiking wasn't working or she had a gut feeling that today would be the day a murderer would pick her up if she tried thumbing a ride. She drove the car to the street in front of the station, pointed it at that big glass front window, and, in a move that she managed with far more grace than she would ever have expected, simultaneously gave it a rev and rolled out. The sedan heaved forward, then rolled on momentum, slow enough that everyone could get out of the way but fast enough to be unstoppable. It entered the front window with a pop and came to a rest there. A lot of the cops ran after Sylvia, which she knew would leave the station empty for Keisha, great!, but also meant, oh shit, there were a bunch of cops after her. There was no way she could outrun them, but she had planned a route to a hiding spot down a side street. Her one chance was to get to the spot before any of her pursuers turned the corner and saw her hiding. She couldn't waste time looking back and so she dove behind the wall she had picked out and crouched there, praying to whatever was out there, praying that none of them had seen her. All of them ran by. She put her head against the wall and closed her eyes. Now it was all up to this woman she had met only a couple days before.

Keisha heard the car and was immediately on her feet, stomping on the skylight until it gave and her body went with it. She landed hard on her side in a shower of glass and found she was somehow unharmed. The cops were all either out front inspecting the damage or failing to catch Sylvia, and so she was alone in a room with five desks. She wasted a good thirty seconds finding the one with Ben Campbell's nameplate. By that point she had no time to look at what she was grabbing. She seized every scrap of paper on top of and inside of his desk and threw it into her bag. It was time to get out of there.

Which is when it occurred to her, with the usual stab of disappointment in herself, that she had not fully thought through this plan. Because get out of there how? The front was a swarm of uniforms, the back door was blocked, and the skylight was high above and rimmed with vicious broken glass. She was trapped. Panic welled up her neck, sloshed around her brain, made it difficult for thoughts to connect. Giving up felt like a reasonable option, but she shook that off, tried to find determination or at least manufacture a simulacrum of it. Every second she stood there, the probability of getting caught ticked toward one. She tried jumping, but the skylight was way too high for that. She scrambled around for a miracle. But there was no miracle. There was only her, and her body, and whatever she would be able to do with that body.

So she clambered up on Officer Campbell's desk, turned, and, without giving herself time to think, hurled herself from the desk up at the skylight, sucking in her stomach in a half-assed attempt to keep from bleeding out on the glass.

Her hands slapped onto the roof, and her chest slammed into the edge and that did some bad things, but there wasn't much glass where she hit, so she avoided getting completely skewered. Even with the excitement of the car, there was no way a bunch of cops wouldn't notice a woman jumping off a desk and half landing up through a skylight. She had to move fast. Her chest was on fire, and her hands were painfully sliding on the sandpaper roof, about to lose grip. Footsteps, louder and louder. Shouts. In a few moments, there would be a hand around her ankle. She thought again about a parking lot in Kansas. About an arm on her throat. And she dug her hands harder into that roof, pulling with whatever she had and ignoring the pain as her chest slid along the edge. In a moment, she was off the roof onto the ground with a brief, awkward stop on the dumpster that didn't so much slow her fall as roll her ankle. And so, bleeding and limping, she tore as fast as she could away from the station.

She ran until the world flickered at the edges, until she could hear the hollow of her breath. She made it back to the truck where Sylvia was already waiting. They were about a half hour out of town on the highway, the long slashes on Keisha's chest no longer bleeding, her ankle throbbing, when she started laughing. She laughed and laughed, and Sylvia started laughing too. Every time they glanced at each other another wave would come. They laughed until there was no sound, only shaking, and Keisha had hiccups for the next two hours.

11

Fourteen months ago. Keisha's friends, and yes, she had once had friends, even though that idea seemed as distant from her current life as every other part of her past, were worried about her sudden obsession, and especially her plan to become a truck driver.

"Do you know how hard those things must be to drive?" said Margaret, the last friend she hadn't fully pushed away with the utter focus on finding a wife they all believed was dead. They were in a kitchen that had once been Keisha and Alice's kitchen, and soon would be no one's kitchen, a kitchen in a house that would stand empty month after month.

"I'll learn," Keisha said. She didn't want to talk to Margaret. She didn't want to talk to anyone.

"You'll learn." Margaret sat at the counter. "Keisha, how long has it been since you were in therapy?"

"Too busy."

"I know." Margaret tried to make a compassionate expression, which really pissed Keisha off. "Finding Alice."

"Yes, finding Alice. Yes, that's what I'm doing. Because my wife isn't dead. And as long as she isn't dead, I will use every moment of my life finding her. And I don't need therapy for that. I need support. And if you can't give me support, you can give me my fucking quiet morning back."

And that was the last time she had spoken to Margaret. Margaret did return, five days later, to try to make amends, to try to find some better way into the maze that Keisha was running inside her head, but by then no one was home. Margaret would check the house once or twice a month, to see if Keisha had come home, had decided to get better, but eventually Margaret realized she hadn't checked the house in a couple months and then she never did again.

Keisha and Sylvia stopped in a parking lot off 95 and went through what they had taken.

A lot, and mostly crap. Reports. Department memos. Printed-out emails. Because it became apparent that Ben was the type of person who printed out his emails to read them. Which would have been amazing luck if his emails had been anything but the dull minutiae of his job. Ticket quotas. Reminders of policies. Automatic emails to let him know that someone had responded to his comment on Huffington Post. Even the emails that might hold interest didn't have enough information to lead to further investigation. Emails to a library near Tulsa with questions about a flooding incident they experienced as a result of burst pipes over the winter, and questions about papers there belonging to someone named Cynthia. Repeated delivery failures from Ben's attempts to email a variety of addresses all with the domain of praxis.edu. Keisha paused at those, but his sent emails contained nothing but short greetings, and none of them had gotten anything but an automatic error reply.

"Do any of these places seem important to you?" said Sylvia, after nearly an hour of tedious reading in which they had both learned a lot about Ben's opinions on *Star Trek* canon.

It was a list of cities, handwritten on the back of one of the printed-out emails.

VECTOR H

~~Everett~~
~~Kingston~~
~~Waco~~
<u>*Victorville*</u>
~~Paw Paw~~
~~Burnt Prairie~~

Vector H. Keisha felt the swoon of grief. One of the phrases from Alice's secret papers.

"Yeah," she managed. "This is definitely something." She considered the crossed-out names and the one that had been underlined. "Of course it had to be the one on the complete other side of the country."

She had been getting frantic calls from Bay and Creek, about the missing travel-sized deodorant shipment, about the missing truck, about the missing her. She had ignored them. So she probably didn't have a job now. That was fine. After everything she had lost, what was a job?

"This is going to be a long drive," Sylvia said. "Do you have an iPhone hookup in here or something?"

Keisha considered this teenager whom she had only known a few days. The girl was so young. And so fucking brave. She was so much braver than Keisha. Smarter too. Faster. Stronger. By almost any measure, a better person. And, knowing this, Keisha knew what she had to do.

Sylvia didn't take it well. Immediately reverted into arms crossed, slumping back, an angry kid with a bargaining mother.

"Well, you can kick me out if you want," she said. "Be a dick move after everything, but I'll find another way to get there."

And Keisha believed that she would. Sylvia had gotten a long way on her own, and she could get a whole lot further. It wasn't a question of could, though, but should.

"It's silly, what we're doing, Sylvia," she said. "Maybe even it's wrong. But you and I, we can't not do it. Right?"

Jaw set, a slight nod.

"Right," Keisha said. "We'd be out here no matter what, even though whatever is waiting in that town, it's not good. Maybe it's the kind of thing a person doesn't come back from. And, Sylvia, I am a foolish, foolish person. Because I'm going to go. No matter what, I'm going to that place."

"And I am too," Sylvia said, in a voice soft as stone, gentle as a knife.

"But you're not a fool," Keisha said. "The Thistle Man, the Hungry Man, whoever else is doing all this, they should be terrified of you. Because I think you're going to be the one who stops it. No, I mean it. I think you haven't even grown into the force for good you could become. But you won't stop anything if you get killed poking around some town that may or may not have any answers. That doesn't have to happen. Because, no matter what, I'm going to go there. Whether you go or stay, it's too late for me. I need you to be smarter than me. I need you to lie low, and keep trying to hear what you can hear, and I need you to grow and get even smarter and more powerful than you are now. Let me be the fool. You be the one who lives."

It was only when the drops reached her mouth that she noticed she was crying.

"Whatever needs to be done in that place," she finished, "I will fucking do it. I really will. And if I fail, then you will be right here, alive and ready."

Keisha didn't say please. Didn't try to touch Sylvia or make any gesture. She sat and she waited. Either Sylvia would agree with her or she wouldn't. The girl was old enough to know which. Sylvia's glare faltered at the edge of her eyes. Her arms loosened. And then she pulled Keisha into a fierce hug. She shook through the hug, and so by transposition Keisha shook too. Sylvia's tears soaked into the shoulder of Keisha's T-shirt.

"Ok," Sylvia said. "Ok. Ok. Ok."

12

She crossed into California north of Lake Havasu. Then into the Inland Empire. Land that would hardly be populated if it weren't for the tempting light of LA over the San Gabriel Mountains, a daily commute for those who want a house more than they want the hours of their day. Land that would be uninhabitable if it weren't for the water brought in by canal, portioned out to farmers, who then sell their portions to the thirsty cities, making them nothing but water farmers. Foreclosures and cabbage and Vons supermarkets.

Victorville is a city of about a hundred thousand people, named after a man born in Ohio who died in the Inland Empire working as a manager of the California railroad. If a person is not from Southern California, it is unlikely they've ever even heard the name of the city. And somewhere in it was the secret that had destroyed Keisha's life. Or so she hoped. It was thin evidence, the fact that the name had been underlined while the others were crossed out. Maybe it merely meant it was next on Officer Campbell's list to investigate. And who even knew where he had gotten his information. What his sources were, and whether they were telling him the truth.

She had left Sylvia at an Extended Stay America in Arkansas. Keisha had paid for a couple weeks in cash. After that, Sylvia would have to figure it out. Most likely she would disappear out onto the roads again. Keisha wasn't worried about her. She could take care of herself. Ok, Keisha was a little worried about her.

She left the truck outside of town and bought the cheapest used car she could find on Craigslist.

"This barely runs," the man said, as she picked up the car from his driveway. "Won't last a year."

"Who's thinking that far ahead?" she said and drove off, after a lesson on coaxing it into ignition.

The issue was where to even begin. Victorville is small, but not that small. A slice of suburb too far from the city to be a suburb. Strip malls and industry and agriculture. Keisha started by randomly sampling the city. Trying local businesses. Eating pizza, getting her nails done, buying shoes at Kmart, and everywhere trying to make idle conversation. Gently poking her way through to anything strange that maybe people noticed, or that they forced themselves not to notice. But it was only a city, only a place where people lived and worked and died.

Until the Burger King, where the guy behind the counter saw her copy of the third volume in the comic series she was reading, *Perla la Loca*, which she had brought in to read with lunch, and said, "*Love and Rockets*! That's my shit!" and she explained that it was very much her shit, too, and they started talking about the series. He was getting worked up about a recent story line she hadn't gotten to yet, and somewhere in that explanation, he referenced "the other town" as though it were a place in Victorville. She let him wind his way down, and when things seemed as friendly as they were going to be, she asked: "What other town?"

He blanched and tried to recover. "Huh? No, no other town. Or, like, Apple Valley, I guess. It's right there, you know. The other town. So."

She tried to keep the conversation going by talking about one of her favorite panels in *Perla*, the one with the dog that was actually the devil, but he muttered down toward the register that he had to get back to work and gave her the order number. After she ate she said good-bye. He only nodded slightly. But now she had a phrase. "The other town." And with that phrase she returned to the places she had already been to.

At each business, she worked the phrase into conversation. Never as a direct question. But as though it were a piece of knowledge she already had, and she would place it out next to a few innocuous statements and then watch how people reacted.

The man at the hardware store was stoic but excused himself a minute or so after she said it and never returned.

The woman at the nail salon winced. "I don't want to talk about it," she said. "They leave us alone. You leave it alone." She wouldn't be drawn back to the subject, and she rushed Keisha's appointment.

The woman at the bike shop got angry. "Don't even say that in here. You don't say those words in my store. You'll bring him in."

"Who?"

"Get out."

By the time she was at a party supply store, it was well after dark, and she was the last customer before they closed. The teenager behind the register shuddered. "Jeez, dude. You can't talk about that."

"Why not?"

He glanced out the front windows. "Because when you talk about the other town, there's a tendency for him to show up. You haven't been going around talking about that, have . . . oh shit," he said, looking again out the window.

"What?"

"You need to hide right now."

Given her experiences up to this point, if someone thought she needed to hide, then she hid. She crouched behind a wire bin of cheap inflatable balls. The door chime rang.

"Hey, Mike," said a voice that was not a voice she knew but had a familiar tone. Like the hollowing of the wind.

"Oh, hey, man, so," Mike said, in a high-pitched waver.

"Son, no need to be worried like that. Heard that someone might be asking around about the other town."

"Oh?"

"Yeah, seen anyone like that?"

"Not that I remember?"

"Don't you think you'd remember if they mentioned the other town, son? Wouldn't that stick out in your memory?"

She shifted slightly so she could see around the edge of the bin. The man was wearing a dirty polo shirt. His fingernails were yellow below the surface. His skin stretched oddly over his face.

Keisha had never seen this man before. It wasn't the Thistle Man. Or, more accurately, it was *a* Thistle Man but not *the* Thistle Man she knew. There were more than one.

13

Her mind was in a race with her heart and both were losing. If there was another Thistle Man, then he was not a monster but a species. How many of these Thistle Men were out there? How many families with a quiet space where once a life had been lived among them? How many people died looking into dull eyes and a gaping yellow mouth, rimmed with sagging flesh? Keisha couldn't put her jumbled thoughts together. Her heart pumped blood madly through her shivering body.

"Uh, no," the kid at the register said, his voice lost in a quaver. "You're right, no. Definitely no one asked about any other town."

This new Thistle Man was silent for a long while. From where she crouched, Keisha couldn't tell what was happening. She could only see the strange crooked posture of the creature, as though gravity for him was slightly up and to the left of the rest of the world. She could only see the deep fear in the teenager's eyes as it occurred to him, maybe for the first time in his life, that no breath came guaranteed.

But the next breath came, both for the kid and for her.

"Pfft," the Thistle Man said. "Whaff. Narn." His wet lips smacked. Then this other Thistle Man turned and ambled crookedly out of the store. Keisha waited until she was sure he was gone and came out.

"Thank you."

"Just get out of here," said the kid.

She did, and despite everything both mind and heart were telling her, she followed after this new Thistle Man. He crossed the empty road, desert wind blowing hot down the street divided by a planter of yellow flowers and waxy leaves grown with borrowed water, and the Thistle Man stomped over them. The two of them crossed a massive parking lot, almost completely empty, and entered a Vons.

The swish of the door opening, the swish of the door closing. Quiet warm darkness replaced by blaring light and air-conditioning, and the murmur of music designed to shop to. There was no sign at all of her quarry. Or perhaps she should think of him as her hunter. Cautiously she walked past the aisles. There were no customers, only the lines of logos receding into a vanishing point of dairy refrigerators. Back again along the aisles. Where were the customers? Where, even, was the staff?

She turned a corner in frozen foods and there he was, only a few feet away. Back turned. His shoulders bouncing like he was laughing, but the sound was more like a man drowning, thick, desperate gasps. He shouted, no words, just sound, then back to gasping. A Vons employee, the first other person she had seen, turned the corner on the other end of the aisle, saw the man, and immediately walked away. Keisha retreated a few aisles down, trying to stay out of sight.

Now that she had caught up to him, she realized that she didn't have any clear idea of what her plan had been. Once again, she had pointed herself in the direction of trouble without thinking through the consequences of finding it.

But the Thistle Man did not turn. He stopped gasping and thrashing and started walking again. Every few feet his right leg would give, like it had no muscle or bone, and his entire body would stoop to the side and then unsteadily lurch its way back up with his next step. She stayed on the opposite ends of the aisles, tracking his movement. He circled the store once and then went back out the exit, never looking around him, although she didn't know whether that meant that he hadn't seen her or that he didn't need to.

Out in the parking lot, he got into a car, a silver Toyota a few years old, relatively clean. As it had happened, she had left her car in this same lot, because it was central to a number of the businesses she had been going to. But the lot was big enough that she still had to sprint at least a quarter of a mile, trying to reach her car in time to follow him. Keisha turned the key and only a faint cough happened and she thought, *No, no, no, I've come this far and I won't have the world fail me*, and she turned the key again, relieved to hear the unsteady whine of the starting engine.

The Toyota turned left out of the shopping center and she followed. She tried to keep a distance between them, but few cars were out in a town as quiet as Victorville, and so it was hard not to be visible. At first they were surrounded by strip malls, but then the right-hand side of the road fell away to desert, where the darkness was near total. In the distance, some sort of factory, all glow and smoke. Sweating, breathing human beings on a night shift inside that factory, and on every side of them, darkness and sand.

They hit a T intersection and made a left, past the bus station. A bus was pulling out, on late-night departure to who knows where. On the other side of the road was the Route 66 museum. A museum to road tripping, to distance, to how big and spread out America is. As Keisha drove, in order to distract her nervous mind from what she was actually doing, she thought about how her country was a place defined as much by its distance as its culture.

Sand drifts on the road. They were fully outside of town now. Stacks of boxcars. An outpost of the Los Angeles Department of Water and Power. Wires emanating from it, almost invisible against the sky, carrying the lights to Hollywood, the air-conditioning to Malibu. Here there was no glamour, only the machine.

They turned again. A road called Gas Line Road that intersected a block away with Powerline Road.

And finally, a military airport. Barbed wire and hangars. They drove along the fences. The road was completely empty, and so Keisha switched off her headlights and drove only by watching his car and trying to mirror its movements. It felt dangerous, but also somehow restful and quiet, like swimming underwater. In the dark, with the thrum of the engines, she could almost let her natural anxiety fade into an undercurrent that wouldn't intrude on her thoughts.

The Toyota slowed, put on a blinker (signaling to whom?) then turned through a hole in the fence into the airport. The hole was rough, with wire hanging loose around it, looking innocently accidental, but was also exactly wide enough for a car.

A small plane came in for landing, and as she drove toward the entrance, she watched the entire landing happen. Red lights blinking their way down, and then finally touching earth and she realized she hadn't been breathing, and then she hit the curb and screamed.

14

Keisha stopped the car on the road, undecided for a moment, but then made the turn. If he noticed her, he noticed her. She had gone too far to be able to make any other decision in that moment. She was always afraid but did what she needed to do.

As she passed through the fence, a shape loomed down at her from the dark. She swerved instinctually, fishtailing for a moment. The shape was huge, with a snub-nosed face and weird shadows crisscrossing from light passing through the fence. She squinted as she drove around it and saw a broad wing, like an arm reaching out for help, and she understood. A passenger jet, a double-decker giant, designed for international flight. Company name painted over. The plane was silent and earthbound.

Her eyes adjusted, and she saw there were more of them. Line after line of retired jetliners. No sign of any other car. She drove slowly past the skeletons of flight. At this point, with her engine coughing loudly in this silent graveyard, she had given up any hope for the stealthy approach. Now it was likely he was stalking her. It would be so easy for him to circle around behind. Perhaps that was his intent on leading her to this place. Perhaps she had driven willingly into a Thistle murder site. She passed under a wing, and its elongated shadow lingered over her car.

Under the belly of one of the planes, she thought she saw movement, and she turned the car toward it. The machines around her had avoided disaster again and again only to end up here, in this desolate place, grounded forever. The omen was not lost on her. All luck runs out eventually. Otherwise it wouldn't be luck.

Keisha opened her window so she could hear the night. The night sounded only like her car and like the wind. Some of the small port windows on the airplanes had been knocked out. She thought about what the inside of these dead airplanes must look like. All fixtures gone, only hollow metal filled with moonlight and rattling in the wind.

When the brake lights came on, her mind didn't have time to react but her body was already slamming her foot down. The belt went tight as her car gritted to a stop on the gravel. The Thistle Man's car was a hundred feet or so in front of her. It was idling. Waiting for something. She switched off the engine, got out, and left the beater behind, running across the hardpacked dirt. The night beyond his Toyota shifted, and she realized that what she had thought was sky was a high wall, and a gate was opening in it. She couldn't see what was on the other side. The Toyota pulled through, the gate slid closed behind him, and the wall became invisible again against the hills.

The wall was featureless, except for a small sign by the gate. It was understated, even elegant, more like a sign for a fancy restaurant than US military property. The sign said THISTLE. She put her hand on the fence, and it was cool, even in the hot night. She tasted sour acid in her mouth and took her hand away. There was something terrible behind this wall, and despite herself she needed to know what it was. She circled around it, but the wall was unbroken, well maintained, and clean. A lot of money and time had gone into keeping whatever was inside this wall hidden. Giving up instantly on the idea of scaling the smooth expanse, Keisha looked around for another option and saw a nearby hillside that appeared to rise above the wall. She had to crawl under the fence to get to it, and the wounds from the skylight in the police station opened up again. Her shirt went wet with blood, and this mixed with the dust into a red paste that covered her as she scrambled her way up the hill. The brush was thick and thorny, but she picked her way through until, panting and bleeding, she turned to see if she was high enough. She was.

Inside the wall was a little town. The other town. Houses. A market. A gas station. Even at this hour, the town's population was out in force. Every one of them was a Thistle Man. A town of nightmare creatures. Loose skin, boneless legs, jittering movements. None of them talked to one another, although sometimes one would laugh, long and loud, and then return to monastic silence. And there was him, the original him, the Thistle Man, the Hungry Man. He was leaning on one of the pumps at the gas station, reading a newspaper.

An entire city of them. Creatures so dangerous, so powerful, that a single one of them had almost destroyed her. And here there were hundreds. Were all of them serial killers, uncaught, living together, hidden in this airplane boneyard on a US military air base?

A US air base. She could have fooled herself that there were some corrupt cops involved with whatever the horrors of Thistle were up to. But this was beyond a few cops. This was a system of violence and laws that protected Thistle from the likes of her, five foot three, a gash down her chest, and a constant fear that she wouldn't recognize a heart attack if it came because it would feel like her panic attacks. The imbalance of power wasn't merely unfair. It was monumental in a literal sense of the term. It was a monolith of disparity and she could almost laugh at the sheer lopsided span of injustice she was contemplating now from that shrubby hillside.

Not that long before, on a highway in Georgia, a wife she hadn't seen in over two years had left a billboard with some advice, and now she was going to listen to it. Who was she to fight a war this lopsided? Her wife had perhaps decided to fight it, and her wife had disappeared. She wasn't as strong as Alice. She wasn't willing to disappear. She was sorry to have failed Alice, although this was what Alice had wanted. She was even sorrier to have failed Sylvia, although she knew that Sylvia would be fine on her own. But this was beyond Keisha.

She got back in her car, left behind the secret town of serial killers on a US air base, drove to her truck in a lot outside of Victorville, then straight through the night to a house that had stood empty since she'd left it, and she stepped through the door into the stale air that smelled like a different part of her life, and she was home for the first time in over a year.

15

When a person leaves their home for a long time and then returns, the furniture, books, and appliances are all exactly how
they had left them. This doesn't sound weird, but it is. There was,
after all, once a person who left those things in those places, and
then months of life change that person, and this changed person
returns to all the same stuff, still there. A person lives always in
the remnants of the life they've led up until the present, making
do with whatever they've left behind for themself.

Keisha felt all this strongly, but most of all she felt defeat and
shame. She didn't get out of bed except to shop for frozen meals.
After her time away, she didn't feel capable of getting her hands
into the correct gestures and timing for cooking, but the micro-
wave still worked as expected and didn't require more from her
than she was able to give. Mostly she spent her time looking at
her bedroom ceiling as though it were a landscape, which in a
way it was, a landscape of texture that changed with the position

of the sun. Shadows made their way from this corner to that, and she followed their journey for hours.

The truck lurched and then stalled. Keisha had never even driven manual before and now she was trying to learn an eighteen-gear rig, having to deal with the idea of a clutch, and an H pattern shifter with a splitter, and timing it all with RPM, a dial that had always been on her dashboard but that she had never for a moment in her life thought about.

"You're trying to shift her, not stop her," her instructor said between wheezing laughs that smelled like every cigarette he had ever smoked.

"I'm fucking trying," she muttered and that made him laugh even more.

He was an old-school trucker, had been doing it since the '70s up until two years earlier when he had retired and opened a driving school. While women driving trucks was not as uncommon as it used to be, he found the idea amusing and took every mistake she made as proof that he was right about everything he had ever thought about the world.

But as obnoxious as it was, for her the only way out was through. Her way into the life she had decided to have was on the other side of this driving school. And while she grappled always with anxiety, and certainly having this old white man laughing at her from the passenger seat was not helping her anxiety one bit, she also contained a great capacity for stubbornness. This entire endeavor was born out of that. Why else would she choose to take on such a hopeless mission, crossing and recrossing the country searching for someone who most likely didn't want to be found? In any case, she set herself to learning how to drive this stupid machine and she would not stop to take any kind of break until she had gotten her clumsy hands to do what was asked of them.

"Yeah, now you're getting it. That was right on it," her instructor said. He had gradually shown more respect as he saw how absolute her insistence on learning was, how little interest she had in what others thought of her.

"You don't have to tell me I'm getting it. Old man, I know I'm getting it."

This is what it was, then, to have a single driving mission and then lose it. Bay and Creek continued to try to get in touch with Keisha. Obviously, she no longer had the job, but they did need the truck back. She had ditched the trailer a few hundred miles from Victorville, far enough that she hoped no one would make the connection, and then she had parked the cab on her back lawn, where she hoped it wouldn't be visible from the street. She didn't want any remnant of her life before to taint whatever it was her life would become next.

Gradually she found her feet, getting out of bed and moving around. Taking walks through the neighborhood, as people from their yards squinted at her with the feeling that they must know her from somewhere but couldn't quite put their finger on where. She started buying groceries that were ingredients, food that other food could be made from, some of it not frozen. Her hands regained the gestures and timing of cooking. Days passed. Then two weeks. She felt like maybe she could do this forever. That it would never be ok, but that she could make a list of activities each day, and then go through that list, and when the list was over the day would be over and she could sleep fitfully before starting again.

A life does not need to be satisfying or triumphant. A life does not need to mean anything or lead anywhere. A life does not need a direction or a goal. Ultimately, a life merely needs to be lived until there is no more living left to do.

The house had a deck upstairs, off the master bedroom, that faced an identical deck on the neighbor's house. A thoughtless bit of subdivision design, mirroring houses so that the entire neighborhood would not look so uniform but ending up with this accidental bit of intimacy. Keisha had never known much about her neighbors' lives, but they had often ended up a few feet apart on summer nights, eating dinner outside, smelling each other's food, half in and out of each other's conversations.

So she was unsurprised when she sat out in the warming weather and one of the neighbors, Sheila, appeared.

"Keisha! I saw lights on in the house but I didn't know if it was . . . how are you?"

Keisha nodded, as though saying yes to a different question that wasn't asked.

"It's good to see you again, Sheila. It really is." She gave her best smile, her most carefree wave. "You have a nice day now."

Often at night she found herself looking out her front window. There was no reason for this, only a lingering instinct to be aware of her surroundings. She got to know the people in her neighborhood better than she had in her years of living there. The people who took runs in the dark or walked their dogs after coming home late from their jobs. Once or twice she saw a person in a hoodie, based on their size probably a teenager. A bored teenager hanging out in a boring neighborhood. Then, a few nights in, she noticed the car. An old Mustang, with a hood that was a different color from the rest of the body, and scratches and dents all down the sides. One of the tires looked low, flabbing out onto the asphalt. It was not the kind of car seen often in her neighborhood, and she watched it intently, night after night, but no one ever came for it, no one else ever looked at it. Sometimes she thought she could see movement through its darkened windshield. As though there was always someone sitting inside, night after night, staring right back at her.

16

Once she had decided to live the rest of her life, Keisha started looking for a job. The kind of job she had held down before everything about her old life had ended. No one knew what to do with her résumé. Middle-tier white-collar work and then this long stretch as a truck driver and now back to searching for office jobs.

"Was this, uh, about finding yourself?" the interviewers at job agencies would ask about her work history.

"It was about finding someone, sure."

"Mm. Ah. Well, we'll call you."

Keisha also tried gingerly to reach back out to friends. Margaret answered the door with a look somewhere between happiness and loss.

"Keisha, dear, I thought I had . . . ," and then she took Keisha into a hug that crushed Keisha's nose into Margaret's collarbone. It had been so long since Keisha had had a friend like this, and she had trouble finding the center of gravity in the conversation.

Margaret asked gentle, probing questions about the missing time, and Keisha deflected them with questions about Margaret's life.

"My life is the same as it ever was," Margaret said. "If you knew me then, you know me now." She cocked her head. "I suspect the same can't be said of you."

"I suppose not," said Keisha but would not elaborate. Finally she made an awkward good-bye and they made plans to hang out again. Keisha desperately wanted to but found herself delaying reaching out again.

Now that she was home, she started going through Alice's things in a more organized fashion. She separated every item she found into two categories: unrelated and possible evidence. The possible evidence pile got bigger and bigger. Eventually everything went into it. How could she know what misplaced grocery list was actually a coded message? It had to be kept, in case she found its concealed meaning someday.

There were the words she remembered from her first time through. Bay and Creek. Vector H. Vector H was referred to in heavy, malignant terms, with words like *fatality incident* and *handled.* None of what she found connected in a way that made sense to her. And so she returned to that beating heart at the center of each person's life. She started going through Alice's laptop.

Every day, at 3:15 p.m., a police cruiser drove by the house. Keisha tried to believe this was a coincidence, but no one has much control over what they believe.

She was asleep when she heard the thump and the gurgle. It sounded like a drainage problem, or a person trying to breathe with a collapsing lung. The sound came first in her dream. She dreamed she was in an immense room, like the ballroom in an old-fashioned estate. The walls were lavish but distant, every decorative detail dwarfed by the scope of the architecture. And scattered all over the space were rolling cots and curtains, all of them unused. A field hospital for a war that hadn't started yet. There was a huge basin of clean water in the center of the room, and she understood that soon the water would be full of blood and pus from all the wounds yet to be inflicted. She bent over the basin, and the water bubbled up at her with a thump and gurgle. She stumbled backward, understanding that something terrible was crawling up from the water. Another thump, another gurgle. A hand with badly burnt skin, peeling and charred, splashed up out of the basin. She started awake.

She sat up in bed, warily eyeing the dark corners of the room. With her blurry, half-awake vision the darkness seemed to heave and pulse. That sound had been so distinct and real and she felt certain it had entered her dream from the real world. She listened for the sound again. After half a minute, there it was, a thump and a gurgle, from somewhere in the house. She didn't know what to do. Or she knew what to do and could not bring herself to do it. She waited and heard the sound a couple more times, and then nothing. She went and checked the bedroom door. Still locked. She never used to keep it locked, but now she always did. She sat up in bed for hours, waiting for the sound to come again, but it never did and she drifted back to sleep as the sun began to rise.

Back out on the deck that afternoon, and Sheila came out with her partner, David.

"Oh!" said David. "Sheila mentioned you were back, but still such a nice surprise."

"It's nice to see you too," said Keisha over the book her sleep-deprived mind had been grappling with for the past half hour.

"Well, don't let us bother you," said Sheila, and the two of them lay out on their deck chairs, not talking to her or each other.

Keisha gave up on the book and returned to Alice's laptop. But there was nothing. Alice's laptop was as blank and inexplicable as her disappearance. It gave up none of her secrets.

Keisha decided she would keep trying, day after day, letting the television play her old sitcom episodes while she methodically went through each folder in the laptop until it dead-ended in a worthless batch of system files, and then she would back out and try again. After two days of this, she found what was labeled as a temp directory full of folders that were named with randomly generated series of letters and numbers. Within one of these, she found a subfolder that contained ten subfolders and one of them contained a hidden folder disguised as a system folder, and that one contained years of pay statements.

Keisha went through the statements one after another, but it only took a few to understand what she was looking at. They were payments, to Alice, from Bay and Creek, going back years. Alice had been working for Bay and Creek since around the time she and Keisha had moved into this house.

She closed the laptop and tossed it next to her on the couch. She had found what she had been looking for and felt not even a little bit better.

Before going to bed, she went back to her deck, half hoping that Sheila or David would be there so that she could have some sort of human contact to recenter herself, stop her mind from going through the years of her life that she had so completely misunderstood. But neither of them were out. The sliding door into their bedroom was open, which was odd. The contractors had put no screen on the doors to the decks, and so no one left their sliding doors open in the buggy seasons, which were most seasons. Keisha tried to look through the door without looking through it, since staring into their bedroom seemed creepy. But there was something wrong about what she was seeing, and she was trying to isolate what it was. Then she noticed a white tube near the bottom of the door. What the hell was that? It was a leg. It was Sheila's leg, sticking out of the doorway and onto the deck.

Keisha lost track of her breath and fell backward against a deck chair. And that was when she noticed a second shape, which had been standing the whole time in the darkest corner of her neighbor's deck.

It was a Thistle Man, a skinny one with missing patches of hair and a head that was lolling around like he didn't have control over his neck. His smile arced crookedly up around his yellow teeth. He stared at Keisha from the shadows.

"Shumf," he murmured gently. "Woo."

17

She had murdered her neighbors by just trying to come home, and there was no to-do list she could work her way through the next day that would make that something she could live with. She was used to not sleeping, one of the side effects of her constant anxiety, but she wasn't used to not sleeping for a good reason.

At around four in the morning she heard haphazard, arrhythmic clapping. Adrenaline seized through her, but she stood and with shaking legs left her bedroom. She crept down the stairs. *Slap slap* came the sound. There was a flickering in her living room. *Slap slap.* The TV was on and muted, showing a local weather-woman describing a hurricane that would never come anywhere near the area Keisha lived. Against this weather report, Keisha saw a blurred reflection. A strange bent shape, swinging loosely back and forth. *Slap slap.* She smelled tilled earth, and she smelled her own sweat, and she smelled cleaning chemicals and the sharp funk of a gas station bathroom.

"WOOP," the shape said. "WOOOOOP." *Slap slap. Slap slap.*

She leaned around the living room door with as little of herself visible as possible. A Thistle Man, not the one she had first met, and not the one she had followed to the town, and not the one from her neighbors' deck, but another one still. He was bent horribly backward, like his spine was broken, and he was loosely swinging his arms back and forth in a circle so that they slapped his chest and back. *Slap slap. Slap.* He gurgled. "WOOOP!" he shouted. "WOOOOOOOOOOP!"

She ran back to her bedroom, making no effort to be quiet, waiting any moment for a hand to encircle her ankle, but she made it up the stairs, slammed and locked the door, and then finally, after all the events of the last few days, she cried. The slapping had stopped. It was silent in her house. She waited for the door to break down, but nothing else happened, except, eventually, morning.

The truth was manifest to her. They would never let her escape. They would never let her disappear into a life, no matter how quiet. They had come for her. These weren't warnings, the murder of her neighbors, the creature in her house. Because there was nothing left for them to warn her away from. She had given up, and here they still were. This was them playing with their food before they ate it.

They left her with no choice. If they wouldn't stop coming after her, no matter how fully she had given up, then she could not give up. She instead would have to be the one to come after them. She was ready. Fuck the Thistle Men.

She would have to be patient. This was not an enemy to approach in haste. There would need to be a plan. The first step, obviously, would be to disappear again, return to the roads where they might have a more difficult time tracking her. She would do her best to switch cars regularly, not take any of the same routes twice, sleep mostly in her vehicle unless she couldn't avoid it. Then she would need to turn the tables on them and watch them. There was that hill above their town. In her head she could see a lean-to, a camouflaged place to sit and watch them. She would take all the time she needed. They would not rush her to oblivion. She would sit on that hill peering into binoculars until her eyes were strained and her nose was pinched. There would have to be a weakness. And, if it took her the rest of her life, she would find it.

Once she had found their weakness, she would gather the forces needed. There must be like-minded individuals out there, like Sylvia, but with more power. More ability to put an end to this nightmare for good. Keisha would find these people, if it took her years, and it might take her years, and she would show them the weakness she had found in her long solitude of surveillance, and they would help her make a plan that exploited that weakness ruthlessly, and then finally she would win, she would crush them, and maybe it would be decades later, but on that day she would come home and once more live in peace.

It was a long and difficult battle she was pledging herself to, but she saw the hard years before her and welcomed them as companions. Let them come. Let her age. Someday she would have her revenge.

She decided all this and it filled her with satisfaction and rage, and then she heard a slow knocking at her door. Like a wind-driven branch tapping inconsistently against a window. Looking out her upstairs window, she saw no one anywhere near the front door, but there was a note, nailed to the door.

Creeping downstairs, holding a heavy book as some token of a weapon, Keisha peered out the front window. No one in sight. She opened the door, tore the note off the nail, closed and locked the door again. The note was short and unequivocal and it made her throw out every plan she had made.

Instead that night she made several frantic phone calls and then, three days short of a month after coming home, she walked out into the darkness, got into her truck, and drove it out onto the street. She had spent no time preparing. She had taken nothing with her. She would only make one stop on the road ahead, to pick up a couple items that she wasn't sure would be helpful. But she couldn't second-guess herself. She was driving directly to Victorville, and she would face these monsters head-on. The note lay unfolded on her passenger seat, and each time she glanced at it, the spike of fear acted as fuel to keep her awake through the long night's drive.

18

The first blue of morning crept up on the airplane graveyard. Keisha sat back in her seat and considered the gate of the other town in front of her. There would be no return from what she had to do next, but hadn't she learned in the last few weeks that there had never been a return possible? This had always been a one-way trip, only now she knew it for sure, and so she could stop denying and come to terms with it.

Her cab was full of a smell so strong it left her dizzy, but whatever helped. She had gotten little help in her life. Now the time for help had passed, had maybe never existed for a person like her. Maybe she had spent her life alone, the only advocate for herself, and she had just never fully realized it. She put her hand on the ignition. She breathed in. She breathed out. She closed her eyes. This was it then.

Her passenger door opened. She opened her eyes and didn't understand what she was looking at. She couldn't breathe in or out. She couldn't do anything even though she wanted to do so many things.

"Chanterelle," Alice said.

The rush of anger on hearing Alice speak put the voice back into Keisha's chest. "Let's stick with Keisha," she said.

Alice looked as she had on the day she had disappeared. Keisha didn't know whether she hated her or loved her or if there was any difference in that moment.

"I'm sorry. I . . . I don't know what to say. I shouldn't have done it the way that I did," Alice said.

"A higher calling?" Keisha said, refusing to look at her.

"A lower one, I guess. The lowest, darkest places. You know. You've seen them."

"Thanks to you."

"Keisha, the world is teetering. I'm trying to keep it sliding in the right direction. Either way a huge and terrible change is coming. But if it slides too far toward them"—she gestured at the Thistle gates—"then it's all over for people like us, people in love, people who feel."

Keisha kept both hands on the wheel. She didn't trust her body to support itself otherwise.

"They'll kill you," Alice said.

"Maybe."

"Keisha, they will kill you to an extent you didn't know a person could be killed. You don't know how dangerous they can be."

"Oh, Alice. I know. I know. I *know*."

"Ok. You know."

"Got your message, and thanks for that, but I can't go home. I tried that."

"I heard," Alice said. "I wish I could protect you. But I need to stay lost for a while. You have to respect that. You have to respect me enough not to look for me."

Keisha turned finally, faced Alice fully. Her eyes streamed, and she made no effort to wipe it away.

"You want to talk about respect?" she hissed.

"Someday, Chipmunk . . . Keisha, I will come back, if you will let me, and we will live out the rest of our lives. I promise that. I promise that. In the meantime."

"In the meantime, stop looking."

"Yeah," Alice said. "Yes. I'm sorry."

Keisha could have hit her. Could have killed her, honestly. Let Alice finally actually be dead if she wanted to be dead that badly. But what she did instead was pull her toward her, and their lips met, and it could have been the day they met, could have been the day they got married, could have been any weekday evening before she disappeared. Keisha felt love, right where she had left it, and kissed Alice so hard that it hurt both of them, because what she really wanted to do was to find her way into Alice's chest and live there among the bones and blood. She wanted them to be one person, but also to be two people; she wanted so many things, most of them contradictory. She pushed Alice away.

Alice couldn't find breath to speak.

"I won't look for you then," Keisha said. "But it's not about you anymore."

"I know," Alice said. She sniffed at the air and smiled a little. "You've made some good precautions, at least. I don't know why it works, but I think it does."

"That's what I'm hoping. It's all about hope now."

Alice put her hand on Keisha's leg, and Keisha stopped herself from flinching away. Alice didn't deserve the touch, but Keisha did, and she wanted it.

"I'm going now," said Alice.

"I am too."

"Please don't do this."

"Get out of my truck."

Alice, one lingering moment of hand on leg later, did.

My hands are shaking, Keisha thought, and then realized that she was wrong. Every part of her was shaking. There was not a muscle in her body that wasn't quivering. She tried to find steadiness, but that was no longer a possibility, and so she tried to find resolve and she didn't have that either. But she did have stubbornness and desperation, and those would do in a pinch.

The conversation hadn't changed anything. She still had to do what she had to do next. Because it hadn't been for Alice, or even for Keisha. She picked up the note and read it again. It had one word and one number. The word was *Room*. The number was Sylvia's room number at the Extended Stay America where Keisha had left her. Keisha had called the room over and over, but there had been no answer, and Sylvia's phone refused texts and went to voice mail when called.

There was no mistaking the message. And so Keisha no longer had the luxury of time to plan, or watch, or gather support. She needed to end this for Sylvia's sake before anyone else got hurt, even though there was no way for Keisha to do this and walk away. She knew she wouldn't live to see the morning that the horizon was promising, and she had become ok with this. She tried one more time to call, this time the front desk at the Extended Stay.

"Anything strange?" said a sleepy-sounding man. "Nothing but this call, lady. I'm not going to go knocking on my customers' doors in the middle of the night because some rando says I should."

So much for that. No more hesitation. No more waiting. She started the engine and felt the vibration of it roar up through her feet. She was still shaking, but now it felt like she was shaking with power instead of shock. It made her feel like she might be able to pull this off, even though she knew the chances were minuscule.

Parked under the belly of a dead jetliner, Alice watched Keisha start the engine. She pulled out her phone and made a call to a person she had never wanted to talk to again.

"I need a huge favor," said Alice. "You really, really owe me."

She was right. The person on the other end really, really did.

But Keisha didn't know anything about that. Her world had focused to the gate in front of her, and her foot on the gas pedal. She put down her foot and the truck surged forward, using the long stretch of gravel to slowly build up velocity, bracing herself the moment before her truck slammed through the gate of the Thistle town.

19

The gate tore off with a sound like the yelp of a strange animal, and Keisha had to scramble for the brakes to avoid being carried through to the gas station. Hundreds of men with ill-fitting skin and yellow polo shirts. The mob surrounded the cab, sneering. One had been hit by her truck as it entered, and he picked himself up and limped to join the others. The skin of his face had been torn off by the collision and underneath was a mealy yellow fat, dripping down over his chin. There was no sign of bone. Keisha tried to find any calm within herself. Her skin glistened. She couldn't smell anything but herself, fortunately, but she could imagine a smell like tilled earth, like green things gone putrid. A whole glob of yellow fat fell from the injured man's face and landed on the ground where he slipped on it. He laughed as he fell, a choked, broken sound.

Tied to a streetlight near the gas station was one of the men. He leaned into the ropes that bound him. His whole body was covered in long narrow wounds that bled viscous trickles of mildew and must onto the rope, but his eyes were alive and focused.

"Get her," he croaked. "Get her."

The crowd parted. There was the original Thistle Man. The Hungry Man. The man who had eaten an omelet and thrust her into a nightmare. He lurched through the crowd.

"Oh, you can get out," he shouted. "None of us are going to hurt you right away. And you aren't any safer in there."

She fumbled the door open with slick hands.

"Look at you," he roared. "Sweating like a scared child. You're nervous."

"I'm always nervous." The other Thistle Men had backed up, formed a circle, leaving the two of them alone in the center. She was his mess to handle.

"You're serial killers," she said.

"We're freedom. Freedom can be good or bad. There can be terrible freedom." She shuddered to hear her own words thrown back at her. He grinned at her reaction. "We are the terrible freedom."

"You're murderers."

"We are creatures of the road. We feed on distance, on road trips, on emptiness. Bodies by the side of the highway."

There was a sound like applause, but softer. The crowd of Thistle Men were sucking in and out on their cheeks, creating a faint sound of flesh.

He grabbed her arm. She didn't know how he got that close, but he was there, and he took her arm like a dance partner, gentle but insistent, and then he pushed her up against the truck. His arm was on her throat. Fear branched through her like lightning, starting from the gut and ending with a thunderclap in her head.

But he couldn't do it. He couldn't push down, and he was wincing, his face wrinkling in disgust. He stepped back, wiping frantically at his arm. She gestured to her drenched face, neck, torso.

"Heather oil. Poured a few bottles right over my head. Tip from a friend."

The Thistle Man growled, and it reverberated out from his chest like a creature ten times his size. "You think that smell will protect you?" He slapped her. The world went white on one side. "It will hurt me, but I will hurt you more."

She reached out before he could realize she was moving. She grabbed his face, wrenched open his rotting, gummy mouth, and shoved in a huge fistful of dried heather.

"I also brought this."

He choked, heaved, his skin turned purple as though his entire body was bruising, and she couldn't make herself believe what happened next. He turned frantically and ran.

The other monsters froze. The tied-up one, glop still oozing from the wounds all over his body, moved his mouth like a fish, saying, "Fuh, fuh, fuh."

In the moment they were frozen, Keisha took off after the Thistle Man. The only way out, as always, was through. As soon as she moved, the others moved too. She broke through a gap in their circle, but she could hear the off-kilter rhythm of their running, and the thick, moist gasps of exertion from all around.

She chased the Thistle Man into a diner. The Burgers 'n More. The inside of the diner was full of rotting food. Milkshakes and hamburgers, covered in mold and maggots. Only the glasses of soda, unable to rot, watery with melted ice, still looked like what they were.

He was already in the kitchen, headed for the back door. She put the last of her energy into a sprint and crashed into him, sending both of them sprawling into the walk-in cooler. She slammed the door and pushed one of the low, heavy shelves in front of it. He flopped around on the ground, spitting out heather, his skin still an angry purple. After the heat of the night air outside, the walk-in made pinpricks on her skin. It focused her, like sobering up from a long night of drinking. She glanced back to check the door, and when she looked again at him, he was on his feet.

"That bought you some time, didn't it?" he burbled. "I wasn't expecting that. You got me to panic. Got me to run."

His skin blotched back from purple to faint yellow. He stretched and flexed, his strength returning. The walk-in was small. A soft patter of hands pawed on the outside of the door, and on the walls on both sides.

"But then what?" he asked. "What weapon do you have to finish the job?"

"Nothing," she said.

"Nothing?"

"Just me. I'm going to kill you."

He laughed, the deep laugh at the end of a good joke.

"You're going to kill me. Oh, Keisha," he said with tenderness, and in the same moment he came for her.

He was stronger even than she had remembered. It was like being hit by a car. Mass without pity, only brutal physics. She didn't feel pain. She was so full of fear that there wasn't room for anything else. She had never been so afraid, terror in every part of her. It froze up her limbs, locked up her joints, made her thoughts simultaneously too slow for planning and too fast to follow. She wasn't a person anymore, just a container for fear.

Keisha thought of Alice. Of believing Alice was dead and then knowing she wasn't. She thought of Earl outside that diner, dying alone, as decent people ate waffles not ten feet away. She thought of a father in a Target parking lot, calling the police, under the belief that the police would help. She thought of a line of billboards with names, a murderer's legacy on an ugly stretch of highway. She thought of a teenage girl, doing her best, and how great her best was. She thought of a bus pulling out of Victorville in the middle of the night. She thought of Sheila and David, an ordinary couple living out an ordinary series of years until their neighbor got them murdered merely by coming home. She thought of home. She thought again of Sylvia. She thought again and again of Alice.

Through all these thoughts, a buzzing anxiety. Anxiety like electricity. Keisha knew, in that moment, that anxiety is just an energy. It is an uncontrollable, near infinite energy, surging within her. And as the Thistle Man started to kill her, she stopped trying to contain that energy. She told her heart to beat faster and her panicked breath to become more labored. She demanded that fear overtake her. *Make me more afraid. I'm not afraid of feeling afraid. Make me more afraid.*

All that energy, she turned it outward, pushing it into her arms, her legs, her teeth. *Fuck the Thistle Man.* When he hit her again, she hit back. Pounding at his face. His chest. Biting. Letting the wave of terror inside her crest over him.

The Thistle Man laughed when she hit him, and kept punching, as thoughtless and inhuman as a rockslide on a highway. But she kept hitting, too, and he stopped laughing. Keisha clawed at his face, and his skin started to go, and that yellow fat oozed out. He grunted, growled, flailed. He was no longer toying with her, he was fighting for his life, but she stayed on her feet with all the fear that animated her. He was the one who finally fell, his teeth mashed into his cheek, shouting meaningless syllables.

She fell after him, knees first onto his chest. She hit, and hit, and hit. And then he was dead.

The Thistle Man was gone.

Adrenaline pounded through her; she couldn't turn off the energy she had found in herself, and she was in pretty bad shape. Bruises, probably a broken rib, definitely broken teeth. But the Thistle Man was a pile of fat and pulp that smelled like mushrooms. She threw up, half on the floor and half on his body. The smells of heather, and her vomit, and the ooze from the body mixed horribly. But with her own hands, she had ended this. She had won.

A patter of hands on the walls. And she remembered all the others.

20

"Let us in, let us in," a ragged voice sang, each note in discord with the note before.

The lights in the walk-in clicked off. In the darkness, she could hear moaning and whispering. A voice sounded like it was inches from her ear. "Fuh, fuh, fuh," it said. Keisha slid to the ground against the wall, and she waited to die.

Then a new sound. She felt it in her stomach first, a bass tone that hadn't been there before. Gradually it slid from her stomach to her ears, becoming audible. Engines. Car engines and then gunshots. The whispering stopped. There was scrambling outside the walk-in, like a dog slipping on hardwood.

Then nothing. Nothing but her and the darkness.

Then light. The door burst open, knocking over the shelf holding it shut. A woman holding a battering ram, a rifle slung over her shoulder, an angry scar, perfectly vertical, along her left cheek. Keisha had never seen this woman before.

The woman looked at the body on the floor. "Holy shit," she said. She examined Keisha again with more interest and then clicked on the radio on her belt.

"You're not going to believe this," she said, "but Vector H is down."

There was an exclamation of disbelief from the radio.

"I know, but I'm looking right at him. Vector H is definitely dead." The woman clicked it off before the person on the other end could reply. "Come on out. Those things have run for now," she said. She gave Keisha a respectful distance, glancing again at the Thistle Man, the Hungry Man, the corpse.

The woman ushered Keisha through the rotting diner and out onto the streets. They were full of armored vehicles. Women and men in uniforms sweeping house to house with perfect precision. But the uniforms did not look like any military she knew. Navy blue jumpsuits, with a logo on the chest. She squinted, but everyone was running around too quickly for her to understand the logo. They moved out of the way of the woman with automatic deference, and Keisha understood that she was the commander of whatever this group was.

"Who are you?" she asked the woman.

"You did a good thing today, Keisha. A very good thing." She shook her head. "Maybe amazing. But now it's time for you to leave."

"Who do you work for?"

"Who do *you* work for?" she said. She was wearing one of the jumpsuits, too, and stopped so Keisha could finally see the logo. Bay and Creek Shipping. The same logo as the door of her cab. Keisha didn't know what to say to that.

"You're lucky Alice called me. We have a new truck for you. It's parked outside the wall. This one is, well, it's a write-off, got in a bad accident with a gate, but we won't take it from your pay-check."

Keisha stood there, feeling like a drained battery.

"So I still have a job?" was the best she could manage. The commander laughed.

"Ordinarily, no. You really fucked up the whole being-a-trucker part of your being-a-trucker job. You stole company property, and seriously messed up affairs with a big client of ours. You, in short, didn't do good. But"—she nodded back at the town of horrors—"as you can see trucking is only part of our concern. And you put an end to Vector H with your own hands. We've lost a few of our own trying to bring him down, so . . ." She put a hand on Keisha's arm, and Keisha flinched at the rare human contact. "We're gonna let this one slide. But don't steal and then wreck any more of our rigs, ok?"

Keisha nodded, grappling with all the information of the last few minutes.

"Keisha, listen," the commander said, "they ran when they saw us coming, but they won't be gone for long. It's truly incredible that you handled one of them, it really is, but you need to go before the rest come back."

She gestured to the truck. Keisha opened the door and stepped up into the cabin. It looked like her old one, except, of course, none of her stuff was in it. All her clothes and books, lost in a wreck, in a secret town, on a US government air base.

"Good-bye, Keisha," the woman said. "You'll hear from us again, I'm sure. Until then . . ." She thought for a moment, shrugged, and said, "I dunno, I guess keep doing what you've been doing. It's kept you alive this far."

Keisha started the engine. Left the Thistle town behind her. She was alive and she hadn't expected to be. She didn't know what to do with that. A couple hours later she pulled off the road just south of the Nevada border, next to a vast field of mirrors reflecting light up to a strange black tower. It looked like an alien starship, landed by a major highway an hour or so outside of Vegas.

If Alice didn't want Keisha looking for her, then she wouldn't for now. But she wasn't done. Because she had been looking in all the wrong places. Why did a trucking company have a private army? Why had they been secretly paying Alice for years? What was Bay and Creek? She had no idea. But she sure as hell was going to find out.

PART II

BAY AND CREEK

WHY DID THE CHICKEN CROSS THE ROAD?

Because the dead are born, because the dead grow and eat,
because the dead make bad decisions and good decisions,
because the dead love, because they love, that's why, but also
because the dead work and make things for the rest of the dead,
and then the dead slow and relax and lean back onto the time
that's given to them, and when there is no time left,
they allow themselves to stop and the dead finally die.

21

Alice hadn't been her first. There had been Mindy Morris in high school. Mindy and Keisha were friends and then knew they were more than friends and didn't know what to do about that and then figured it out. Keisha wanted it to be a secret, Mindy didn't. They kept it a secret. A lot of people knew anyway. Keisha was sure that she had successfully fooled her parents, but her parents knew. Except in some ways they didn't know. They knew, but didn't like it, and so made a choice to not know. People are capable of that, of knowing but choosing at the same time not to know. Eventually Keisha would tearfully tell them, and they would have to know then, and they were more ok about it than either they or Keisha had thought they would be. Later they would be completely fine with it. In between there was a period of adjustment. Not everything can be alright all at once.

When Keisha went to college, she and Mindy were still together. They would talk every day on the phone, and then every few days. And then it had been a while and they both realized they weren't together anymore, but still hung out on breaks when they were both back home. Toward the end of freshman year, there wasn't even that. In that moment of clarity that she was single, Keisha thought: *This is good. This is good. It's time to be single for a while. Learn more about myself. I'll stay single for at least a few years, and then see what happens.*

Two days later she ended up in a study group with a student named Alice. Remembering it now, it was possible she had thought nothing except that Alice was interesting and funny, and cute when she ran her hands through her hair. But Keisha chose to believe the version of her memory in which she had seen Alice the moment she had walked in and she had thought about her plan to stay single, looked across the table at Alice, and thought: *Well, shit.*

And now: routes and deliveries. A few cents a mile. Eating at truck stops. Sleeping in her cab. Back to the rhythm of existence as it had become for her in the last year or so. She needed a break from the mystery. A break from yearning. For now she would just go about her job, a job that recently she had thought was over for her. She had thought all things were over for her. Now she would stay out of trouble and try to live something like a normal life for a little bit. The mystery would be waiting for her whenever she was ready. There was no rush, now that Alice didn't want to be found. Keisha could be a human being for a bit.

Sylvia had reached out the morning after Keisha's night in Victorville. The night before, in the Extended Stay, she had felt a plummet in her gut, as though remembering a terrible event, but also knew with inexplicable certainty that the terrible event she was remembering hadn't happened yet. She didn't know how she could remember something from the future, but she had learned to trust herself and so she hid out in the parking lot, and that's where she had been hiding when two Thistle Men had opened her door as though the door were not locked at all, and then they came shambling back out and went to talk with the wide-eyed guy at the front desk. She thought it best if she disappeared back into the roads, but she left Keisha a few phone numbers of people who might be able to get to her if needed.

Keisha, meanwhile, saw the Bay and Creek commander not two weeks after their first meeting. The woman who had led a heavily armed team into the Thistle town was dressed like a truck driver, was driving a truck for the company. Was, Keisha supposed, actually a truck driver. At what point of pretending to do a job do you end up just doing the job? Keisha wondered for a moment why Bay and Creek hadn't kept their routes separate, but Keisha must have been below the company's interest. Perhaps even below the company's notice.

The commander was chatting with a warehouse worker at a distribution center outside of Omaha, at ease, a truck driver on a smoke break, talking, flirting maybe. As she winked at the warehouse worker and tossed her cigarette on the ground, he handed her a piece of paper, which she slipped into her pocket without reading. No, these two were not flirting. There were those dark currents again, surging under the precarious layer of Keisha's day-to-day life. She had a choice. The correct way forward, she decided, would be to forget this, to pick up her delivery, and scatter out to the Kmarts and supermarkets of the land.

Keisha had always found it difficult to do what was correct. She told her supervisors she needed a break, and they gave her one without comment. After all, they didn't pay her if she wasn't working, and like at any company, if she wasn't being paid, then she no longer had to be considered. *Go as long as you want*, she was told. *Let us know when you want to make money again.* She bought another cheap civilian car, using up the little bit of money she had earned since getting back into the life, and she waited outside that distribution center in Omaha. A week later she saw the commander again and followed her truck. Together they went to Chicago, where the city starts an hour out from the city limits, and then back up across the rolling green of Wisconsin over to Minneapolis, where the people retreat into tunnels during the fierce winter, and still none of the stops the commander made were unusual. No suspicious activity. Until she drove south and south until they reached the desert east of Los Angeles. She hadn't picked up a new shipment. There were no distribution centers in that region. She was driving an empty truck into empty land. Keisha followed.

Dead stop traffic in the San Fernando Valley. High above, way up there, on a power line, three tiny birds. They swayed as the line swayed; at any moment they could take off.

An hour later, over the hill into a plain of suburbia. Orange tiled roofs and the signs for Targets and Walmarts arrayed out into the distance like the flags of nation-states. Acres and acres of lot for every acre of store. Entire medieval cities could fit into one of these parking lots. At night, in the least lit corners, teenagers learned the best secrets of being an adult, before trudging, the next day, to their cashier jobs in the Target or the cell-phone stores to learn the worst secrets of being an adult.

Past Palm Springs, and south toward the Salton Sea. An expanse of salt water created accidentally by a flood and maintained by agricultural runoff. With no natural flow of water in or out, the sea is destined to die, evaporating back into salt plain and, because of the fertilizers in the runoff, subject to algae blooms that cause mass fish die-offs.

When Keisha was a kid, she lived near a good deal of agriculture, and from the road she and her friends could see a pond near the edge of some fields. The pond had a little island in the middle and trees all around it. The water was bright green. One day, they had snuck under fences, through fields, and to the pond. The pond bottom was lined with black plastic, something she realized only now was because they didn't want whatever was in that pond seeping into the groundwater. They swam for a couple hours. Then they went home, showered, and agreed there was something wrong about the water there, and never went back.

That's the story of the Salton Sea. All of California spent the '50s and '60s sneaking into a sea of agricultural runoff, and then realized that there was something wrong with the water and they should never go back. The resorts died, crumbling away or buried in mud.

And still the commander drove, into an area where there was no industry, where there were few people at all.

22

The sun was setting over the Salton Sea when they turned off the highway in a town called Niland, at the hollowed-out ruin of a corner store, still advertising beer prices on one of its remaining walls. In the ruin, there were a dog, a pony, and a horse all hitched together against a broken wall. Past this there was a scattering of houses and trailers, and then an electrical substation, bright lights and heavy security, and then some railroad tracks, and finally a concrete pillbox spray-painted with the words *Slab City. The Last Free Place.*

Slab City is a squatter's city. A mixture of gutter punks and anarchists and artists and retirees looking to make their pensions stretch. Anyone who wants a patch of land without worrying about paying for it. The last free place. The commander's truck rumbled ahead. As they moved into the barren places and the roads got emptier, Keisha let her get farther and farther away. A truck like the commander's would be easy to spot leaving. There was only one road into and out of Slab City.

It would have seemed to Keisha impossible that her life could be changed in the next few moments. But flashing blue and red lights cut through that night. She swore and pulled over. The old fear again, layered with new and fresh fear.

Several minutes passed. The lights flashed behind her. She stayed parked in the dry dirt, waiting. The slam of a door. The woman who got out of the police car was small, a wisp of person, flickering toward Keisha through the lights. When she reached the window, she stayed back. She had no bright flashlight in Keisha's eyes. She seemed almost meek, with her hands in her pockets. Her face was disjointed shadow, an eye here, the corner of a mouth, but no cohesion.

"Hello, I'm Officer . . . Clock," she said. "Do you have any idea how fast you were going?"

"I think I was . . ." Keisha had been driving in a dark desert on poor pavement. She had been driving at or below any possible speed limit. "How fast was I going?"

"I don't know. That's why I asked," the officer said. Her voice had a sigh to it, like it took her more breath than most people to talk. "What's your name?"

"Keisha. Uh, Keisha Taylor."

The cop nodded. Her hair was over her face. Nothing about her posture read cop. She seemed unsure. Like someone who had been dressed in a costume and shoved onstage without knowing which play she was in.

"No problem, Keisha. I'll need your license and registration, please."

"Sure. Right." Keisha gave her a fumble of paper and license, and the officer snatched it out of her hand like a bird pecking gingerly at feed.

"Ok. I will run these through the system. Sit tight." The woman flickered her way back through the lights and disappeared into the car.

The longer Keisha waited, the more convinced she was there was something deeply wrong about what was happening. Deeper than the usual terrifying dynamics of a situation like this. The officer's uniform had been loose, sloppy. Details in the wrong places. And the badge. The badge had looked plastic, like a child's toy. What would happen if she just started driving, driving out into the last free place? She put a toe on the gas, rested one hand on the keys. The road invited her forward.

"You can have these back." Keisha had not seen or heard the officer return. Her paperwork was thrust back through the window. The cop made no comment about Keisha's hand on the keys, and Keisha lifted her hand and accepted the proffered items.

"Thank you," Keisha said.

"Did you get a chance to visit the beach?"

"What?"

The officer gestured with a tilt of her head. Her neck was limp, not set correctly.

"Of the Salton Sea back there. Weirdest beach ever. The sand isn't right. Not the right texture."

The cop still had no flashlight, was slouched in a shadow between headlights.

"Then you look closer at the sand, you know, of the beach? And you realize. The sand isn't sand. It's fish bone. The beaches are made of bone here."

"Is there a problem, Officer?" A cliché but Keisha wanted this encounter to move into cliché. To make any kind of sense.

"I used to have this thing as a kid." The woman was whispering now, but even from a few feet away Keisha heard every word clearly. "I didn't like uncovered windows. At night I thought there was something out there watching me. Even if only a sliver of the window was uncovered. I would picture an eye pressed up against it. Then during the day it was different. I would imagine a monster shuffling around the house, and the monster would be arriving in that window soon and they would see me, but worse, I would see them."

"Was there a reason you pulled me over?"

"You were going fast." The officer leaned forward now, putting her thin arms on the car door. Keisha could feel the woman's breath, and that drove a spike of anxiety through her chest without knowing why. There was a detail her body had noticed but that her mind hadn't picked up on.

"I was going over the speed limit?"

"No idea." The woman laughed. "You were going fast. It's exciting. Anything moving fast, you want to chase it."

"What department do you work for? Are you a state trooper or . . . ?"

The officer glanced back. In silhouette her face appeared to be entirely made from straight lines.

"I'd have to check the car. I forget what it said when I got in it."

"When you got in it?"

"It was dark. I've gotten more used to the dark. I've grown as a person. I would have thought you'd be proud of me."

Keisha put her hand back on the keys.

"I need to see your badge."

The woman giggled. "Sure." She held it out. Keisha had to lean to see it.

"This doesn't say any department on it. And it says that you are a Police 'Instigator'?"

"I could take off both your arms."

An engine roared to life in Keisha's body, a thrum she felt from scalp to sole, but still her fingers stayed frozen on the ignition.

"With my own hands. No tools. I could take them off. I've done it before. It was easier than I thought it would be."

Finally Keisha found movement and the car came to life, but before she could shift the woman's hand darted out and shut the car off again. Her torso was in the car and here finally Keisha saw her face. There was no fat and her flesh was so thin as to be nearly transparent. Her eyes were sunken, her nose was tight around the cartilage. She seemed a paper person, every movement a paper movement, but her strength in forcing Keisha's hand on the keys had been unmistakable.

"Driving away would be an error."

"What do you want?"

The woman unfolded her torso back out of the car. She was the same size as before, but she no longer looked frail. She was an animal wound up to pounce.

"You know, it's been so long since anyone asked that. I was just thinking about it, standing on that beach made of bone, near a town with its cheery '50s resort sign still up, a woman on water skis in a bikini, and now the whole town's settling its way into the silt, and I was standing there thinking, what do I want? I don't know what I want. So let's instead think about what you want. You want to be careful. You've seen things. We don't like people who have seen things. I would say it makes us nervous, but we don't have the capacity for nerves, so more it makes us agitated. Makes us wild."

Keisha leaned out of the car now, thrusting her own body into the other woman's space.

"I've faced fiercer dangers and walked out alive," she said with a courage she did not feel but could sure as shit project. "You want me scared? Officer, you have no idea. I'm always scared. You think fear is new to me? You think fear is the novelty that will change my behavior? For me, fear is living. And I've lived this long, haven't I?"

The woman cocked her head, said nothing. "Haven't I?" Keisha repeated.

The officer crossed her arms over her chest. Her arms were much too long for her body.

"I like you. You're the most interesting one yet. I can see why they sent me."

"Who sent you? The police?"

Again that laugh, like porcelain falling on tile.

"You think the highest it goes is some thugs in blue? You think the Thistle Men could live in peace on an air force base because some state troopers are in on it? The police don't understand. I feed on the police."

"Try to feed on me. You wouldn't be the first." Keisha had made the decision that she wouldn't be afraid, no matter how afraid she got.

"I could dismantle you with just my teeth. I've done that too." The officer patted the car and walked away. She called as she went, not looking back. "My name is Officer Steak. I'll be seeing you around, Keisha. This is going to be a good time, I think. Isn't it so nice, you know, when you love your job?"

The cruiser started up again. It turned and headed perpendicular to the road, out into the desert. About fifty feet away its lights switched off and it was invisible, undetectable except for the fading hum of its engine.

Keisha laughed. She couldn't stop laughing. Every part of her was so afraid and she couldn't stop laughing. The Thistle Men had been hungry. But this woman was something else. Something a whole lot smarter and more powerful.

23

An entire day spent waiting and searching. Slab City, for its initial appearance of emptiness, was crowded with life and art. A sculpture garden made of discarded junk. A library tucked away among sage and trailers. A towering monument to Jesus made of hay and latex paint. A particleboard shack on a hill with a big yellow eye. No truck, though. No woman from Bay and Creek. The commander and her vehicle had disappeared into the homesteads and the squatters.

Keisha, still rattled, still rattling around inside her head, decided to give up the chase for a bit. Head north. Lie low and see where the commander resurfaced. If her routine was anything like it had been, it wouldn't be long before Keisha found her again. And she had no interest in staying anywhere near the woman whose named changed midconversation and who was definitely not a police officer.

She went up the West Coast for a couple long days of driving, going until her eyes went bleary and the road in front of her duplicated itself and she knew she needed to rest for a bit. Eventually she came to Cape Disappointment, a couple miles north of the Oregon border, and decided it was isolated and beautiful enough to stop.

The beaches were broad and solid enough that the locals drove on them. When she walked on them, she was often the only person in sight. Waves repeating themselves at the tide line, clouds of birds fluttering up and resetting. It made her feel safe being so alone. Then she thought about earthquakes and tsunamis. Both were coming for this region eventually. This area would have to pay for being beautiful lowlands by the ocean. Everyone just hoped the bill would come due after their life span.

As she walked, Keisha thought through the timeline. First the dogs would bark. They'd know before any human. Then she would have six to fifteen minutes. Ten to thirty seconds after the dogs start barking, the ground would shake. Six to fifteen minutes later the tsunami would come.

If she began running when the dogs started barking, could she make it through the grassy dunes and up to the hills? No. She could see the route to safety, but she couldn't outrun the wave. Six to fifteen minutes after the dogs started barking she would die. That's what would happen.

Each day, she finished her walk still alive. When what was coming for her would finally come, there would be no warning.

Her break wasn't entirely rest. She went to libraries and city halls and university archives, took the time to talk and to listen and to read. She kept her eyes on the margins of the highways, the weird places that people saw and then later believed they had misremembered. The things people know but choose not to know. She searched out stories that could easily be discounted and she didn't discount them.

She heard about a town called Charlatan that was encountered by different travelers in completely different parts of the country. A town unchained to geography. She heard about a black barge on the Columbia River, always floating at the same point, never moving with the current, crewed by the lost souls of the people who had unwisely searched for answers about it. She heard about a factory in Florida, on a remote beach, right on the water, that thrummed with activity but never seemed to have a single worker.

The country was full of these stories, often told but rarely listened to. She listened to them.

She heard something else too. A name she thought she had heard before. Praxis. No one seemed to know what Praxis was, what it stood for, if it was real or a fiction whispered by drunks with their elbows propped on sticky bars off quiet roads where once the mill traffic had passed. But wherever something was off in the country, there, too, was the name Praxis. A mystery hiding behind all other mysteries. She heard the name from dive bar regulars and from microfiche archives dusted off from city filing rooms and written in drooling spray paint on underpasses.

"Yeah," said one of those dive bar regulars, a woman named Mallory who would, three weeks later, slip and hit her head on the wet floor of a cereal aisle and find when she awoke that she could no longer stand the taste of alcohol, a change that she would think later likely saved her life, or at least her marriage, "I know Praxis."

"What do you know about them?" asked Keisha, who was growing tired of having conversations that always went a bit like this.

"They're unknowable, aren't they?" muttered Mallory as she got up and headed toward the door, skidding a bit on the freshly mopped barroom floor. "It is not for us to know. It is only for us to believe."

Keisha went north, drove until she hit Seattle. Following an instinct she didn't understand, she drove to the Fremont Troll. A huge piece of public art designed to rehabilitate the area, run off the lowlifes and drug dealers, bring in the tourists. But all had not been peaceful around the statue. Less than ten years after it was built, a man murdered the driver of a moving bus on the highway above, sending the whole bus, full of passengers, flying off the bridge, and crashing next to the troll. A few years later, twelve sheep skulls were found placed in a nearby yard. No one knows why. A prank, probably.

Or, Keisha thought, staring up at its concrete face and its hubcap eye, *worship*. There was worship here, she could feel, but she didn't know what was being worshipped. *Not the statue*, she thought. There was movement in the shadow by the troll's hand, and Keisha realized a person in a hoodie was standing there, watching her. Their hood was pulled far over their face. Their hands rested in the front pockets of the hoodie. Keisha could feel great power, as tangible as the giant concrete hands, as the gray hoodie.

And then the person was gone. Against every instinct, Keisha rushed forward, but no one was there. The sidewalk was visible well in each direction. The person in the hoodie had vanished. She thought again of the power she felt from them.

Yes, there was worship here. Worship of a being perhaps well worth worshipping.

24

Even as Keisha began to date Alice, she still thought of herself as committed to staying single. She didn't allow herself to understand what they were doing as dating. They were friends who sometimes had sex. They went on dates but weren't dating. Being with Alice felt better than anything, but there could always be something better. Never accept what she already had. Reach for what she could theoretically someday have.

She tried to be honest with Alice. "I'm not a good person to like," she would say. "I don't want a relationship right now."

"Sure," Alice would say, like Keisha had made an offhand comment about the weather. "Hey, let's drive to the beach."

The beach was cold and kind of miserable, but they took a walk anyway. Between a pile of rotting seaweed and an inlet where water poured from a metal pipe, Alice took Keisha's hand and spun her out and then back so that the two were facing, and they kissed for a long time. The beach smelled sharp, like milk about to turn, but neither of them could smell it. Keisha completely belonged to Alice at that point but hadn't realized it yet. Maybe Alice already knew.

It was Alice who said "I love you" first. They had been talking on the phone, and Alice got to class and needed to hang up. "Ok, I love you, bye," she said. Then she texted. "I think I said I love you. I do."

"I love you too," Keisha texted back and realized that it was true.

All this happened, no matter what happened after.

With no experience in corporate research or the structure of companies, little knowledge even of the basics of how a business was organized, Keisha did her best to trace the history of Bay and Creek. She searched the internet for public records and quickly found a seemingly endless number of layers, shell company after shell company. Some of the records, registered in sleepy, rural counties, had yet to be digitized and those she had to drive out for, make small talk with clerks at town halls that looked like residential houses while the clerk shuffled through a stack of paperwork that no one had ever needed anything from.

"What's all this for?" the clerk would ask, and Keisha would shake her head ruefully and give them an underling-to-underling look.

"Hell if I know," she would say. "My boss sends me after all sorts of weird things. Not my job to ask why."

"I gotcha," the clerk would answer, and then there would be ten minutes more of small talk before the record was found. But it only ever led to another shell company. Some companies seemed to, through several layers of other names, own the companies that owned them. A closed loop of corporate record keeping.

Keisha also looked for any record of an organization that went by the name Praxis. There was no sign of them in registered businesses. Whatever they were, they kept everything they did off-book. They did leave evidence, though she wasn't sure if this was intentional or not. Going back decades, even into the last century. Local legends that included the name Praxis. One story from the Civil War, a vision of motley-dressed dancers seen in the sky above a bloody battle, led to an academic paper no one had requested in over forty years that mentioned agents of Praxis carrying out missions of uncertain purpose during that war. Even which side those missions were meant to support was unclear, and the authors of the paper dismissed the reference to Praxis as a distortion of history through years of retelling. But Keisha believed in these agents of Praxis. She just didn't know what they wanted.

Risking discovery, she made tentative posts on a few message boards related to conspiracy, the kinds of places she would never have opened before her life became more complex than the most grandiose of conspiracy theories. Mostly her queries went unreplied to or were met with links to Wikipedia articles about strange cults or out-of-place artifacts, or, if the replier was lazy, aggregated lists with titles like "The 50 Creepiest Articles on Wikipedia (Number 16 Made Me Cry Out and Reach for My Partner in the Middle of a Sleepless Night)." But a few posters on a forum dedicated to government overreach mentioned that some of the terms Keisha was using reminded them of a woman named Cynthia O'Brien who used to post on the board but who had stopped abruptly a year or so before. Cynthia had been one of the names on the billboards in Georgia. A victim of the Hungry Man. Maybe Cynthia wasn't a random victim after all. Maybe none of the victims were random.

After three weeks of research across the country, Keisha was in North Carolina, leaving the library at Duke, where a reference to Praxis had been gathering dust for decades in a misfiled index that had taken three days to track down, and she saw a person in a hoodie down the road, peeking out from behind a low concrete wall. The hood was pulled low over their face, but the direction of their body was unmistakably oriented directly at Keisha.

"Hey," she shouted and ran for the person. It wasn't that she wasn't afraid. The only way to be brave is to first be afraid.

The person in the hoodie stepped back behind the wall. Keisha got to the wall a few seconds later. It was a small alcove for dumpsters, no outlet, and it was completely empty. She spun around, looking for where the person could have gone, and she saw them, impossibly, another hundred feet away, leaning against a tree in a parking lot. This time she sprinted, arms pumping. As she ran, the person casually pushed off the tree and stepped behind it.

"No, you don't," Keisha said, going full speed at the tree, and slapping her hands on the trunk to slow herself down. But again, there was no one there. At this time of night, the parking lot was mostly empty. There were no nearby cars, nothing for anyone to hide behind. She looked carefully around, but there was no sign of the person in the hoodie. As she started to walk back to her hotel, she looked up and felt all the sweat on her skin go several degrees colder. An old tobacco factory a quarter mile away. Tall stacks that emitted no smoke. On the roof of the old building, barely visible, but definitely there, a person in a hoodie with their hood pulled low over their face.

"What the fuck are you?" she shouted at it, and to anyone who happened to be in the area.

The figure in the hoodie didn't respond. Didn't move. So Keisha just kept walking toward her hotel. When she looked again a few moments later, the roof of the factory, and the street all around her, was once again empty.

25

After they graduated, Keisha and Alice lived in a tiny apartment in the Bay Area. The apartment was basically a kitchen with a bed in it, the bed itself barely big enough for the two of them. It was the only furniture they had and so they spent all day in it. They slept, ate, and talked, all on the cheapest mattress a small amount of money could buy. When they finally upgraded to a midrange bed, the guy who collected it said it had sagged more than any mattress he had ever seen.

Moving in together hadn't been easy. There were fights, discomfort. Two people with two lives figuring out how to shrink those lives to fit a tiny bed in the corner of a kitchen. Gradually Keisha realized it wasn't a constriction, but a rearrangement of terms. There was infinite space in that tiny apartment, if they could reorient themselves to find it. Soon they settled into this new way of living, and the two of them became a unit. It was the first step to having a life together.

The realization that their life as a couple could have the same length as the lives of their bodies didn't come until Keisha's father died. They stayed for a couple weeks in her mother's house on a guest bed that was bigger than the one in their apartment. Keisha was still in shock, and her head didn't feel attached to her body. One morning they lay facing each other, the sunlight lighting half of Alice's face. Keisha said, "I could spend my life with you." And Alice said, "That would be nice." They wouldn't get married for another few years, but that was the moment that the possibility of forever revealed itself to them.

Keisha returned to work. Miles meant pennies meant dollars meant a paycheck. But she didn't stop investigating. She reached out to friends at Bay and Creek. Forming friendships with co-workers in a workplace so diffuse was obviously tricky, but there were the folks at the distribution centers, and sometimes the shipments took a bit to work out and you'd hang and chat. That's how she had come to know Lynh. Lynh was a dispatcher, monitoring the routes and making sure every delivery was being made in the most efficient way possible. Bay and Creek had a complex proprietary software that tracked the route of every truck and calculated how to make the most money with the least amount of fuel and driver costs.

If Keisha wanted to know what was happening at Bay and Creek, access to that software system would be momentous. A picture of everything the company was doing at any given time.

"I'd love to settle down. Get off the road, get into dispatching, you know?" Keisha said.

"Sure," said Lynh, a little suspiciously. Keisha had gotten her to meet on the pretense of a friendly catchup but this was sounding awfully professional.

"But I don't have any training in that kind of thing, you know?" said Keisha. "If I could borrow your login, I could watch how it all works. That would give me the advantage I need the next time there's an opening. I promise I wouldn't touch anything. I just want to learn."

"It's not worth my job, sorry, dear," said Lynh. She sighed. She liked Keisha and had been looking forward to hanging out with her. Everyone wanted something from everyone, or at least that was Lynh's experience over forty-nine goddamn years of life.

"I'll give you two hundred dollars," said Keisha.

"Two hundred dollars still isn't worth my job. They take access to their system very seriously."

"A month. I'll give you two hundred dollars a month to let me watch how it all works."

Lynh eyed her over a bottle of light beer. "Why would you be willing to spend that much for this?"

"Because when I get a good job, I'll make back more than that. Help me out, Lynh. I don't want to drive a truck forever."

Lynh frowned but nodded at the same time. She didn't believe a word Keisha was saying. "I'll give you a training login. It allows you to watch but not change anything. Don't tell anyone at all. And don't let them know that you're looking to change roles. Companies these days. They value absolute loyalty from their employees but show no hesitation in dropping anyone at any moment."

"Thanks, Lynh."

"Don't mention it. And don't be silly. Two hundred dollars a month is ridiculous. I couldn't accept that."

"Well"—Keisha put her hand on her chest—"I really appreciate—"

"I'll take a onetime payment of four hundred dollars. Cash, please."

That was how Keisha got the access to monitor the entire Bay and Creek delivery system. She would stay up late, watching dots move across the country, the flow of fuel and pallets. More specifically, she found the truck the commander drove and followed its assignments. None of them were unusual. She wondered if Bay and Creek had noticed they were being watched and so were being more careful. Or if the commander's side trips weren't noted in their official system, which was more likely. Keisha wondered if this was all a kind of busywork for herself. Like in the grief groups, she was still trying to describe the shape of the monster that was devouring her. She watched the Bay and Creek system until her eyes went dry and red and heavy, and she fell asleep despite herself.

26

Jerry Morrisette had been a medic in Vietnam, an alcoholic, a monk. He was hired by Caltrans to run a maintenance crew at the Crystal Springs Rest Area in 1990. He parked a decommissioned ambulance behind the bathroom and lived in it. At the time, the rest area, convenient to San Francisco, but also conveniently rural, was a popular site for drug trade and gang conflict.

Jerry tended the grounds like they were his own garden, because that's what they became. The bathrooms were always impeccable, with vases full of flowers on the sinks. Eventually he moved out of the ambulance into a Caltrans maintenance shed. To help keep crime away, he painted some of the parking spots with "Reserved for California Highway Patrol" and it worked. The drug trade and the gangs moved. Jerry went on living, unknown to the State of California, in a rest area he sometimes referred to as his monastery.

A few years later, the state found out and tried to evict him. But the people of the Bay Area fought for him, and Jerry was made official. The state put up a trailer for him and he moved in, with two dogs, Butch and Spike. And the bathrooms were clean. And there were flowers in the vases.

Keisha smelled the garlic from ten miles out. Gilroy, California, is where the nation's garlic is grown, and the smell permeates the whole area. From Gilroy, Keisha followed the 101 through the town of Coyote and up toward San Francisco. About a half hour out she had to pee and laughed at the thought of trying to stop a truck in the city and find a toilet. As though an answer to that specific prayer, she saw a sign for the Crystal Springs Rest Area and flipped on her blinker.

Even though the lot was full, the bathroom was empty. There was a glass vase full of fresh flowers on the sink. Keisha chose the stall in the back corner. She had read once that the first stall, most visible to the rest of the bathroom, is also always the cleanest because people choose it less. She didn't know where she had read that, had no way of knowing if it was true, but had spent the rest of her life believing it.

"What have you seen?" a voice asked from the stall next to her. The stall had definitely been empty when she had walked by it moments before. It wasn't empty anymore. The voice sounded like an MP3 from the early 2000s. Flat and faint. "Two of you, like now," the voice said, "but two of you. Later. Soon. Or already. I can't tell." The feet in the stall next to hers shifted. The person was sideways, facing the divider.

"I'm sorry, I think you have me mixed up with, uh . . ." Keisha didn't know how to finish that sentence, then realized she didn't have to and so left the stall and headed for the sink. The stall next to hers was open, and empty. She stared at it. Someone had been in that empty stall. And as she thought that, the stall stopped being empty. A person in a hoodie, the hood pulled over their face.

The person was slumped, looking at their feet, whispering to themselves. Then they were standing. Not that they stood, but that they were sitting and the next moment were standing. Then they were at the sink, running their hand over the flowers in the vase, still whispering. And then they were looking at Keisha. Their hands tearing at the petals. They murmured louder. Keisha sprinted for daylight like it was her next heartbeat, and as she did she was able to pick out one word from the whispers.

"Praxis."

It started with the death of a dog. Spike died, and Jerry Morrisette started drinking again. His work suffered. He phoned a Caltrans supervisor who he believed had poisoned his dog and threatened him. Police came, his trailer was searched, three guns were found. Why did Jerry Morrisette have three guns? Well, he did live in a parking lot that once was frequented by drug trade and gangs. Or maybe it was because he lived in America, and so for better or worse, or worse, or worse, he could.

The state began eviction proceedings. Insult of all insults, they didn't let him clean his bathrooms anymore, brought in another worker to do it. The state even cast doubt on the most fundamental aspects of his story. Maybe there hadn't been so much crime at the rest area before. Maybe Jerry Morrisette hadn't done much more than be real good at cleaning. His single-handed transformation of a troubled place into a peaceful garden might have merely been good PR.

An article from 2014 said he moved to a trailer in South San Francisco. As of that article, he had been given six months to live.

Cancer, of course. Always cancer. There is no more sign of Jerry Morrisette on the internet after that. Presumably he died, but this story does not contain that certainty. These are the only facts that this story contains: there was a man who had gone to war and come back, and gone to religion and come back, and who turned a rest area into a place of worship for a few years, and then his dog died and it all ended. There's no moral to this story, but there is a real human life.

Keisha's first instinct was to drive until the tank was empty. Instead she climbed a trail from the rest stop up the hill behind it. At the end of the trail was a statue of a man, bulbous and ill-formed, pointing at the highway like he was scolding the passing cars. The plaque said it was Father Junípero Serra. He was lumpy and squat with a drooping face, the shape of a human, but not put together right, and stuffed into skin that wasn't the correct size. It was, she realized, a statue of a Thistle Man, pointing at all his potential victims in the passing cars. She descended the trail and, without letting herself hesitate, went back toward the bathroom.

A family of laughing women from three different generations went in right before her. At least she wouldn't be alone in there. But the bathroom was empty. The air felt different from the air outside. Much cooler. A smell like a slow river, somewhere between clear water and algae. There was a vase with flowers on the sink. She examined each stall. Empty. Movement behind her, and she turned to see a man with a long graying beard, wearing an orange safety vest, carefully arranging the flowers in the vase. "Excuse me," he said, the details of his form lost in the dimness. He nodded slightly and left.

She looked back at the stalls. The person in the hoodie was sitting in the middle stall, folded over at the waist, and whispering at the floor tiles.

"Hello?" Keisha said.

The whispering got faster, more urgent.

"Hello?" she tried again.

"You again," said a voice to her left. The person in the hoodie was sitting on the sink, legs dangling. They were barefoot and their feet were filthy. "Or is this the first time?"

"Who are you? What do you know about me?"

"I am an oracle. In hidden places on the highways, in the bathrooms at gas stations, behind the painted scenery of roadside attractions, in vans parked far out in the grassland. There are oracles on these roads."

"You can see the future."

"You misunderstand me."

"You said you were an oracle. What did I misunderstand?"

"You misunderstand *me*. You don't understand what I am."

"Why don't you help me understand?"

"I want to help you," they said. They were back in the stall, flopped backward against the tile like a person unconscious. "You are in danger."

Keisha snorted. "Some prediction."

"You don't understand the danger," they said.

"There's a war."

"Yes."

"And I'm caught between the sides."

"Yes."

"So that much I understand."

"You don't even understand the most basic shape of it," they said.

Keisha asked the question that seemed to be the heart of all of it.

"What is Praxis?"

The person in the hoodie rose, hanging limply from their up-stretched arms as though held on invisible hooks. "Many dead at the hands of Thistle."

"Yeah, they're serial murderers."

"Killers without direction. Without purpose. Or so they'd like you to believe."

They came toward her, bare toes dragging on the pristine floor. When they were close, she could smell, unmistakable and over-powering, heather.

"One of their murders holds a secret."

"Which murder?"

"I can't tell you," they said.

"Why can't you tell me?"

"Because," the oracle said. "I didn't. Because in this moment I don't tell you. I am always here, and I am always not telling you. I'm sorry." They put their hands on Keisha's shoulders. "The pipes burst in the library in Oklahoma, but all is not lost. It wasn't lost."

A library in Oklahoma. Burst pipes. There had been a mention of that in Officer Campbell's emails. Keisha couldn't remember the details.

The oracle leaned close and Keisha saw for a moment, within the hood, two human eyes, and the wet-reflected light of tears falling from them.

Laughter. One of the women from the family was coming out of a stall. The other two were at the sink. They were laughing about the brother of the woman in the stall, who had insisted on buying a number of paper maps rather than using his phone but then couldn't even read the maps correctly. Keisha stood shivering against the sink. One of the other women side-eyed her but didn't ask if she was ok. The three left the bathroom. There was no vase on the sink, no flowers. The floor was muddy and trod on, hadn't been cleaned in a while. She stayed there a long time, trying to put some version of herself back together again, and then shaky, but her, she stepped out into the light.

27

Keisha had to pee again and there were no towns in this part of Death Valley. But there were also no cars. The dark clouds lingered. She pulled her truck onto the muddy shoulder. It was strange, squatting by this highway, and looking for miles into the distance, and seeing no one. She enjoyed the absolute silence of distance. She was alone here.

It was in this area that Cynthia O'Brien's body was found. It wasn't where she lived, but she was murdered on vacation, while staying at one of the hotels in the national park. Later her papers would be moved to a library near Tulsa, where they were destroyed by a burst pipe, and then asked after by Officer Campbell. Keisha had no idea if this was the murder that the oracle had meant, and if the place where the murder had happened held any significance at all, but still she had come. Here she was, trying to approach the mystery.

Not far away, Officer Floor watched. She had been following Keisha since the Salton Sea. Here there were no towns, no watchers to watch her watching. Pull a little off the road, cut the lights, and a person becomes invisible. To take a few uncertain years from someone's life, is that so much of a crime? What are those years worth, and would Keisha have even gotten them anyway? Isn't it better to die in a purposeful, clear way than to stagger on until a superfluous organ starts making its cells wrong?

Of course, the officer might choose to not even provide the generosity of a graceful death. How humiliating, for instance, to die peeing in the dirt. But instead she lay back on the hood of her car, enjoying its warmth, and looking up at a sky promising rain, a sky as gray and blank as slate. A sky about to break into violence.

The officer closed her eyes and waited.

If she had a name, her name was Thistle. But she had no name. There was no separating her from Thistle. She and it were born in the same instant. Even she could not explain her history. Her first memory was of clawing out of mud after a long rain, but perhaps that was not her first birth. There may have been earlier births in simpler forms that she does not remember. Back then she didn't need to look human and so she didn't. She took all sorts of forms: a bird of prey with long white feathers, a burrowing creature with long white teeth, a plant with thorns that broke off and putrefied in the flesh. Her name and form did not interest her. What interested her was the effect she could have on the world.

Once humans came, she mimicked them, seeing in them a unique opportunity to cause new pain. It is difficult to track her history once she blended in with people. Which were acts of isolated human cruelty, and which were influenced by her whispering?

In 1873, a traveling doctor and salesman of cure-all medicine arrived in the town of Okmulgee, Oklahoma. The sign on his wagon said THISTLE MODERN MIRACLES OF HEALTH! He spoke and sold in town for a few days and moved on. His assistant, a small woman who introduced herself variously as Miss Wheel and Miss Night, took the coins and offered in exchange vials of a dark blue and bitter medicine. Three weeks later, everyone who had tried the medicine died of a lingering and painful condition that manifested first as a red bulging in the skin and then incurably infected the brain. The town doctor died himself before he could give an educated opinion of the plague, having disbelieved in the medicine but having sampled it for his own edification, and by the time another doctor was allowed to see the bodies, they had disintegrated into a marshy sponge that smelled peppery and sour.

The inconsistently named officer, who in this moment called herself Officer Arm, continued after Keisha. Past the larger towns were the mining towns, a few houses and a school attached to a quarry, and a processing plant. It was dusk and the plants were still churning. Busy workers, for now, until their jobs went too. Everyone's jobs are expendable, except the officer's. That kind of violent hunger is always in demand. She could sleep a thousand years and wake up to a world that needed her.

A man stopped his car to take a picture. The expanse was majestic. The officer stopped too. She put him into the bushes and left him there. Then she got in his car and pulled it back on the road. Always a good idea to switch vehicles.

She could taste bitter on the tip of her tongue and she tried to hold it there. Tried to make the bitter taste linger. There was a coyote up ahead. The coyote was waiting for the officer's approaching car, standing in the middle of the road, calm. The officer slowed her car and held the animal's brown eyes with her own, and they understood each other. Low creatures, taking blood where they could, as natural as the salt flats, as natural as a rock face. They kept quiet eye contact for several minutes. When people saw her, they tended to look away. They recognized that she was not something they wanted to know. But the animal met her gaze blankly. The officer winked and told the coyote that she needed to get back to her own prey, as she was sure the coyote needed to get back to hers. As she drove away, the coyote watched, unmoving.

1901. Chicago. Thirteen missing children over one summer. Disappearances traced to a new shop. Thistle Goods and Butchering. Staff and owners disappeared before questioning but were described by neighbors as a crew of oddly shaped men acting under the orders of a small, frail woman who called herself Madam Tile. The evidence found in the shop required the complete demolition of the structure, as the horrors there made it beyond rehabilitation.

1955. Missoula. The only synagogue in town burned down by a group of men with faces that no one would admit they recognized as their friends and neighbors. A federal investigation of the crime was cursory, and most of the witnesses were deemed unreliable due to their repeated insistence that a woman was seen walking through the flames in the building, passing through the heat and singing. The case was closed with little investigation. Most of the Jewish community moved away. People didn't talk about the burning much, and soon even the witnesses wouldn't say that they had been there. Many saw the woman from the fire again and again, drinking in local bars, talking in low tones with groups of local men.

Most of the buildings in Death Valley Junction are still in ruins. A former dormitory for employees at the borax mines. Then in 1967, a ballet dancer named Marta Becket broke down in the town and stumbled on a small abandoned theater that the employees once used as a community room. She moved from New York City to this town, where she and her husband were most of the population, and she began ballet shows in the desert three times a week. Many performances, no one would show up, and so over the years she painted an audience on the inside of the theater, so that there would always be someone watching. She died in 2017, but there is still a ballet dancer who does a weekly show to guests at the attached hotel.

Cynthia O'Brien's body was found five miles from town, on a highway leading to the nearest casino. Keisha drove out to the spot, or as near as she could figure it. It looked like any other spot on the road. Miles away, a cloud cast a shadow directly down onto a low round hill, and to Keisha it looked perfect, like a landscape painting. She wasn't used to being able to see this far in the distance. She stood in the place where Cynthia was found, or where she thought Cynthia was found, and then she drove away, not knowing more than she had known before.

Keisha stayed at the hotel by Marta's theater, with its musty carpet and Marta's paintings on the wall. There was a café that was only open a couple days a week but was surprisingly good. She didn't know how they made money with a restaurant open only two days a week in the middle of nowhere. But she felt grateful for people who come to places like this and do things like this: dance, and make food for strangers. Good people deserve good things.

The officer curled up inside one of the ruins of the town. She enjoyed how cold it got at night. It was time for her to switch cars again, so when a tourist couple pulled into the unlit lot, she helped herself to them and then to their vehicle. She felt grateful for people who come to places like this.

A hundred years ago, and fifty years ago, and ten years ago. "Perhaps we can help each other," said the woman with many names, to the government official who frowned. He didn't ask how she could help him. He knew. There were always troublemakers. People who didn't go with the program. Communists. Civil rights agitators. Even plain old liberals. A government can only do so much directly against these degenerates without risking the title of democracy. But a band of serial killers with this woman at the heart of them? They could cause all sorts of useful chaos. "Perhaps we can help each other," said the woman with many names, and the government official felt his skin crawl, but he nodded. "Yes, I think we can." She smiled. She had this conversation with many government officials, over many years, and they always said yes. No one could resist the terrible freedom she offered.

Her side of the bargain would be providing an excuse to take care of enemies and troublemakers. Their side of the bargain was to merely stand aside and offer no obstacle as she sowed the kind of freedom she hungered for.

• •

Keisha just wanted to make it to the next dry place. Lakes formed suddenly. Soon all of the land on either side of the road was water, waves lapping at an asphalt shore. Keisha's truck made it through this and up the mountains into a narrow pass. The rain was worse. The only way out was through.

A few miles from the flatlands, Keisha eased around a precarious corner and had a moment of, *What is that in the road?*, and then a bang and the bottom of her cab was dragging. A huge rock. She pulled the truck to a stop. There was nowhere to move it on a road so narrow, so she only had to hope her lights would prevent collisions.

She got on her stomach and crawled under the cab. She was downhill of the wheels of her truck, and she thought, *Ok, so this is how I die.* The rock was jammed into the bottom of the cab. She tried pulling on it, but it didn't budge. A car whipped around the corner and swerved to miss her. Mud all down her body. She turned her head and felt her heart skip as she saw a pair of legs standing by the driver's-side door.

"Hello," she shouted and crawled out, banging her head on the front bumper. "Did you stop to help?" as though anyone had ever done that for her. But no one was there. She got back in her cab and started driving, the rock scraping on the road, sounding like the cab itself was coming apart. And then one last terrible ripping sound and the rock fell away. She stopped at Stovepipe Wells, a motel dressed up as a western village. There was a terrible smell, like burning rubber. And she thought, *Oh, my engine is fucked.* But even away from her truck, the smell persisted. The wind was saturated with it. The next morning she realized that she was smelling mesquite trees.

Almost. The officer wiped a little mud off her shoe. *That was almost it. Smell the sage and the mesquite. It could be peaceful as you went.* She smiled fondly at Keisha in the distance. Another time, then. The officer was in no hurry.

1983. Olive, Montana. Elizabeth Harris, one of the last children to grow up in a town that would soon fade from existence except as a name on a map. She was playing in a field near her house when she came across a deep hole she had never seen before. Peering into the hole she saw at the bottom a small, frail woman. The woman's face was covered in blood, and her eyes were looking back up at Elizabeth. The woman began to sing, in a sweet, high voice. "O, martyrs," she sang. "O, soldiers of a lower cause." Elizabeth turned and ran. She would not put together until later that evening, but subsequently would be unable to forget, that as the woman sang she had been slowly floating up out of the hole toward the surface. Elizabeth moved away from Olive as soon as she was old enough and dreamed of that woman's song and the whites of her eyes floating slowly upward at least once a month for the rest of her life.

28

Keisha spent weeks watching the commander's routing in the Bay and Creek system, but none of it was out of the ordinary. The only way forward was the tedium of comparing the routing in the system to the commander's actual physical movements. This time Keisha didn't bother switching to a car, just did her best to be inconspicuous in a truck, which on crowded highways was not difficult. After all, the sky is pretty big but people still go whole days without noticing it.

Soon she realized that, sure enough, often the commander's route strayed from what was set out for her in the efficient routings of the system. Not by much, but little detours that made no sense, that definitely slowed down delivery. Any point where these detours happened was a point worth investigating, but Keisha only had one body and one life and so she chose a stretch of farm road in Georgia that the commander often took even though the highway would save her over an hour.

Keisha researched the properties along that farm road. There weren't that many to research, as the acreage of each was sprawling. Most were old family farms that had been bought out by a larger company that merged with another company and then was bought again and so were the property of the agricultural division of a corporation with a main business of manufacturing hard drives for laptops, or other similar corporate clusterfucks.

But one farm was different. It was owned by a company that was owned by another company, which also did business under the name of a third company that was owned by the original company. A perfect, impenetrable ring of shell ownership, the source leading back to itself without giving away anything true. Keisha had seen this before. That farm belonged to Bay and Creek.

On her next off-week, she went to the farm, bumping over the drive that had reverted to a groove in the tall grass. It didn't look like a tire had touched this ground in many years. The house itself was half reclaimed by plants, a tree growing through into the second floor, windows gone or boarded up, walls shrugging themselves back into the ground. The front door had fallen down and the frame itself was buckling. *Please don't collapse on me*, she thought.

Inside, everything was covered in dust and pollen. A few cans in the kitchen, corn and beans, and a half-empty Yoo-hoo container. In the bedroom, a mattress, mostly rotted away, leaned on the wall. She was afraid to climb the stairs. She wouldn't trust them to hold. She sat on a faded green couch in the living room, hoping that nothing was living inside of it. Here was only abandonment. A family who staked their lives on the health of the fields only to be undone by age or disease or bad loans. Or, more probably, never a family. Every broken plank of wood, every sagging wall, a reconstruction, a fake.

And if it was a fake, then it was a fake for a reason. It was a hiding place. She got up and went back over the debris, carefully looking for any sign of disturbance in the heavy layers of dust. But there was nothing. She went through the unbroken grime of the kitchen with her flashlight. This time, she noticed that the dust covering the stove looked different from the rest. She ran her finger along it, and her finger came back clean. She leaned close, saw the lack of depth to the dust, and felt the slow dawning. The dust was painted on. The rest of the dust in the kitchen was real, but on the stove it was painted. And also on the floor, she realized, in front of the stove. Fake dust. Fake grime. She examined the stove inch by inch. On one of the dials, over the painted dust, she found a fingerprint. She felt such fear then. All she wanted to do was go away from this place, to run back to the truck and drive until the state line was behind her. But instead she put forward her shaking hand and turned the dial. There was a click and the stove swung toward her. Behind was a staircase.

The staircase had a switch at the top. She flicked it and a series of fluorescents popped on. It was a clean, industrial staircase, with a blind turn at the landing. She made her way down, ready at any moment for a shout, or a gunshot, or some strange creature of the roads to come up from the depths and meet her. But when she turned the corner of the landing, she saw one last flight and then a large metal door. She descended to it and tried the handle, but it was sealed shut and looked impervious to any force she would be able to muster. There was no way in for her. But she knew one of Bay and Creek's secrets. And she would hold on to that secret until she could understand how it could be useful for her.

29

They were married long before they were married, which is a common enough story. For straight people, too, these days, Keisha guessed, but that's a choice on their parts. There was a bit of triumphant defiance in calling Alice her "wife" without the official paperwork. *We don't need your say-so to be enshrined in love. We only need our own.* Still, the rights of two women together are fragile enough. Without the auspices of marriage, who knew what would happen if one of them ended up dead or in the hospital. It was easier and clearer to set everything into the lawbooks.

And she found that even though she hadn't given much thought to the wedding, as she went through the process it did end up meaning something to her. They were married in their living room, by Margaret, who would one day be the last of their friends to stick around for Keisha after the rest had been driven away. Looking back, Keisha didn't know if Alice had been planning her disappearance even then.

They honeymooned in Hawaii, spending more money on the honeymoon than the wedding. Which were they more likely to remember, after all? A big dinner party where they were stressed out and tired, or a trip that was the two of them exploring a place they had never been? They lay out by the adults-only pool of the resort and were given complimentary alcoholic popsicles by the pool staff and rode horses together, which Alice loved and Keisha most definitely did not. Riding horses was just like walking, she decided, only to go anywhere you first had to persuade a gigantic toddler that they wanted to go there too.

This was still a happy memory for Keisha, despite the pain that came after. Happiness is not negated by subsequent pain. But it does make the possibility for future happiness seem dimmer. Every good moment is shadowed by the question of that moment's longevity.

Keisha hadn't heard from Sylvia since making sure she had escaped from the Extended Stay, and it seemed a good time to get in touch and compare what they had found. She looked through the information Sylvia had left her. A patchwork of, not friends, but friendly faces of people she sometimes crashed with. Gutter punks and squatter houses, leftist co-ops and college students with old rental houses in neighborhoods near the campuses. Keisha emailed and phoned, but most of the contact information was out of date and she came up again and again against mailer daemons and sympathetic recorded voices, explaining to her that she had gotten something wrong and so kindly fuck off.

Then she got through to Tanya, who ran an anarchist study group in Chattanooga. He (Tanya was a man, but he liked his birth name. His mother had named him before she died, and he didn't see why societal expectations of gendered names should make him change it) was suspicious and said that even if he knew where Sylvia was, he couldn't tell a caller he didn't know. "That girl has some dangerous elements after her," he said. "Boy, don't I know it," said Keisha. "Then you understand," he said. He did offer to pass on Keisha's name and current contact information.

"Not directly, you understand," Tanya said. "Don't get any ideas that I have a line on her. But I can ask around to the right people."

"Thank you so much," she said.

"Yeah," he said. His voice changed, became softer, and a little worried. "I don't know who you are, what you're doing. But if you're on the same path as Sylvia, please be careful. We need every one of us."

"I'll try. Best I can do."

"Best any of us ever can. Ok, Keisha. Good-bye now."

That night Keisha got on the CB radio again, for the first time since Victorville. It had made her sick, knowing that Thistle had heard her. But she liked talking into it more than she cared if Thistle was listening.

"There's a sense of family," she said, "that forms between people who have to travel a lot for work, no matter what that work is. Corporate suits flying to sales meetings twice a week. A drummer who sits in the back of a van eight months out of the year. People like me, driving our trucks."

She leaned back in her seat, looking up at the stars. The volume on the radio was all the way down. She didn't want a conversation, especially now that she knew who was listening. She just wanted a place to put her thoughts.

"You can recognize the look in the other's eyes, this feeling of having seen too many miles in too short a time. You can compare stories about Cleveland and about Ann Arbor and Birmingham and Fort Lauderdale. They know the romance and they know the despair and so you don't have to talk about either. You can ask them how the Hampton Inn is in Madison, Wisconsin, and they'll know exactly what you mean."

She turned the radio off, went to bed. Sylvia called three days later.

"I'm in Upstate New York," Sylvia said, jumping past any how have you beens, are things going oks. "I need you to get up here."

"What's there?" asked Keisha.

"An answer, maybe. I want to find out who really killed my mother." Sylvia hung up. Five minutes later, she texted Keisha an address. Keisha tried calling back, but it went to voice mail.

30

Sylvia saw it first that night. A man twitching near the dumpster. She thought he had been injured or was a drug addict. Her stomach bottomed out as she realized it was a crouching man, thrashing at a person below him. Sylvia saw but could not comprehend that the man was eating the other person.

"Mom," she had whispered. "Mom." And her mom turned, and, bless her forever, she did not run like Keisha once did. She set her jaw, said, "Sylvia, honey, you get inside the station and find somewhere to hide." And she pulled out her phone to call the police.

Sylvia told Keisha all this in a motel room in Saugerties, about forty minutes from the gas station, which was still open, although it had recently changed brand names. Keisha found her there, waiting on her bed, door cracked open. The motel was only one floor, a line of doors with a parking space in front of each. The room smelled like furniture polish and wet leaves. When Keisha stepped into the room, Sylvia cried out and launched herself from the bed. It had only been four months, but they had been a long four months for them both. They hugged and Keisha felt again how small the girl was. It wasn't fair, her having to go against the whole world like this.

"But it wasn't only the Thistle Man," she said. "There was a second person there. I want to know who they were. I want to know who killed her."

Her luggage was a trash bag full of a mix of clean and dirty clothes. A mostly empty bottle of heather oil. She had a toothbrush but had run out of toothpaste a couple days ago and hadn't had a chance to buy more. A copy of *Penny Century* by Jaime Hernandez.

"Thanks for introducing me to *Love and Rockets*, by the way," Sylvia said, nodding at the book. "Need stories like that when you don't have people around you."

"Sylvia, have you been taking care of yourself?" Keisha knew that she sounded like a mother, but maybe that's what Sylvia needed. Sylvia looked like she couldn't decide whether to be annoyed and instead smiled gratefully.

"I'm alive, aren't I? We're both alive, and that's no small achievement."

"No, I suppose it isn't."

"I don't even know what taking care of myself would look like at this point." She shrugged at her bag of things. "Probably not this, I guess. But I don't have more, so it has to be enough."

Keisha sat down in the armchair by the window and immediately wished she hadn't. It smelled like a mouse had recently died on it. She got up.

"The two of us have done a lot of settling," Sylvia said.

"Our lives are a compromise," Keisha agreed.

"But maybe someday, they won't have to be."

Sylvia looked so earnestly hopeful that it broke Keisha's heart.

"Yeah," she said, with the most hope she could muster, "maybe."

The Taconic State Parkway is beautiful, a road that meanders. It feels like taking a walk in the woods. But taking a walk in the woods is something best done slowly, on foot, not speeding in a car. It is a dangerous road. No streetlights. Sharp turns. Long stretches with no shoulder, just a rock face on one side and a thin barrier on the other. If life is a balancing act between beauty and danger, then the Taconic is paved right down the middle.

The Sunoco station where her mother had been killed was off the Taconic. Sylvia walked around the station, putting on a show of careful investigation, but with shaking fists clenched tight at her sides. This place, for her, was a wound.

"We're not going to find anything here," she said.

"No," said Keisha.

"It's been years. There wouldn't be any physical evidence left."

"No."

She nodded, put her hands on her hips.

"Her name was Sylvia too. My mom. People got so confused about her making me Sylvia Junior. Women aren't supposed to do that. They'd think they misheard. There was like six months when I was fourteen that I hated it and insisted on being called Ace, but I got over it."

She turned away from the crime scene that was a few years too late to give up its answers.

"Well, shit," she said.

. .

Sylvia had come back out when her mother started shouting. The lights had dimmed on that side of the station. There was no sound of police coming, of anyone coming, of any help at all.

"You wanted to see," the Thistle Man said, in a voice that oozed out of his throat. He dragged one leg forward, the rest of his body leaning backward. "Now you will see."

Sylvia stepped toward them, but her mother caught her eye. And her mother put up one hand. *You stay away. You hide.*

"And I did, I guess. I don't remember what next, it's all sorrow and blood, but I do remember a couple hours later, huddled up in the brush on the other side of the Taconic, hiding. I remember footsteps in the leaves nearby, I guess the Thistle Man looking for me, but he never found me. Still hasn't."

But that was not the whole story. Someone else was there with the Thistle Man. Sylvia remembered a person wearing a hoodie, standing next to her mother, right at the end. In the darkness, Sylvia couldn't pick out any more details. Just the Thistle Man, and the figure in the hoodie, small, faceless, with their arms out toward her mother. Someone helped the Thistle Man kill her mother.

Keisha thought about a bathroom at a rest stop south of San Francisco. The smell of heather. The jittering movement. Who were these oracles, haunting these roadside places, and what cause did they serve?

Unsure of what else to do, they went the next morning to the Dutchess County Sheriff's Office in Poughkeepsie. The woman at the front desk seemed friendly. An older woman. Definitely not police anymore, if she ever was one.

"Can I help you?" she asked. A good question that Keisha was unsure of the answer to.

They explained they were looking into a murder that happened a few years ago. Gave the details. She did some searching on the computer.

"Huh," she said. "This isn't right."

"What is it?" asked Sylvia.

"The case was closed. I don't know why that would have happened. It's a murder investigation, double homicide, only a few years old, and no suspects arrested. Why would they close this?"

She frowned, reading through the notes they had on file.

"Why would they close this?" she said again. Her tone wasn't confusion, but despair. She knew exactly why they had closed it. She looked up at the two of them, lips half open, holding what she had to say next uncertainly in her mouth, and then finally let it slip.

"Go have lunch, at the Palace Diner. It's around the corner. Food's good there."

They thanked her and went to the diner, a twenty-four-hour institution, with a sprawling parking lot and its own in-house bakery. The kind of diner impossible to find outside of the Northeast.

"Hey," said Keisha, after they had ordered. "Have you ever heard the name Cynthia O'Brien?"

Sylvia shook her head. "Why? Is she important?"

"I don't know. She was murdered. I think by the same people who murdered . . ."

"Oh." They didn't talk after that.

Sylvia was halfway through a chicken salad sandwich and Keisha was stealing Sylvia's fries when the woman showed up, holding a filing box.

"I want you to know," said the woman, "that there are some of us who don't believe in it. Who believe that this is wrong, what they're doing. I want you to know that we are not all on their side."

The woman looked around briefly, felt satisfied that no one was paying attention in the crowded diner, and put the box under the table.

"There isn't much, but take it. Not me. At least not me."

She turned and left without waiting for a response. The waiter asked if they were ok on their coffees. They were ok.

31

There are vineyards in the Hudson Valley among the apple or-
chards. A serious effort to create a wine industry. New York wine
is so-so at best. But as the climate changes, who knows? Certainly
the areas famous for wine will lose their climate, and so one of
these places that are a laughingstock among wine snobs will
become the new Bordeaux. Either that, or everyone will be too
busy being refugees from the drowned cities to worry about wine.

Keisha and Sylvia drove past vineyards to a motel room in
which they were two of fifteen living creatures. The box was almost empty. No real investigation done on the case. The police
knew who the killer was, and so officially had no leads. The bare
minimum of paperwork, which is still a lot of paperwork, but
none of it said anything. Restating basic physical facts of the
scene. Describing actions taken by the responding officer in a
step-by-step style of writing designed to intentionally repel the
reader through tedium.

But there was one item of interest. A manila envelope, folded over and mummified in packing tape. Keisha performed surgery with the knife from her bag. Inside was a videotape.

"Camera at the gas station?" she said.

"Oh, god, I hope," Sylvia said. She frowned at it. "How do we play this?"

"Jesus, you make me feel old."

The area was full of high-end antique stores run by transplants from Manhattan. They skipped all those and went to the grimiest secondhand store they could find, a basement shop with a window display cluttered with childlike paintings of animals flying kites and riding skateboards. There was a taxidermy moose head well on its way to falling apart by the door, and, in the back, for fifteen bucks, there was a VCR/TV combo.

"Had this exact one in my dorm room."

Sylvia nodded. "I used to think about what my dorm room would look like." She left the rest unsaid, and with that they returned to the motel. Sylvia pulled the drapes while Keisha set up the TV.

"Let's hope this works." She stuck the tape into the slot. There was a worrying thud, but the image sprung to life. Warped colors and digital static resolved into a wide shot of the side of the gas station. Sylvia's mother against the wall. The Thistle Man stepping toward her. Not the same Thistle Man that had followed Keisha, but just as misshapen and toothy. And there was Sylvia, coming out of the door, seeing what was about to happen, screaming. The Thistle Man seeing the younger Sylvia, breaking into a half-melted smile. Even through the low-quality tape Keisha could see his skin bulge and writhe.

"That's not what happened," Sylvia said. "I hid. She gestured for me to run. He never saw me."

On the tape, the Thistle Man turned back to Sylvia's mother. His hand was on her throat. The person in a hoodie was there. They didn't walk up or emerge from anywhere. First there was nothing and then there was a person in the shadows. It was impossible. But Keisha remembered Crystal Springs and knew that she didn't understand impossible anymore. The person in the hoodie flung themself toward Sylvia's mother. On the tape, Sylvia made a sobbing scream that the Sylvia in the motel couldn't hear because the tape had no sound.

Before anything else could happen, the Thistle Man snatched his hand back, and there was something wet in it, and Sylvia Parker Senior had a gaping wound where her throat had been. He had taken it, like someone might take a box of cereal off a shelf. Now the Sylvia watching the tape was screaming, too, and Keisha held her, hoping no one at the motel would decide to call the police today.

Back on the screen, the person in the hoodie put their arms around Sylvia's mother. They eased her to the ground. The dying woman stared deep into the face of the person, completely obscured from the camera by the hood, as though she had seen a sight more astonishing even than her own death, and then she was gone. The Thistle Man tossed what he had taken from the woman onto the ground, and just as casually picked up Sylvia Junior. He held her aloft like a parent looking at a baby. He was laughing, his jaw wobbling wider and wider. The person in the hoodie got up from their crouch and took hold of the Thistle Man's head. They yanked backward and their strength must have been incredible, because the Thistle Man flew like he weighed nothing. Sylvia fell hard and lay senseless or stunned. And then the person in the hoodie took the Thistle Man apart. Tore off his arms and his legs in two easy movements, crouched down and whispered to him as he wriggled in that oozing puddle of yellow fat coming out of his body, and then popped his head off. It was over in a few seconds. Keisha thought about how much it had taken from her to fight off a Thistle Man. What was that figure in the hoodie? Certainly not human. The creature in the hoodie picked up the unconscious Sylvia and carried her out of frame. The footage went to black.

Sylvia touched the screen. Tears ran down her face but broke against the determined set of her mouth.

"All this time, I thought they helped the Thistle Man kill my mother. I thought I had gotten away on my own. But they saved me."

"Whoever they were, they were very, very strong," Keisha said.

"Yes. And they are on our side."

"So what now?" Keisha meant this for herself as much as for Sylvia. Wait until whatever those creatures were in the hoodies saved the day? It had its temptation.

"I need to find that person in the hoodie. Whatever they turn out to be. There is a powerful force of good somewhere. Before I can find the evil that destroyed my life, I need to find the good that saved it."

She hugged Keisha, and Keisha hugged her back, fiercely.

"Anxiety bros," Sylvia said, smiling into Keisha's shoulder.

"Anxiety bros."

"You'll see me again."

"I better. Goddammit, I better."

32

Keisha went back to the one clear lead that she had, the abandoned house with its hidden staircase and locked steel door. Any time she could find a moment between her deliveries, she would rent a car, drive to Georgia, and stake the place out, watching for movement. But the location seemed as abandoned as it had been made to look, and she wondered if her poking around had caused them to avoid it in preference for other entrances. She was almost to the point of giving up her vigil when a truck pulled up, trailer and all, and someone—she was too far away to tell who—hopped out and entered the house. Keisha followed them inside.

The interior looked exactly as it had before. The same sense of abandonment. Dust over everything. A feeling that the structure of the house was uncertain of its physics and ready to settle into rubble. But she didn't hesitate on any of these details. She understood them as window dressing. Instead she made directly for the kitchen. The stove was already swung aside, the staircase exposed. Why would they leave the entrance visible like that? It was possible that they simply did not expect anyone to enter this long-abandoned farmhouse on this specific afternoon. This was one of several possibilities that occurred to Keisha.

Still, she didn't see any other option for herself. She had set her own trajectory long ago, and now could only follow wherever it led. So she made her way down the stairs, ready for the ambush from whoever had laid this trap for her. Instead she made it to the landing, turned, and saw that the steel door had also been left open. Beyond it was a sterile, steel corner, with the same institutional fluorescent lighting as the stairs. This was of course a trap. This was a bad idea. She hurried down the stairs and through the door before she could listen to all the shouted warnings in her head.

The corridor was short and lined with cameras and ended at a second steel door. Here was where any who entered were vetted and either let through or trapped between the doors until they could be dealt with. Keisha didn't know whether this meant life in some black site prison, or poison gas hissing out of the walls. She did know that the door at the other end of the hallway was ajar. She approached it slowly, giving them plenty of time to slam it shut and end her investigation forever. But it remained cracked open. She pushed and it swung silently inward.

On the other side was a balcony overlooking a colossal underground space. The space was full of equipment and offices, training areas and storage. It was an entire base, buzzing with activity. Hundreds of workers, many visibly armed, bustled around. Overlooking it all, next to Keisha on the balcony, was the commander. The commander didn't turn to look at Keisha as she joined her.

"My name's Lucy," the commander said instead. "Impressive, isn't it?"

"It's unbelievable."

"Bay and Creek is fighting a very dangerous enemy. You know. You've met them."

"Thistle."

Lucy nodded. "Thistle indeed." She turned to face Keisha. "I understand your curiosity, I truly do. Bay and Creek has many secrets, and secrets invite uncovering. So here. I have let you through the doors. I am letting you see the secret at the heart of this war. A war almost everyone you've ever known has had no idea was happening in their country. Here it is. Here are the good guys."

"How long has this war been going on?" Keisha said, picking from one of a thousand questions.

"How long has America been going on? It's a shadowy line, but the conflict gradually formed as the nation did. Listen, Keisha, you can't keep following me."

"Ok," said Keisha. She didn't know what else to say. Given what Lucy had done for her that day, it seemed a reasonable request.

"I'm showing you this because I need your curiosity sated. But you can't come back here. Ordinarily, an outsider who saw this, they wouldn't make it back out into the world. But something in me says you won't be an outsider to this war for long, if you ever really were one."

"I've been fighting in it this whole time and I didn't even know," said Keisha.

"Exactly. Well, now you know. What you do with this information is your business. But you need to walk out of this base now. Go back to your deliveries. Go back to the towns and the highways. You can't come back here. And you can't keep looking into me. Do we have a deal?" Lucy reached out a hand. "I like you, and I know Alice loves you, so please take my hand and tell me we have a deal."

Keisha took her hand. The name of Alice had made her tremble, and she knew Lucy could feel it.

"Thank you, Keisha. Now it's time for you to go."

So Keisha went. Back to her truck, and back to her life. As she drove away, she went over all the new questions this revelation had given her. Just what was Bay and Creek? Where did it get the funds for enormous underground bases, designed to fight a war with monsters? Monsters who had the police in their pockets, and apparently at least parts of the military, if not the entire government? And why in the world would she be allowed to see all that and get to walk away? That was the question she kept coming back to, because it did not make any sense to her. Given what she knew, why was she still alive?

33

After the wedding, Alice got a new job. It had a better income, and soon they were able to make a down payment on a house. Alice hadn't been sure that buying a house was worth it anymore. The future value of a house was so uncertain, and dependent on the gambling of rich investors who could never lose their own money, only lose everyone else's. And a homeowner always has to look fearfully for cracks, leaks, mold, mice, and any number of things that were no longer anyone's responsibility but her own. Rental, that was where it was at.

But Keisha had had enough of rentals. Of not being in control of the place that she called home. Subject to the whims of landlords who might decide on a change in tenants or any other number of things that would affect their living situation. The breaking point for her had come from a landlord who without warning or compensation turned the entire rest of the building into a gut renovation. Abruptly their life in a place that they had thought of as home became a series of hanging plastic sheets and leering men in their hallways and sharp bangs and drilling starting from six in the morning.

"Never again," Keisha said. "A house. That we own. We're putting down roots."

Of course, the irony was that in order to put down those roots Alice would need to take this new job, which involved a great deal of travel. She would be gone two or three months out of the year, cumulatively, but the pay was so much better that she couldn't turn it down.

"Absence makes the heart grow fonder and all that shit, Chipmunk," said Alice. "This way we'll never get tired of each other."

And for a while she was right. There was the pain of the separation, but the pleasure of the reunions was intense. Where others talked about marriage as an uphill walk, a struggle and a negotiation, they were just in love and that was that. Maybe it was all that time away that did it.

About a year into Alice's new job, though, that changed. She came back from one of her business trips different. Keisha didn't know how else to put it. On the surface, Alice acted the same. Same smile. Same easy way of moving through the world. Someone who didn't know her that well wouldn't have seen any difference at all. But for Keisha the difference blared. There was something new buried in Alice's personality. Keisha couldn't figure out what, and she certainly didn't want anything to be different, so she pretended it wasn't. She took what she knew and put it in the highest, most remote corner of her mind, and hoped it could sit there gathering dust forever.

• •

It was a hunch that saved Keisha. She was sleeping in a truck stop that met only the barest minimum of the definition. A spot where she could park the cab and sleep, near a bathroom hut with a few lights and a couple bored security guards in a booth near the bathrooms. But it was enough. In her life, at this point, space and time were all she needed. She settled back into her cot. Usually she listened to music or podcasts on her phone, anything to misdirect her mind long enough to perform the sleight of hand of sleep, but today she lay in silence. The revelations of the day, all that the underground base implied, should have kept her up thinking, but instead they made her indescribably tired, and she knew that her mind needed no distracting that night. It had thought itself out, and the moment she was lying down, the world started to drift away from her.

Then came the stab of panic. There was no stimulus. The night was as quiet as before. No movement. No sounds. No suspicious shifts in the light. But her body filled with anxious energy. For a moment she was frustrated. Not now. Not when she was finally approaching something like rest. Then she thought of a walk-in cooler, where that anxiety had manifested itself as a weapon, one that had saved her life. She decided to trust it. She got up from her cot. Felt the cold air and decided to take the blanket with her. She walked away from the cab, stood in the big empty lot, where the other rigs hunched like hibernating animals. Where to? She let her anxiety lead her, followed the spikes of her panic toward the bathroom hut, where there was a bench in the lights. The bench faced the guard hut. She sat on the bench and looked across at the guards, who looked at her bemusedly and then turned back to their television. She ignored them, watched her truck.

For a long time there was nothing, and she considered that anxiety was irrational, and listening to it was like listening to a child. It's not that they are never right. It's that the correct info is mixed in with a lot of imaginary things, and, like a child, anxiety can't tell the difference between the two. She wrapped the blanket tighter, preparing to stand and return to her cot, a little ashamed at herself for giving in to her stupid gut, when she saw the movement by her truck. A figure was capering around it. Small, frail even, dancing sideways around and around it. It was the woman who had pulled her over near the Salton Sea. Keisha sat back down, looked again at the guards, wondered if they could possibly provide enough protection. The woman crawled into Keisha's cab. The door had been unlocked, but she wriggled in through the passenger window. A minute later she wriggled back out again and considered the truck with her hands on her hips. Then she turned and saw Keisha and even from across the lot Keisha could see a broad smile cross her paperskin face.

34

"Not the smartest move, waiting in plain sight," she said, sitting down next to Keisha. She was still wearing her motley imitation of a police uniform. She didn't smell like the Thistle Men had smelled, but she didn't smell human either. She smelled like rock being crushed to gravel, like earth and the burning smell of friction. "Maybe you remember me? Officer Cloud."

"I figure if you wanted to find me you could."

The woman looked over at the guards. They stared hard at Keisha, but when they looked at the officer, their eyes slid away quickly, as though they might be injured if they looked for too long.

"You know that they can't protect you. Not if I decide to kill you now. I wouldn't think twice about taking them with you."

Keisha nodded. "Sure, I know that. I also know that I don't need protection."

The woman laughed. "Boy, I love your spirit. One gets so tired of mewling and tears. But you have something different in you, don't you? You're not afraid."

Keisha met her strange, unfocused eyes. "You got me really wrong, Officer Whatever. I'm always afraid. Life makes me afraid. And if I'm already afraid of life, then what are you?"

"Certainly not life," said the woman, her voice low and earnest. "But I think you misunderstand your situation. I'm not a . . . what do you like to call them? A Thistle Man. No low monster looking to feed. Go ahead, punch me in the face if you want." She leaned in close. Her face was a patchwork of shadow in the off-center lighting over the bench. Her breath smelled like ferment and mud. "Hit me as hard as you like. Do you have heather oil on you?"

Keisha hesitated. Pulled the small bottle out of her pocket.

"May I see it?"

What difference does it make at this point? Keisha thought. She handed it over. The officer opened the bottle, sniffed it, then put it to her mouth and took a long pull.

"My boys, anything that reminds them of those oracle freaks and they get weak in the knees. I'm not so easily impressed." She handed the bottle back, looking straight ahead and leaning back against the wall. "That tasted disgusting." She smacked her lips.

"So you're who Thistle sends when their regulars can't get the job done."

"Thistle doesn't send me anywhere."

"Well, I'm going back to bed, Officer . . ."

"Table."

"Officer Table, it was nice talking to you. My regards to Thistle." Her heart pounded and her head felt light, but she forced herself to stand and walk steadily back to her truck, then inside and onto her back and waiting with her eyes open, but the woman did not follow.

As Keisha drove on the next morning, she went over again the questions that these last days had left her with. Starting with: the Bay and Creek secret base. Why in the world had she been allowed to see it and then allowed to leave? There couldn't be a fundamental objection to killing in order to maintain the secret. That base was huge and well staffed and she suspected there were others. For a secret that big to have been so well kept, blood must have been shed in the past. An organization with absolute mercy would eventually have faced leaks, and Bay and Creek had stayed under the radar for who knows how long. They would have no moral objection to killing her.

One theory was that Alice was protecting her. But again, this went against how well Bay and Creek kept their secrets. If a person not wanting their loved one killed was enough to keep that loved one safe, then the secret of Bay and Creek would have been leaked years ago. Not even Alice, no matter how high she was in the organization, should have been able to protect her like this.

As Keisha thought about this, she noticed a fellow truck, painted an eye-peeling yellow, driving erratically. It shuddered past, pushing its engine to a whine. Covering the entire passenger-side window was a series of cardboard signs. All of them said, in handwritten scrawl: "I Not Bad Boy." She couldn't see the driver. Soon she lost them, and filed it away as possibly dangerous or possibly just another oddity of the road.

The only conclusion she could draw was that Bay and Creek wanted her to see that base and walk away alive. And the only reason they would want that was if it helped their cause. If it helped them fight Thistle.

And then there was the question of Thistle. When it had only been the Thistle Man, the sole creature, it could have been dismissed as merely a predatory animal taking an interest in possible prey. But this had moved beyond that. When the Thistle Man had failed, then this officer had arrived. They were determined to see her dead, once they had tired of playing with her of course.

Bay and Creek wanted her alive, and Thistle wanted her dead. She must have a role in this war, one she couldn't see yet. She was meant to be useful somehow. She only needed to stay alive long enough to figure out what her role was supposed to be.

She stopped at a Cracker Barrel to pee, and when she came out, that yellow truck was there. Every inch of its windows plastered in those signs. "I Not Bad Boy." The doors were open. Standing on the hood of the cab was the woman in the ramshackle police uniform. Her chin was stained with blood, and when she saw Keisha, she started howling. Not like an animal. Like an alarm. "WOOP, WOOP." No change in her expression, her eyes locked on Keisha's and that high, mechanical howling, "WOOP WOOP WOOP." Keisha ran for her cab, and the officer didn't chase her. Keisha fumbled into first gear and got herself out of the parking lot. The officer stayed on the hood of the cab, dripping blood onto the yellow paint, howling, and watching Keisha go.

35

For all of Alice's traveling, she and Keisha only ever took one road trip together. Keisha had always preferred to stay home. With her anxiety, it was the one place where she felt halfway safe. But her anxiety was why they had gone. Two years after the change in Alice, there was a summer where Keisha's anxiety had gotten so bad that air had stopped working for her. She would breathe in and breathe out and still feel like there was no oxygen at all. She was in a perfect vacuum of panic. Alice found her sitting on the shower floor, not having done anything but let the water wash over her for twenty minutes, and Alice said, "First off, Chanterelle, there's a drought, and second, let's go on a trip."

Keisha was terrible at being on a road trip. The long miles. The way the miles related directly to the hours in a ratio that could be bent but not broken. This was normal to Alice, but horrifying to Keisha. Every minute seemed to stretch so long, and the scenery was repetitious and blank. Keisha had to stop and pee every hour or so, which she could tell annoyed Alice, but Alice would never say, and anyway Keisha was happy, because what Keisha hadn't noticed was that she was bored. And bored was a big step up from dysfunctionally terrified.

The second night they stayed at a motel where the rooms were themed, the Sea Captain's Room and the Forest Room and so on. They chose the Wildlife Room. There was a lamp shaped like a wolf's head. Keisha had discovered, to her joy, that one of the four channels on the TV was PBS, when Alice got a call. Her conversation was casual, "sure, sure" and then she hung up, and, like it was an unrelated thought, suggested that she might drive down to the supermarket, get them a few things for dinner. "Do you want to come?" she asked, but Keisha had had enough of sitting in a car, and *This Old House* was on, so she shook her head, sat cross-legged on the bed with a pillow clutched to her chest.

Alice was gone for a long time. Over two hours. The fear returned. Keisha stared at the curtained window, wanting to go outside, to get help, to do anything. But she could only wait, and wait, and wait for Alice to come back. The air stopped working again, and Keisha gasped uselessly against the anxiety. Because she knew her wife would never come back.

Her wife came back. "Supermarket was closed," she said. "I looked all over," she said. But only the gas station was open, so she bought a feast of gas station snacks.

Keisha hid her anxiety. Didn't want her wife to feel the pressure of knowing how much Alice being gone had destabilized her. They sat out on the balcony. The sunset over the parking lot, and the self-storage center next door, it was beautiful. They ate their gas station feast. It became one of Keisha's favorite memories.

The two of them with almost nothing, and still they had everything.

But Alice was gone a long time. Way longer than fit her story. She had lied. Keisha had known that. And Alice had seen immediately how anxious Keisha was underneath her pretended calm. They had both smiled and worked around what both of them knew.

On an impulse, Keisha pulled off the last exit before the Mexican border and parked her truck at a gas station. She hadn't picked up her latest shipment and so she had no trailer now, only her cab. Driving without a trailer felt light to her, which was silly in one sense, because it was still a big lumbering machine, louder and heavier than any car she had ever owned. But all feelings are relative, and now she felt something close to flight without all that tall bulk dragging behind her.

The woman from Thistle was never going to let her live. Keisha had a role to play in this war, something that made her too important for Bay and Creek to dispose of, and too dangerous for Thistle to let escape. So she had decided to do the only thing she could. She would drive her truck over the border, ditch it somewhere, buy a car with cash, and through a series of those transactions, each more south, she would find some new life to live. Not forever. She hadn't given up on happiness for herself. But somewhere quiet and safe where she could wait it all out. Until her role in this conflict was clear and she could return, do whatever it was she was supposed to do, and then maybe, finally, impossibly, return home.

A car full of college students pulled up next to her, two of them getting out and jogging into the station. A family in a minivan laughed at a joke that would make no sense to anyone outside of the family. She watched the cars pass on their way to Mexico. It was going to be easy to let herself follow that current. To drive until the dusty hills grew wet and lush, until she reached another border, and then another border after that. Until the weather grew hotter and then colder again. Maybe very cold. Who knew how far she would go?

It wasn't fair that it was going to be her who played this role. But then, was it fair for all the victims of the Thistle Men? Killed by the caprice of bloodthirsty creatures for no better reason than that the people happened to be there when the creatures' hunger rose. At least she had a purpose to their hunting of her that all those other victims had lacked.

Or most of them. That name came to her again. Cynthia O'Brien. One murder held a secret, the figure in the hoodie at Crystal Springs had told her. Had Cynthia been like Keisha? Had she had a role to play, a role that had been successfully suppressed by Thistle?

Without thinking about it, Keisha already had her phone in her hand, idly searching Cynthia's name again, while still believing entirely in her flight from the country. Cynthia, she already knew, had been a local historian who had been researching a number of government records involving an eminent domain issue when she had been unexpectedly murdered. The issue had been small and quiet enough that no one had connected her work to the tragic randomness of the attack upon her. But Keisha couldn't help wondering what Cynthia had found in her research that left Thistle with no choice but to target her.

All of Cynthia's papers had been donated to her local library, outside of Tulsa. The oracle said something about a library in Oklahoma. So did the email from Officer Campbell. Keisha looked at the address of the library for a long time. She looked up as the car full of college kids pulled away and turned on the road toward the highway. Keisha, too, pulled away onto the road, but she joined the current of cars moving away from the border, heading back north, as she started the long drive toward Oklahoma.

36

Keisha parked outside of the Lillian Adler Memorial Library. The building was a converted house, and the parking lot was a patch of gravel in what had once been a backyard. She felt the gravel crunch under her feet as she approached the door. There was a dangerous piece of knowledge inside this small converted house. She entered.

A young woman smiled up at her from the front desk. "Hi there, can I help you?"

Automatically Keisha scanned the room for escape routes and danger. The room didn't offer much of either. While the library technically had a second exit, it was only about ten feet from the main door. A dodge around fire code by a lazy builder. There were a few other patrons, an older woman absorbed in a thick novel, a schoolkid studying while waiting for a parent to get home from work and pick him up, no one who looked like they were likely to be spies for Thistle. But then, she couldn't afford to make assumptions.

"Yes, hello," she said to the librarian. "I'm Keisha and I was hoping you could help me . . . uh . . ."

"Mercy."

"I was hoping you could help me, Mercy. I had read that the papers of Cynthia O'Brien were moved here after her death. I'm a genealogical researcher hired by the O'Brien family and I was hoping that I could take a look at them?"

As soon as Keisha said Cynthia's name, a flicker crossed Mercy's face, but a moment later she regained her look of friendly concern.

"Well, sure, I would love to have been able to help you on that. I don't know how much help they would give you with genealogy, Cynthia's stuff was mostly municipal records from her research. Pretty boring unless you really care about the minutiae of our town."

"I promise I would," said Keisha, but Mercy's face stayed frozen in bland customer service mode.

"Well, that may be, but unfortunately we don't have her papers anymore."

"What happened to them?"

"We had a bad flood in the library. The pipes. Froze solid and burst. Water went everywhere. We had to throw out half our collection. When we went to check her papers, it was a box of pulp. Ended up in the garbage, I'm afraid."

"In the garbage."

Mercy's customer service smiled widened as her brow furrowed. It was an unconvincing combination.

"That's right."

Keisha considered how best to approach this. After all, Mercy herself could be from Thistle. What better way to protect whatever secret was here than to plant one of their own to squat over it, with a friendly smile and a watchful eye, quietly taking out anyone who asked the wrong questions. In that scenario, the papers had probably actually been turned to pulp and discarded, leaving Thistle to pick off any loose ends who were dumb enough to walk through the front door. It was entirely possible, maybe it was even likely, but what good was it to worry about that? If she was going to die, she would die. She leaned in close and dropped her voice past library quiet into a whisper.

"There's a war," she said.

Mercy frowned. "Pardon?"

"There's a war, and Cynthia knew something about it. I think you may know something about it too."

"There are a lot of wars, ma'am."

"Please, Mercy. This war took my wife from me. It took my life. It took every moment of every day for the last few years." She was crying and tried to control herself, then decided it might be useful and let herself go. "I need to understand why all this happened to me. And I think the answer is in Cynthia's papers. I don't think they were destroyed. I think you've been keeping them safe. And, even if you didn't know it, I'm the one you've been keeping them safe for. Please help me, Mercy. This is my last chance at understanding."

Mercy looked at her for a long time with a neutral expression, then sighed.

"I shouldn't do this. I shouldn't. Wait here. If anyone needs help, tell them I'm on break and will be right back. Mostly no one needs help."

Mercy walked past her. Keisha stood at the desk. No one in the library paid any attention to her. About ten minutes later, Mercy returned holding a box.

"Soon after Cynthia's estate passed these to us," she said, "we started getting weirdos coming by asking to see them."

"Weirdos asking to see them?" Keisha said, smiling.

"Not your type of weirdo. Strange men. Real creepy. Others who I think were government types. See, Cynthia had been researching a conflict with the government, and it got me thinking that maybe they were trying to destroy her work."

"So you pretended the job had already been done."

"I had to. I didn't think we were safe as long as we had these papers. So I turned off the heat. Let the pipes burst. Hated to do that to the books, but I figured if they were government, they'd be able to check on something like a flood. I took the box of her work home, put it in a closet, and hoped no one would ever ask about it ever again."

She put the box in Keisha's hands. It was light, only half full of paper.

"Don't tell me what it says," said Mercy. "I don't want to know. But I really hope you find what you need. I do." She kept eye contact with Keisha for a second, then said, "Ok," and returned to her desk.

37

The papers all were related to an eminent domain case in which the federal government was trying to build a power plant in a mostly unpopulated area. The power plant appeared to be related to the military, or in any case there wasn't a lot of public info available on the technical details or where the power would be going. To build, they needed to move out the occupants of about ten houses scattered through the area. But they hadn't counted on how fiercely the occupants would fight for what was, to an outsider's view, a not tremendously valuable piece of real estate. There was a court proceeding, one the government was guaranteed to win because no judge wanted to start any sort of precedent threatening the mechanism of eminent domain.

This is where Cynthia had become involved. She had a lot of experience through her job of the careful and tedious task of sorting through government records and she started recording and monitoring this case, looking for any details that might be helpful for the occupants. This archive Keisha held was the result of that research, a pile of contracts and technical diagrams, zoning maps and court filings.

Keisha had felt such momentum going into this moment and found herself fighting off the despair of the crash. She didn't know what she had expected. A note, handwritten, perhaps, saying, "Here is what Thistle is and here is what it wants." Or an incriminating picture of the president handing a pile of cash to a Thistle Man. But of course, they were government records. That's what Cynthia did. She collected them and pored through them. So Keisha did her best to see them as Cynthia did. She grabbed papers at random and looked through them as slowly as she could, trying to make herself understand each page completely, or at least as closely as she was going to get, before moving on to the next.

The sun was setting when she found her first instance of the word *Thistle*. It was in one of the government filings, involving a contractor named Thistle Limited working on a specific part of the power plant. Keisha felt her breathing speed up just seeing that word. There was an answer in here, she was sure of it now. She started digging through for anything related to the part of the project that Thistle was listed as working on. And sure enough, again and again, in small references, indexes, in footnotes, there was this contractor, Thistle Limited. So whatever this land grab by the government was, its real purpose was to build something for Thistle. This was proof that at least some part of the government was knowingly working with Thistle. That in itself was huge, of course, but it only confirmed suspicions she had. She wouldn't let herself believe that this was all the archive had for her.

Keisha heard a sound above her and looked up, feeling her body tense, ready to run. It was Mercy. "The library is closed.

I'll let you stay while I finish up a few things, but after that you'll need to leave and come back tomorrow." She gave a small, sad smile.

"Could I take it with me to my motel?" asked Keisha. "I'll bring all this back tomorrow."

"No," said Mercy. "No, Cynthia's things have to stay with me. That's where they belong. But you'll be able to come back tomorrow." She patted Keisha's arm. "I promise, it'll be safe with me."

Maybe so, but Keisha felt herself getting frantic. She couldn't leave this library tonight without an answer. She read back again through every paper with the word *Thistle* on it, looking for what she was missing. And, only a few minutes later, she found it.

One of the documents referring to Thistle also referred to another name, one Keisha knew quite well. Bay and Creek. It seemed to be a mistake, because the mention of Bay and Creek was reiterating an earlier part of the document, one in which the name had been Thistle Limited. It also referenced a contract by number. She dug through, knocking papers on the ground, and found the contract. There it was. The contract was describing the work that Thistle was doing except it wasn't with Thistle. The name used here was Bay and Creek.

It wasn't proof, but still Keisha knew. This was the secret that Cynthia had inadvertently found. This was why she had been killed. Because she had discovered evidence of the truth: Thistle was Bay and Creek. Bay and Creek was Thistle. There were no two sides to this war. Only two organizations pretending to fight each other. She had been part of a play. She had been made a fool.

And then the awful moment, the sinking thought. Had Alice known? Had Alice been part of this lie?

The lights above Keisha flicked off, and she looked up to tell Mercy that it was ok, she had found what she needed. But Keisha didn't understand what Mercy was doing. Mercy was lying on one of the study tables, her back arched awkwardly. Keisha realized that Mercy's shirt had been torn open, and so had her skin, and her rib cage. The entire front of her torso had been pulled apart as though by surgical equipment, and she was lying under the last lit bank of fluorescents like a patient in an operating room. Her face was turned toward Keisha, and Keisha wanted to project fear on her frozen features, but if she were honest there was only the dull glaze of death.

"Keisha, it's time," said a familiar voice. The woman from Thistle sauntered toward her out of the darkness, her arms wet to the elbows with Mercy's blood.

38

"They didn't leave me alive," Keisha said. "They didn't let me walk away. They knew you were coming."

The officer stopped, the fluorescents casting hard shadows across her face. "Oh, is that what you've been thinking? That Bay and Creek let you live?"

"I thought maybe I was useful to them somehow." Keisha wondered how long she could keep this conversation going before the predator that wore the skin of a human came at her. The officer laughed and started to advance again. Not long, then. Keisha considered her options, decided she had none, and bolted into the shelves. The officer continued to move at a slow walk.

"Keisha, I don't believe you've been useful to anyone in a long time," she shouted as she followed where Keisha had run. "Even that wife of yours decided she could do without you, didn't she? No, the reason Bay and Creek didn't kill you is because they already knew I was coming to do it. I get first pick, and I had claimed you. You interested me."

In the small room, the voice echoed off the ceiling and Keisha couldn't tell where it was coming from. She was crouched somewhere in Reference. She pulled out one of the books and tossed it over the shelf to land with a thud in the next aisle, then took off in the other direction, hoping that the creature hadn't been standing on the other side of the shelf, watching her throw.

"You work for Bay and Creek and for Thistle."

"I don't work for anyone," said the creature. "Ah, Bay and Creek. Thistle. Having two sides to a war is convenient, you know, but it isn't strictly necessary."

Keisha turned a corner and an arm thrust out of the shelves, sending books scattering with immense force. She threw herself left to avoid the hand, slamming her shoulder painfully into the wall, but she was able to slip past. Up ahead was the main entrance. If the Thistle creature was in the next aisle, that meant the way to the door was open. Without letting herself consider the drawbacks, she sprinted toward it. At that speed, she was almost to it in seconds and looked back. The creature was leaning casually against the back wall of the library, making no move to follow.

"You won't make it out of this library," shouted the officer. "But please try."

The door was only about fifteen feet away. Keisha lunged. In the corner of her eye she saw the creature spring up from the wall. She had never seen a living thing move so fast. The officer vaulted tables, her feet hardly seeming to touch the carpet. Keisha's hand landed on the door. And then she was on the floor. The officer kneeled on her chest, her knees sharp and digging into Keisha's ribs. She leaned down and again Keisha saw her face clearly. Paper skin. A paper woman with animal strength.

"A war is so useful, Keisha," the creature said. "Lots you can hide in a war. Money diverted. Force and weapons justified. Unhelpful people killed and what are you going to do? There's a war on, after all." She traced her fingernail along Keisha's neck. "Ok, I'm going to kill you now. See if you can pinpoint it, the moment where you start to die."

Keisha felt the surge of survival. *Fuck Thistle.* The energy of anxiety exploded outward into her limbs and she hit with all the strength she had. She hit the officer in her face over and over, hard palms upward at the nose. And she stopped as she heard a noise, a noise that at first she didn't understand, and when she parsed it, she felt complete despair. The officer was laughing. Was laughing at the blows Keisha had landed. And then it was the officer's turn, and her hands were unimaginably powerful, and they were all over Keisha, and she knew that she had failed, that everything she had done up to this point hadn't mattered, and that Bay and Creek and Thistle would continue destroying lives across the country long after her death this evening.

There was a pop, and she wondered what part of her body it was, where the wave of pain would come from. But instead the hands attacking her stopped. There was another pop, and then another. And the officer slid off her and fell lying next to her. There were two streams of blood going down her scalp, running from bullet holes at the top of her skull. Keisha tried to understand. She flung herself up, arms swinging wildly and someone caught her from behind.

"Whoa, whoa. Keisha, it's me." The voice stopped everything in Keisha. She stepped back. It was Alice, a handgun clenched by her side. "I was wrong. I thought I was doing the right thing, but I was wrong and I'm sorry." She slowly put the gun down on the ground, and stepped forward, with both hands out.

"I'm so, so sorry," she said. "Will you come with me?"

PART III
PRAXIS

WHY DID THE CHICKEN CROSS THE ROAD?

Because on one side was everything she had ever known
and on the other side was a future, maybe, and even though
she was afraid to leave everything she had ever known,
she also wanted a future, maybe, and so hesitating,
and then not, and then moving quickly, running, sprinting,
even, desperate, she crossed, and found a future, maybe,
leaving behind everything she had ever known.

39

Alice had two hundred more miles to go that day and she was tired. Her body was tired. Her mind was tired. She was tired of her job, of being away this much from Keisha. Maybe if her job had meaning, if she was working on something she believed in, she would feel differently. But instead she was essentially a traveling salesperson. Oh, there were trappings to it. She showed up in offices, did presentations; "sales" didn't show up anywhere in her job title or description, but she wasn't fooled. She had no illusions about what she did. There was no real difference between her and those tired men from old movies, with worn suitcases, knocking on one more unfriendly door.

Maybe it was this exhaustion with her work that led her to stop at the Amazing Painted Rocks! A Miracle of Art! Or maybe she just had to pee, and the sign for the roadside attraction also promised clean bathrooms. At this point in her day they wouldn't need to be clean. She'd settle for some shade to pee in. The day was hot and only getting hotter and she checked her map again. Still two hundred more miles, as it had been a minute ago.

So she stopped and she paid the five dollars to a bored teenager who was watching a public access channel on an old portable TV. The teenager nodded toward the painted rocks, and there they were. Rocks, and they were painted. Although what had once presumably been bright color had been mellowed by the sun until it was merely a tint to their natural shade. Not what Alice would call a Miracle of Art! but actually a bit better than she had expected.

Painted rocks dutifully viewed, she took advantage of their bathrooms, which were, as advertised, remarkably clean. She was unsure if this was because of careful diligence on the part of the owners or, more likely, a real lack of visitors that might cause any messes. Still, here really was a roadside miracle and she was happy to take advantage of it.

What would normally have happened is she would have left the bathroom, headed right back to the entrance, been nodded out by the same bored teenager, and then driven those two hundred miles to try to sell to another office of bored middle managers. Then the entire rest of this story wouldn't have happened. Her and Keisha's lives hinged on this single moment, in which she decided that she wanted to walk by the painted rocks again. It wasn't because she liked them or felt like she needed to get her money's worth. Honestly, the bathroom had been more than worth the money. She was looking for a delay on the rest of her day and the rocks provided an excuse.

While she was standing there, trying to find the rocks interesting, she noticed movement over a rise behind them. She liked animals and thought there were maybe coyotes or rabbits running along the top of the hill. But she looked closer and understood that she was not seeing a rabbit or a coyote. She saw an arm rise up, and a different person's arm pull it down. There was a muffled scream.

Alice had also struggled with anxiety, but she handled it differently than her wife did. Keisha internalized her anxiety, stuffing it down until it buzzed around wildly in her body. Alice projected her anxiety on the world, seeing a place that was as scared as she was, and this paradoxically tended to make her protective, willing to put herself at risk to alleviate the fears that she assumed in others.

In that moment she saw someone possibly being attacked, and she thought about how terrifying that must be, in this lonely roadside attraction, here behind these stupid painted rocks, and before she had another thought she was already running up over the rocks, over the rise in the hill, to help whoever needed help.

There was a woman on her back. Over her was a man in dirty clothes. The woman was fighting back fiercely, but the man was clearly very strong. Alice kicked him in the head. He made a popping sound with his lips and rolled to the side. He looked up at her. She had never seen anyone like him. His skin was wrong. It sagged and cracked. His lips were crooked. His eyes and teeth were the same shade of yellow. He wore a dirty polo that said THISTLE on the breast. The man grinned his awful grin. The woman on the ground had already sprung up. She started punching at the man, but he pushed her aside. He came at Alice. His hands were unrelenting as they grabbed at her. She kicked him over and over. But he was pushing her. She was about to fall over the edge of the rise, crack her head on the painted rocks. The woman grabbed the man and pulled him off Alice. The man fell backward and without hesitation both women stomped at his head. Over and over. His head didn't crack like a skull. It mushed down into a fatty yellow paste.

Alice couldn't believe what had happened. Had they just killed someone, her and this stranger?

"What is . . . ?" she said. "How is . . . ?"

"Yeah," said the woman, who years later would rescue Keisha from a walk-in cooler outside of Victorville. "I was like that my first time too."

Alice took a good look at the woman. She was about Alice's age, short hair, her clothes scuffed up but otherwise unharmed except for a single deep gash that went in a perfectly straight horizontal line down her left cheek.

"He got you," Alice managed.

"Actually, I think that might have been you, honey," the woman said, wiping her cheek with the back of her hand. "I think you got me good with your nails while we were struggling with him. I'll forgive you on account of you saved my life and I have no real need for unblemished cheeks anyway."

The woman sat down with a tired sigh, started tying her shoelaces, which had become undone in the struggle. She tilted her head at the dead man, or creature, or whatever it was.

"Don't worry. I have some friends that will clean this up."

Alice looked down at the body and could only nod, as though what the woman had said was normal.

"What was that? He didn't seem human."

"He didn't, no," said the woman. She inspected the blood smear on the back of her hand. "Shit. Listen." She got back up, dusted herself off, and considered Alice thoughtfully. "You came in there brave, and you fought well. I would have been dead for sure without you. Thank you for that."

Alice didn't know how to respond to that.

"The organization I work for," the woman continued, "we could use people like you. People who rush in. People who can handle themselves. What's your name?"

"Alice."

The woman held out her hand.

"I'm Lucy. Alice, how would you like a job?"

40

"Hand me that."

"Here."

"No, not that. *That.*"

"You don't have to take that tone of voice."

"Don't tell me what I have and don't have to do."

The space in the back of the cab was cramped. Their things were everywhere. Clothes. Toiletries. Food and food wrappers. The debris of life. But that was only part of the mess.

"Careful."

"Alice, you tell me to be careful one more time."

"Excuse me for not wanting you to get hurt."

"You do not get to. Oh, you do not get to go there, not at all."

The first thing Keisha had done, of course, was embrace her. Right over the body of that awful creature, still flowing what looked like human blood onto the carpet. She pulled Alice tight and didn't say anything. Alice couldn't say much, either, because she was being hugged too tight to breathe. She tapped out of the hug. Keisha held her at arm's length and glared at her, and then the glare fell, and Keisha said, "Fuck." She said it over and over, filling in for anything she might have thought to say if she were given a lifetime of quiet contemplation, like none of us ever are.

This out of her system, she asked the most obvious question. "How did you find me?"

And Alice gave a truthful answer: "Keisha, I never lost you."

The work their hands were doing was delicate, and so despite their frequent disagreements, they pushed forward, putting every part in place. Pouring in the exact measurements. If one element was off, neither of them knew what would happen. They were not experts on this or most other subjects.

"Keisha, do you think we could have a civil conversation?"

"We'll have a civil conversation when you've earned it, even if it takes six years. Hold this steady."

Two months together like this. Friction so intense it would have sent them flying off in different directions if it hadn't been for the complete devotion they both had for their goal. Still they both slept in the tiny cabin, and night after night they ate across from each other in truck stops and fast-food restaurants. They would try to move the conversation toward safer waters but find that there were no safer waters. All subjects led to the great black crevasse that was Alice's abandonment.

"Ok, these are done. Let's get going."

"You're going to have to forgive me at some point."

"Alice, my love, I don't have to do shit."

The two of them decided to not speak for a bit after that. See how that went. Anyway, it would go faster if they divided up. Each of them took a bag and they hopped out of the truck. They were parked down the road a bit, deep in a grove of trees, in the hope that they wouldn't be spotted.

"I've been keeping track of you," Alice said in the library. "From the moment Bay and Creek hired you, I couldn't sleep I worried so much."

"That's sweet," said Keisha in a monotone. She turned and walked out of the library, not looking back at Alice. They needed to be gone. The buzz of the reunion was fading. And had the body of the officer moved?

"I'm sorry, Keisha. I thought I was doing the right thing. I tried to keep you safe," said Alice as she hurried after.

"I don't need you to keep me safe." Keisha was stunned to find that the outside was the same quiet town she had come to just a few hours before. She made herself look at Alice and, despite herself, she would not have traded places with anyone else in the world in that moment.

The motel was creepy. Old abandoned motels tend to be, but this one was also clown themed. WELCOME TO THE CLOWN MOTEL, the sign said. Figurines of clowns still hung from some of the doors. Keisha tried not to look at their milky eyes, the pupils having faded away, as she tried the door and found it unlocked. The inside of the room had even more clowns, lining the shelves. Enormous paintings of clowns on the walls. Everywhere big toothy grins leered at her through red painted lips. She tried to block it all out, just take the package out of the bag, leave it on the bed, move to the next room.

It wasn't until the last room in the row that she screamed. Alice came running up the stairs, a knife pulled out that Keisha hadn't known she had been carrying, a wicked-looking blade designed for violence.

"What is it?" said Alice, scanning the area, blade aloft. "Are you alright?"

"Yeah, I'm fine. Honey, I'm fine." She took Alice's hand and gently lowered it. She pointed into the room, where there was a life-sized statue of a clown, frozen in the middle of a horrible wink.

"You sure you don't want me to start stabbing it?" Alice asked.

"Shut up," said Keisha, but soft and affectionate, as she walked past the horrifying statue and placed the final package.

Quieter, and hand in hand, they walked back out to the highway. They turned and looked at the Clown Motel. It was drifting toward evening, and the clowns painted on the building were going into shadow. The giant sign hadn't been lit in years. This was about to change. Behind the motel was an old graveyard. The scene was weirdly lovely, and Keisha regretted what would have to happen next.

"You want to do it?" said Alice, holding out her phone.

"No," said Keisha. "This was your find. You pull that trigger."

Alice held the phone up. "Hey, this is still how my heart feels every time I look at you." She pressed the call button. There was a whump they felt in their chests. Ten bombs in ten rooms simultaneously went off. Bits of the Clown Motel were blasted up into the darkening sky, a translucent orange against the setting sun. It was beautiful and stupid and sublime and violent.

"Corny," said Keisha.

"Couldn't help myself." They hurried through the trees to the truck before a passing driver saw the fire and tried to figure out what authority should be called about an explosion in the middle of nowhere.

"Thank you for saving my life," said Keisha, back in her truck in the library parking lot. There had been a moment of hesitation from Alice as she automatically headed toward her truck, but Keisha hadn't wavered for a moment and hopped up into the cab in which some of the worst moments of her life had occurred. Alice settled into the unfamiliar position of the passenger seat.

"Of course," she said. "I'd do anything for you."

"And fuck you for following me like I needed looking after."

Keisha started the truck. That familiar vibration of the engine had a calming effect, a meditation of the body.

"I'm not coming with you," said Keisha.

"Oh." Alice looked down at her hands.

"But if you want, you can come with me."

It was Alice's turn to drive.

"Do you think it's actually hurting them at all?" Keisha said.

"Blowing up entrances to their bases?" said Alice. "It certainly can't be helping them."

"So we're at least ticking them off."

"Ticking them off's a start, right?"

"Right, sure," said Keisha.

Sabotaging every possible Bay and Creek or Thistle facility they could find. The press didn't know what to make of them. Blown-up buildings across America felt like it should be covered as terrorism, but was it terrorism when the criminals only blew up old abandoned buildings in parts of the country that had been slowly bleeding population for a long time? They were called the Derelict Bombers. TV comedians referred to them as architectural critics, taking down some of America's oldest, ugliest eyesores. But Bay and Creek would know. Hopefully they were hurting them a little. Any kind of sting at all.

Someday they would have to move past annoyance and really take the fight to them. How they would do that, Keisha had no idea. Alice didn't know, either, but her focus was less on the big picture of the battle. She needed to somehow make up for what she had done.

41

In college, Alice had put up a placid face to Keisha's insistence that she wasn't interested in a relationship, but she would take walks alone in the forest near campus and shout until she had let out her frustration and hurt enough to once more be placid. Unequal affection is cruel. But she sensed the affection was not actually unequal. That Keisha only wanted it to be, so that she could feel a sense of strength after the end of her last relationship. And so Alice waited her out, or at least would for a little while. She wasn't going to wait forever.

When she said "I love you" by accident, it had been an unforgivable showing of weakness for herself, and she wondered if there was a way back from this crack in the façade she had put up, but then Keisha had said "I love you" back and had meant it, and the façade came down for them both. That week they lay in bed.

"I need proof," said Alice.

"Of what?" said Keisha.

"Of us." She hated being this vulnerable. But it had been a tough few months, and she was tired of pretending. "I want proof of us," Alice said. There was a moment of quiet. Maybe she had gone too far. She was the cool one. And this wasn't cool.

But Keisha laughed. "That I can give you," she said. She kissed Alice, and the feeling between them was so evident it was all the proof either of them needed, although they subsequently expanded on that kiss just in case.

It was the night after the Clown Motel. Keisha watched the stars peekaboo behind the shifting clouds while Alice lit a fire. There was never an explicit setting of responsibilities, but Alice mostly did the menial tasks of their new life without being asked, as a way perhaps of atoning for what she had done. Keisha never asked why she did it, and Alice never thought about it. These were the roles that they had given themselves, and they were what they were.

The rig was parked some ways off the highway. Mostly when they could they slept in the wilderness, lighting fires on the side of the truck away from any possible road so they couldn't be seen. Neither of them knew if this would keep them safe. Bay and Creek obviously had a far reach and Thistle had a kind of mystical instinct that neither of them knew the extent of. For all they knew the brush around them teemed with hidden Thistle Men, musty spittle dripping down loose chins.

Weeks now of this new existence. Living as outlaws. Causing damage where they could. Hoping that it meant something. In the evenings, sitting around a fire, mostly not talking, because mostly they didn't talk. Keisha wouldn't even kiss Alice. She slept in her cot and Alice curled up on the narrow floor. They never discussed this sleeping arrangement, but Alice did not dare try to change her position. She would be forgiven or she wouldn't be. In the meantime, there was a greater evil to address than her own past sins. They weren't partners in romance but fellow soldiers in a war. At least for now.

The fire flared up, eating through paper and into the twigs and starting to nip at the larger blocks of wood. Alice used a stick to better arrange the structure. The two of them looked more like weekend campers than truck drivers. But what does a truck driver look like?

"This isn't working," said Keisha. Alice froze.

"Us?" she said.

Keisha didn't respond to that. She kept her eyes on the clouds. After a moment, Alice half-heartedly poked at the fire and then put the stick down and sat next to her wife.

"We are mosquitoes," said Keisha. "We are drawing tiny amounts of blood and all it causes is a moment of discomfort and then they forget about us."

"Mosquitoes are one of the most dangerous creatures in the world. They cause something like a million deaths a year."

"It was a metaphor. We're not giving Bay and Creek malaria."

"So what else could we do?" asked Alice.

"I don't know. I don't know at all. I just know we can't keep doing what we're doing and expecting anything at all to change."

"We have to do something though, right?"

This was the belief that both of them were living on. Even if this wasn't the right thing to do, at least they were doing it. Even if they wouldn't succeed in acting, at least they were acting. It was a personal triumph, rather than one that actually hurt their enemies. And that was the problem. What good was fighting if it was only for the sake of having fought? If they didn't have an end point, then where were they going?

"Do we think the whole government is involved?" said Keisha.

"I don't think so. There'd be too many moving parts. Even within Bay and Creek most people don't know. Parts of the police. Parts of the military. A few of the folks in power. I'm sure there are some who know that they are aligned with Bay and Creek and believed as I believed that they are trying to keep the country safe with the help of a useful organization. And some know that they are aligned with Thistle. Those who see a use for random violence and fear. I doubt there are many who know they are aligned with both."

"How many people, do you think?"

"I don't know," said Alice. "A few bad apples." She smiled.

"A few bad apples, shit. Good apples and bad apples don't matter if the outcome of the system is harmful. A good person doesn't matter if they're working in a bad system."

"As one of the good apples for a bit, I agree. But our intentions were good." She shook her head. "Our useless intentions."

"The mosquito," Keisha said again, but in a different tone of voice, like it was the answer to a question Alice hadn't asked.

"Hm?" she said, facing the fire. Alice was tired. She was so tired, but there was no rest in sight.

"Why is the mosquito such a dangerous creature?"

"Disease. Malaria."

"Yeah," said Keisha. "Yeah, exactly. The mosquito itself isn't dangerous at all. What's dangerous is what it carries inside of it."

"Ok . . ."

"We're like mosquitoes, Alice. We're not dangerous for who we are. We're dangerous because of what we carry inside of us."

"Malaria?"

Keisha gave her a joking slap on the shoulder. "We have information inside of us. They have a secret, right? We need to make it not a secret anymore."

"Huh."

"We need to get that information out of us and into everyone in this country. Then we'll be dangerous the way a mosquito actually is."

"So what do we do? Flyers? Graffiti? Make a website?"

"I don't know," said Keisha. "I think we can't do this on our own. I think we need help from someone who can make people listen."

"Who would that be?"

Neither of them knew. They started looking through major news sites, finding people who seemed to report on national stories and looking up their contact info. And then they started calling them, from pay phones always. There were still pay phones, a few of them, at older gas stations, in the hallways of cheap motels with crumbling walls.

Mostly they got no response at all. Or the person would hang up on them. But then Keisha called Tamara Levitz from the *Los Angeles Times*.

"Who are you?" she asked.

"I am one of the Derelict Bombers," she said. "And I want to tell you why we're doing what we're doing."

There was a pause. Keisha waited for the click. Instead, Tamara's voice again.

"Ok. I'll need proof of your identity."

"That I can give you." She laughed in relief, hoping it didn't make the call sound like a joke. "That I can give you."

42

Alice signaled for the waitress. Three years into this new job, Keisha safe back at home, and still her pulse was racing like it was that first time at the Painted Rocks.

"Yeah?"

"Could I get a little more orange juice?" she asked, loudly.

"Sure thing, hon." The waitress took her glass, winked at her. After twenty minutes in the place, she and Alice were best friends. Alice had that effect on people, an ease that implied intimacy even if nothing was truly shared. She made friends with bus drivers, bartenders, waitresses. Mostly because she went into their interactions with the goal of improving their day and expecting nothing in return. Directly behind her a woman slid out of her booth and headed for the front door. A minute later Alice got up, too, and followed. The waitress was just coming out with the glass of juice. It looked good. Fresh squeezed or at least a good simulacrum. But she couldn't stay.

"Sorry, I got a call. Have to go. Can I pay here up front?"

She had a sip of juice as she waited for her change. There was always room for a little moment for herself. But then she was outside and jogging. Lucy was waiting for her. The wound that Alice had made in her cheek on that first day they met had settled into an angry scar. It felt to Alice like a physical manifestation of the compact between them, this mission they carried out together.

"Took you long enough," Lucy said, already jogging even though she didn't have a direction yet. "No more flirting with waitresses. Where did you see him?"

"Heading through the lot. Around back there. I wasn't flirting. Some of us are just friendly. You might try it sometime."

Lucy angled her jog toward where Alice had pointed, and they both picked up their pace until they were flat-out running across the pavement. It was daylight, and so this wasn't ideal. People would be watching them, wondering what was going on. But Alice had worked for Bay and Creek long enough to know that if they didn't move fast, it was likely their target would be long gone. The Thistle freaks had a way of fading into the walls and into highway traffic. That wasn't going to happen this time. It had been months since she and Lucy had caught anything. They were ending that streak here, today.

Their target had walked right by the window, as wrong a sight in the sunlight as any creature of nightmares, but no one in the diner had reacted. Many of them had seen, some of them might have even known what they were seeing. But they had turned away. Made the safe choice to forget what they had seen. People, Alice knew, were capable of that. Of knowing, but choosing at the same time not to know.

"Don't worry," said Lucy. Her voice was always calm and composed. Even as they sprinted through the heat, she sounded like she was chatting over cocktails. "We're gonna get him."

"Damn right we are," huffed Alice through gasping breaths. She wasn't even calm or composed when she *was* chatting over cocktails, and here, sprinting, the adrenaline for what was coming next building up in her? Forget it. As usual, her anxiety was projected outward and manifested itself as a familiar feeling of protectiveness. Not that Lucy needed her protection.

They came around the corner, and they weren't too late. The hunched, snuffling figure was between two dumpsters, facing the wall. When he heard their footsteps, he turned. Loose skin, yellow teeth and eyes, an earthy sweet smell. His skin bulged and writhed, as though tiny creatures were trying to escape his body.

"Oh, Lucy," he said in a high, phlegmy voice, "you seem to have healed up so well. I'm glad to find you in good health." Lucy touched her cheek reflexively, and then she stepped forward.

"I'm here under the authority of Bay and Creek."

That buzzing laugh, like a colony of insects burrowing up out of his lungs. "I bet you are." He shook his head fondly, and it was in that moment, when they assumed that nothing would start yet, that he came at Alice. Like all the Thistle monsters, he was awkward and shambling, but when it came time to hunt, he moved quickly. He had her flying through the air before she could reach for a weapon or brace her body. Then her arms were pinned under his boneless, heavy legs, and his toothy mouth was lunging at her face.

Lucy kicked him off her with the toe of her boot. He made a wet whooshing noise, like a drain sucking in the last bit of water, and rolled away. But he was on his feet by the end of his roll. Thistle creatures had surprising grace despite the awkwardness of their bodies. He jumped at them again. A headfirst jump that only would be possible for someone absolutely unafraid of injury. His forehead hit Lucy's nose and they both landed against the wall. Lucy had her hands on her nose and her eyes closed. He spun her by her shoulder, slamming her head into the wall. Then he tried to tear a chunk out of her back. So Alice put a knife through his head.

Even a year before, she wouldn't have been able to do that. But she was a different person now. She understood the stakes. The knife went through his head and burst out the ear canal of the other side, spraying the pungent fat along the dumpster.

"Huh, huh, huh," the Thistle Man said, turning toward her as his face split into two and melted toward his shoulders. He fell to the ground where he continued to make a soft repeating sound with his lolling tongue.

As usual, the professionalism in Alice was gone the moment the job was done. She hugged Lucy.

"We got him!" she said, dancing her around a bit. "We got him!"

Lucy danced with her, but there was a stiffness that Alice felt to her movement. She wasn't as happy as Alice, and Alice didn't know why.

"We did it." Lucy smiled slightly back, but the smile ended at her lips. This change had happened a month before, and there had been a heaviness to her friend and fellow soldier in this war.

What Alice didn't know, couldn't have known, was that Lucy had been promoted. This promotion was kept secret because of the process involved. Lucy had been taken into a room where a supervisor had carefully and sympathetically laid out the truth of the war to her. She had been working with Bay and Creek for six years, and she had seen the true horror of Thistle that they had been working against. And here was her supervisor, explaining that Thistle wasn't the real enemy. That Thistle existed because America needed them to exist, so that Bay and Creek could work for a greater good.

"What greater good?" Lucy had demanded.

"War is a powerful force for change," said her supervisor. "Don't you agree there's a lot about this country that needs to change?"

At first Lucy knew she would leave, but then the doubt came upon her. She was a good person, working with good people. She had sacrificed everything, leaving behind a man she loved, leaving behind two children, because she had believed that nothing was more important than winning this fight. And she had found Alice, who had been the bravest and most capable person she had ever had serve by her side.

Surely this work couldn't be for nothing? Even if she hadn't been privy to the details of what they were doing, she knew in her gut that it had to be for the good. So she agreed to keep working for Bay and Creek while she reconciled what she had learned with what she wanted to keep doing.

If she was going to stay, then she needed Alice to stay too. But she worried about how Alice would take that same revelation, if she would understand the way that Lucy had, about that grand plan that neither of them was big enough to see, that if they had been doing good before, then they must be doing good now.

The reason, Lucy knew, was that Alice had Keisha. Alice had a family that she went back to between every mission. Keisha was going to be the reason that Alice wouldn't accept the truth about Bay and Creek, and then she would be killed because Bay and Creek couldn't let people walk away once they knew.

Lucy had become so quiet lately only partly because of what she had learned. What made her even more troubled was what she would have to do next. She would have to convince Alice to leave Keisha behind forever. It was the only way to save her.

"You sure you're ok?" said Alice.

"I'm great," said Lucy. "Let's go tell headquarters the good news."

43

"Everything you've given me has checked out," Tamara said, "but be patient. A few of your stories coming up true doesn't mean I can go to print. Something like this, we need everything airtight."

"I get it," muttered Keisha, but she was impatient. She had been doing this for long enough, and she wanted it to be over, while knowing that it was maybe not any closer to over than when she had started. Alice let Keisha do these calls, even though they both knew that Alice was better at talking with strangers. Patient Alice. Alice doing everything asked of her while she waited for Keisha to forgive her. It made Keisha furious. Why should she ever forgive her? Why did Alice think she was owed that? The nicer Alice was, the angrier it made Keisha.

"Yeah, well," she said, "let me know if you need anything else to verify. Once you're all aboard we can really start working."

"Sure," said Tamara. "But, hey, before you go. A friend of yours passed along a message. I guess she didn't know how else to reach you. She said you've changed your number since she last tried, and she says that's smart. I don't know how she found out I'm talking to you. But . . ."

"Well, put it in the folder." Tamara had established a secure shared folder so that Keisha and Alice could send her information without revealing identity and location.

"Will do. You be careful out there."

"Yeah. You be careful in there."

She flipped shut the old cell she was using that week and flipped open her laptop. The folder had a message from Sylvia.

"Miss you and love you. I'm safe. I'm looking for the good. I will find it. There are oracles on these roads."

And an address in Wisconsin.

Keisha had filled in Alice on Sylvia, and so Alice didn't ask questions, just googled the address. "It's a water park. Or it was. Closed a few years ago."

Keisha nodded.

"If Sylvia thinks we should go there, then that's what we'll do."

"There are oracles on these roads," said Alice.

"Apparently so."

"Do you know what that means?"

Keisha felt some pleasure in knowing something Alice didn't and wondered if she should feel guilty about that pleasure. No, she decided. She wasn't the one who had to feel guilty about anything.

"Yeah, I think so," she said.

They drove in silence for hours, as the scenery shaded greener. It's hard to tell regions apart by the human structures. A CVS is a CVS, a Starbucks is a Starbucks. Every town is built like every town, and so all that changes is the nature that's been allowed to stay. As a traveler heads north, the trees shift from broad leafy canopies to the narrow spurs of conifers, and the suggestion of hills gives way to great structures of rock with sweeping aprons of untouched snow. Or, on another drive, the hills dot themselves away into nothing, until the traveler hasn't seen elevation in hours, nor many trees, only a lot of grass, and a lot of road. Or the traveler leaves behind a wetter, greener climate and the world fades from grass to kindling, to dirt and rocks, and then, like a sign marking a border, the first great cactus, harbinger of the desert.

It's up to nature to tell people that they're moving. Otherwise each Kmart sign looks like each Kmart sign, every Subway sandwich tastes the same.

"How long are we going to be like this?" Alice said, after an hour of silence.

"Like what?"

"Please don't pretend ignorance."

"Mm," said Keisha.

"I left because I thought that's what I needed to do to protect you."

Keisha didn't say anything.

"I thought you were in danger and that the only way to protect you was to leave. And that's why. And I'm sorry."

Still Keisha said nothing. They entered Wisconsin.

It was a rainy, cold day in the Dells, and any tourists who might have been around had been driven into the malls and indoor water parks. No one was on the road, certainly. They arrived at the King Arthur Camelot Splash Zone, which had several letters broken on its sign. The park was inside a dark and boarded-up building; the slides that wrapped around the exterior walls like vines were unmaintained and sagging. If there was a hiding spot for an otherworldly creature in the region, this looked as likely a place as any.

One of the doors was propped open with a bit of cardboard. Maybe from teenagers who came by to drink and skate in its empty pools. Or maybe so this oracle could come and go. The two of them slipped inside. Faint light seeped from between the boards, but it took a long time for their eyes to adjust to seeing anything at all. The swimming pools looked like open mouths. The slides were looming spirals in the air above them. Their footsteps echoed in the cavernous space.

"Shit," said Keisha. Her hands were shaking, but she wouldn't let Alice hold them. "Let's just find this . . . whatever it is."

They walked along the edge of one of the pools looking for something out of the ordinary. It didn't take long. Once they were able to make out details of the space, they saw steam in the center of the room and started toward it. One of the hot tubs was full and bubbling, the water clean, the mechanism well maintained. Keisha felt a crunch under her foot. It had been a piece of candy, still in its wrapper. There were offerings of all kinds around the hot tub. Bills, fives and tens, left on the ground. Some candles. Baseball cards. Cigarettes. Bottles of booze. Candy.

"Offerings for the oracle," said Alice.

"So where are they?" said Keisha.

"Maybe had to use the bathroom."

Keisha looked into the water, through the bubbles, at the concrete benches where once vacationers had sat. Was there a shape there? A mass forming in the steam? She couldn't quite tell what was solid and what was vapor. The shape spread, like ink in water, until it was a cloud of gray, which rose toward the surface, and a person with a gray hoodie pulled completely over their face emerged sitting relaxed with arms spread along the sides of the tub. Their hoodie was dry. The air was perfumed with the smell of heather.

"There are," said the person in the hoodie, in a distant, gentle voice, "oracles on these roads."

44

It was Alice who first suggested they live together, and Keisha
was once again reluctant. Not that Keisha didn't trust the lasting
nature of their relationship, but she had never lived on her own
and wanted to get a sense of what that was like before cohabitat-
ing. Alice knew what living on her own would be like. It would
be lonely and not as good as living with Keisha, and it was stupid
to deny themselves a pleasure so simple and easy as company.
But when Keisha finally agreed, Alice felt some panic. Maybe
this was moving too fast. Maybe it was important after all to see
what it was like to live on her own. She assumed that she knew,
but assumptions were fantasies that had the delusion of reality.
Alice spent the better part of a year making excuses. "You're
the one who brought it up!" said Keisha, and that was true, but
Alice's feelings were also true. She struggled with them for those
months before moving in to that studio apartment Keisha had
found. The first night, sleeping on an unfamiliar mattress, Alice

looked over at Keisha, only a few inches away, and she knew that she had made the right decision in the same way she knew her own name and which vegetables she liked and didn't like. It was innate, requiring no interrogation; even when later they bickered or had quiet spells, she knew that the choice had been right and that their lives belonged together.

"Two lonely warriors in an unbalanced war," the oracle said. "Come sit, lonely warriors. You can put your feet in the water if you want."

Keisha shrugged and pulled off her shoes. Alice put a worried hand on her, but Keisha shook it off and let her feet slip into the water. It was hot enough to sting, and she could feel the muscles in her legs letting go of miles of tightness. Seeing this, Alice joined her, and they both sat with their legs in the water, facing the oracle.

"So what now?" said Keisha. "Do you predict our future?"

"I don't predict the future," said the oracle. "I only maintain it."

"Cryptic," said Alice.

"Some subjects are so complicated," said the oracle, "that even speaking of them plainly sounds cryptic."

Keisha felt dizzy above this pool of heat in the cold room. The overwhelming smell of flowers. Her vision swirled, and against the far wall she saw a flicker in the shadows. She felt that they couldn't stay here long. There was a strangeness to this place that would pull them further and further in, and if they stayed too long, they would never be able to leave. Thinking this, she tried to pull her feet out of the water but found that she couldn't muster the will to do so. Alice was sweating and seemed to be experiencing the same problem.

Enough, thought Keisha. *We have questions.*

"Then ask them," said the oracle.

"What is Praxis?"

"That I cannot tell you."

"Why can't you?" demanded Keisha.

"I maintain the future," the oracle said and offered nothing more.

"What does Praxis want?" asked Alice.

"Praxis is not about wanting. Praxis is about doing."

"What does Praxis do, then?" Keisha snapped. "I don't want to stay here all day." *Or much longer than we already have*, she thought.

"Praxis fights against Thistle, under whatever name they choose to operate," hummed the oracle. "We have always fought against Thistle. For as long as there has been Thistle, Praxis has fought it. For as long as there has been Praxis, Thistle has threatened it."

"War forever," said Keisha.

The oracle shrugged almost apologetically. "There are always bad people. Thistle is merely a focus for that. For the world to move forward, the good people must struggle to organize a better world. Praxis is merely a focus for that. We did not start this struggle, but gave ourselves entirely to it."

Above the murmur of the water, Alice heard a quiet crack, like glass being stepped on. She turned around, scanning the room, but it seemed empty as far as she could see. Much of the room was dark, though, darker than she had remembered it. The sun must have set while they were talking.

"But what are you?" said Keisha, urgently. She couldn't get her legs to leave the water. She felt that the oracle was holding her there, but it was possible that what was holding her was her anxiety. The most pernicious effect of anxiety was it made it difficult to tell what was actually dangerous and what was just a jumpy reaction of the spine. "We have evil inhuman monsters on one side, and mystical creatures on the other," she said. "What kind of being are you, and why are you helping us?" *If that* is *what you are doing*, she didn't say.

There was a patter of feet, far across the space. The oracle lifted themself up, so they stood knee deep and dry. The darkness in the room was closer than before. Keisha could not make out the farthest of the empty pools at all anymore.

"There is not your struggle and my struggle," said the oracle in a voice that boomed out into the dark. "There is only our struggle. We fight alongside you because there is only one fight."

Out of the darkness, a figure walking, then many more. Thistle Men. The one in front was gaunt and stumbled forward with his head turned as far sideways as it could go. His mouth was open and his tongue was lolling.

"I'm sorry, Keisha," the oracle said. "Our time is up. Remember this: No one sees the future. They only ever maintain it."

Keisha and Alice, finding that they could stand, scrambled back from the water. The hot tub was surrounded on all sides by the men. Laughter, coarse and wet, like a person laughing into mud.

"What is Praxis?" said the Thistle Man with the tilted head. "What is Thistle? Tell me what will come to pass, O oracle of the roads." More laughter.

The oracle did not step out of the water. They were standing in the water and then they were facing the Thistle Man, head bowed. The Thistle Man in the lead lunged forward and the others followed, whooping.

Keisha had seen an oracle absolutely destroy a Thistle Man in that low-quality tape in the motel room in Saugerties, but it was another experience entirely to have it happen in person. The oracle never took a step, only was in one place, and then was in the next. They were next to the Thistle Man who had lunged at them, and with a casual twist of their hands the Thistle Man was torn in half straight through the torso. The strength involved was unimaginable, absolutely beyond the realm of human. But many more Thistle Men were coming out of the darkness. The oracle flickered from one to the next, killing as they went, but no matter how many they killed, more came. The oracle had their hands on one of the men when three others grabbed them from behind and one of the men sunk his teeth into the oracle's shoulder. The oracle shrugged the man off, but blood poured down their body. They moved a little slower now, and another group fell on them, dragging them down. The oracle was impossibly strong, but there were too many Thistle Men for anyone. They had the oracle down on the ground, and there was a terrible screaming, the oracle's gentle voice in terror and pain, and the Thistle Men had their hands in the oracle's open chest, pulling and tearing.

The oracle stopped moving, stopped screaming. There was a thud, deep from the earth, and the bubbling hot tub turned cold and emptied, the water sucked directly downward with no spiral. The empty tub was dry and covered in dust and leaves. Alice and Keisha found that their feet were dry, their socks and shoes back on.

The room was almost completely dark now. Keisha and Alice could not see the exits. They could only see the smiles of the Thistle Men, turning to them, one by one by one.

45

Those first years with Bay and Creek were a brutal shock for Alice, a shift into a world of subterfuge and violence. She thought often of running away, but she didn't know what her employers would do if she tried, and she didn't know if Thistle would seize the opportunity of her no longer living under the protection of Bay and Creek. She felt stuck and she felt scared. When she would walk through the door, home from a mission, Keisha would grab her and kiss her and hold her for the longest time. The contact, simple as it was, felt electrifying after the absence.

"You make that money for us?" said Keisha.

"Yeah, Chanterelle, I made that money."

"Then let's go to bed. I got so sleepy waiting up for you."

And as Alice fell asleep with her wife's arm over her, she knew she could never quit. Not because she was afraid. But because Thistle threatened every innocent person in the country, and she had to fight them. She had to fight them so people like Keisha could stay up yawning and give their wives sleepy kisses as they came through the door. She would do it to protect Keisha and everyone like her.

There was no time to coordinate. They could only start running. Keisha took off for the walls that she couldn't see, hoping that reaching them would guide her to the door. She felt a hand grab at her, the musty smell of Thistle, but she pulled away. Behind her, footsteps, but she couldn't tell if it was Alice following her or Thistle. The whoops and gurgling laughs came from every side, and so she concentrated only on forward motion.

A hard blow to her face. She stumbled backward and put her fists up to protect herself. When no second attack came, she realized that she had run into the wall. She unclenched her hands and put them on the concrete that had almost broken her nose. The door they came in should be to her right. She started running again, one hand on the wall to guide her.

"Alice," she shouted. There was no response except the howling of Thistle Men in the dark. "Alice," she shouted again, hoping that her wife would follow her voice, knowing that the monsters would follow it too.

She had no idea how long the building was, and so no idea how long she would run until she reached a door. She didn't reach a door. Instead her feet hit something solid and she sprawled forward onto cold metal. A staircase along the wall.

"Huaaagh," said a Thistle Man, looming out of the shadow toward her. "Huaaagh ha hahahoo." Keisha didn't have a decision, only an imperative. She ran up the stairs and found herself on a bridge over the pools. Along the wall were the mouths of the tunnel slides, perfect black *O*s. She thought about the slides as an escape, but the claustrophobic darkness she would have to crawl down made her entire body clench and she kept running, until she heard "Keisha!" from the room below.

Looking down, the room wasn't nearly as dark as it had been from within it. The evening sun still shone through the cracks in the boards over the windows. Why had it been so dark before? With this light, Keisha could clearly see Alice, stumbling blindly along the bottom of an empty swimming pool. Men lined the sides, cheering and swaying. One by one they jumped in, feet pointed as though breaking water only they could see. Some stuck the landing and others collapsed like sacks of hamburger, but even the ones who had fallen rolled themselves slowly to their feet and advanced toward Alice.

Keisha turned toward the staircase at the end of the hallway but knew she wouldn't even make it to the top of the stairs before they got to Alice. There was no hesitation in what she did next, although there was a great surge of panic. She dove headfirst into the slide leading to the pool Alice was in and started pulling herself down it. The slide was so narrow that she felt her shoulders might get stuck. Why would they ever make a slide so narrow? Or maybe it only seemed narrow in her panic. The walls of the slide tightened around her like a corset and she couldn't breathe. She concentrated on putting one sweat-slick hand in front of the other and pulling herself forward. Her chest burned as it slid on the dry plastic, but she scrambled and wiggled through, until Alice's screams were a few feet away.

"Keisha, oh god, Keisha," Alice screamed, and Keisha was on her way. She pulled and pulled and pulled. She took the energy of her panic and directed it into her hands, every inch an inch closer to her wife.

Then she was out, crawling awkwardly onto the bottom of the pool. She found that now that she knew the darkness wasn't real, it no longer existed for her. She could clearly see the pool, and the Thistle Men seething along it, and Alice caught helpless in the middle. Keisha barreled forward and took blind Alice's hand. Alice screamed and punched her.

"Ow, it's me, it's Keisha, Jesus."

"Oh god, I thought you were dead. I thought we both were. I thought—"

"Shut up and run."

They did. A Thistle Man cackled and blocked their way and Keisha drove into him shoulder first. He swung like a door opening and staggered into the base of the slide. Hands and arms in their way, and Keisha put her head down and ran through them. There was the exit. A Thistle Man in front of it, his head lolling loose like it had become detached from his spine, his arms out in a waiting embrace. Keisha pushed Alice away from her, still holding on to her hand, until their arms were outstretched between them, and they clotheslined the Thistle Man, whose slack head snapped back and pulled his body with it. Then they were outside, where the sun was still up and their truck parked right where they left it.

They ran all the way to the truck and were hurrying to get inside when they realized no one was chasing them. The door to the water park hung open. The dim interior was visible, and there was no sign of anyone in or near the building. Every Thistle Man had vanished.

"I saved your life, Alice," said Keisha. Her face was hot, and she had so much anger she didn't know what to do with it. "I want you to think about that. The next time you justify to yourself that you left and made me think you were dead because you wanted to protect me. The next time you find that excuse making the smallest appearance in your brain. You think about this. I don't need your protection. I never did. I'm not helpless. I'm not weak. I have anxiety sometimes and so you thought you needed to make decisions for me? Well, fuck you. That's what I think of your excuses. Fuck you. Never tell me about what you thought was right ever again."

She started the truck. She got them the fuck out of Wisconsin.

46

"And that's where they found the baby," said Lucy, her eyes shifting right to see how Alice was taking it. "Or at least what was left of her."

"Jesus," said Alice.

"Nope, not even he could save them."

They were quiet for a long time.

"That's horrible, but I can't do it," said Alice. "I can't."

"You could kill her if you don't."

"Anything could kill her. Only one person can love her."

Lucy kept bringing reports of families of employees, targeted by Thistle. Held hostage in exchange for information or sabotage. Or sometimes just slaughtered, fed to Thistle's hunger. The message was clear. Keisha was Alice's family. And her employment was putting Keisha in danger.

None of these stories were true, exactly, but Lucy justified this to herself by thinking that Keisha could well be in danger.

Anyone could be. Certainly this was a dangerous job. Lucy couldn't have Alice bolting when she found out the truth about their war with Thistle, and there was no way to keep her from doing that while she still had her bond with Keisha. If Alice bolted, Bay and Creek would kill her and probably Keisha, too, and so maybe Lucy wasn't even lying, exactly. Keisha really was in danger. This was all part of a good cause. Lucy found that she had been justifying more and more to herself, and the more she had to do this, the more convinced she became of the righteousness of her cause. After all, she was a good person, and she wouldn't be working on the side of evil.

"I'm not leaving her," said Alice with finality. "I'm leaving the job." This was far from the last time she had said that.

"You know that won't work." Lucy sighed. "Thistle will think that it's a ruse. They'll think you're still working for us. And you won't even have the inside information from us to give you a heads-up. If it's just the two of you, without connections, without reinforcements, how long do you think you'd last against Thistle?"

"I don't know. I only know I'm never leaving her."

Lucy nodded slowly, making it clear the subject wasn't closed. "Ok, forget it. Let's go over the mission."

"Surveillance," groaned Alice. She rolled her eyes.

"That's right, it's a sit-on-our-ass mission. They aren't sure of the Thistle movements in the area, and they want to be."

"So we look but don't touch. Try to get a feel for what Thistle is doing in somewhere this remote."

"Got it in one."

"Of course I did, I'm very good at this," said Alice.

The whole foray was somehow even more boring than feared. They didn't see any Thistle movement at all. At what point of watching nothing does one move from surveillance to stasis? Alice thought they were toeing that line.

"They're wasting us here," she said.

"Personally I agree. But who knows? Maybe something interesting will finally happen."

That night Thistle came. Alice didn't even have time to see them. It was Lucy's watch and she dragged Alice to the car, her face tight and afraid. Alice tried to remember the last time she had seen Lucy afraid and she couldn't. Even when they had first met, and it had seemed that Lucy was about to die, even then she didn't look like this.

"I've never seen so many of them at once," hissed Lucy as she fumbled the car into motion. "They have the road into here cut off, we'll have to try to drive deeper."

The asphalt turned to dirt and wound its way up a few low foothills before settling into a valley where a grid of dirt roads had no structures on them, laid out for people and industry that never came. Theirs was the only tire tread Alice could see on the road. Lucy stopped the car and lit a cigarette. They waited, but no one was following them.

"We can't try to leave on our own," she said. "We'll have to wait for extraction."

Alice checked her cell. "No reception."

"Shit," said Lucy. She had driven out here three weeks earlier and double-checked every cell network to make sure none of them reached this spot.

"Alright," Alice said. "They better hurry. Keisha's expecting me home in two days and I'm not disappointing her."

The two days passed. Then another week. No one came for them. Lucy would drive back the way they had come in and return shaking her head, trembling a little in one hand. For someone like Lucy to react that strongly, what she had seen must have truly been terrifying.

"Not a chance," said Lucy.

"Where the hell is Bay and Creek?"

"I don't know." Lucy shook her head. "I don't fucking know."

Bay and Creek didn't come. Three weeks. Alice tried and failed to not think what Keisha must be going through.

"We have to risk it," said Alice.

"You think this'll be better for her if you die?"

No, of course not. So they waited. Another week and Lucy came back frantic.

"The way is clear. I don't know how long. We have to go."

They went. The engine overheating, low on gas, but they made it to a safe house. Alice took out her phone. Lucy put a hand on it.

"What are you doing?" said Alice.

"Think about this. What are you going to say to her?"

"I don't know. She needs to know I'm alive."

"That's right. She thinks you're dead. She'll have a lot of questions. So where have you been? What happened to you?"

"I don't fucking know. I'll figure it out."

She started to dial and Lucy knocked the phone out of her hand. Alice punched her before she even knew what she was doing. She started to apologize, and then didn't.

"What are you going to tell her?" wheezed Lucy from the floor. "You need to have this straight in your head before you call."

Alice picked up the phone and stood with it in her hand for a long time. "Think about it," said Lucy. "Maybe this was fate. You couldn't disconnect. You couldn't do it even to keep her safe. But now it's already happened. And what could you even say to explain it? Let her think you are dead. Do this work. Win this war.

Make it safe for everyone like us. And then, you can come back to her and tell her the truth."

Alice screamed. She dropped the phone and screamed. Lucy let her. But Alice didn't call Keisha that night. Or the next night. She sobbed. Lucy went outside and smoked every time Alice started crying. Alice wasn't sure whether this was to give her space or because Lucy was annoyed by it. Eventually it became too late to do anything. At this point, Keisha would definitely think she was dead. And in a way, she felt that she was. She wasn't a person anymore. She was a Bay and Creek solider. This war had taken the relationship that made her human from her. All she had left was to win that war.

Still, she couldn't ever convince herself that she was as hollow as she wanted to be in order to bear what she had done. Through sleepless nights, she would think of ways to let Keisha know she was alive. And then a Thistle murder, brutal, outside of St. Cloud, Minnesota. April snow on the ground. All of the news vans, telling the grisly story to the world. And like a volunteer in a hypnotist show, who acts as though under a spell but is really doing what they want to do the entire time, Alice stepped behind the reporter and looked directly at the camera.

47

A stakeout is an exciting way to describe falling asleep in a parked vehicle. Alice had nodded off an hour before, and Keisha was on her way. But she kept thinking about the exit from this life. A time in which she wouldn't have to live this way anymore. And that ember of hope kept her from slipping completely into much-needed sleep. Instead she watched the grain elevator. It was wooden with gables and a few frosted-over windows, looking like a movie haunted house that had stretched upward past the scale of human existence. There had been no movement that day, or the day before. But they were sure that this was an entrance to a Bay and Creek facility, and so they had set up behind a line of trees between two nearby fields and they had watched it with a camera. They needed more evidence, more information to help Tamara fill in the gaps.

It was just as Keisha had given up, decided she could afford to take a little nap, maybe an hour or so, that a car pulled up to the grain elevator. Four men got out. All were wearing tactical vests, black caps pulled down to their eyebrows, machine guns on their backs. She slapped Alice's shoulder. "It's torn!" Alice cried as she woke up.

"What?" said Keisha.

"I don't remember. Something in a dream."

"No one cares about anyone else's dreams. We have something."

The men did a cursory sweep of the area, but it was a rural region, a hundred miles from anything that could be labeled with the word *city*. They weren't expecting to find anyone, and so they didn't. Then they filed into the grain elevator. Keisha and Alice sat in silence for thirty or forty minutes. Neither of them moved even to check the time. It felt like they were close to something, and moving even an inch might ruin it. The men returned from inside. In the center of their group, occasionally shoved along by one of the men in the back, was a frail man in an undershirt. He had a cloth bag pulled over his head. He was barefoot. They put the man in the car and drove away without checking the area at all. They were confident in their secrecy. Keisha and Alice gave it another couple minutes without moving or speaking, then Alice leaned back in her seat and sighed.

"I think we were right. Bay and Creek brig. That seems worth reporting on, right?"

Keisha checked the camera. "I hope so," she said.

As they drove to the next spot, she flipped back on the CB radio. She turned the volume off, as she always did. She had listened enough in her life.

"This constant road trip has done something to me. It's changed time. Used to be an hour-and-a-half drive felt like a while, the kind of drive you'd need to gear up for, the kind that would make you dull and listless with the length of it. Now four or five hours move by with a real pep to them. I've learned that all it takes is sitting and existing. Do that long enough, and anything will be over."

She glanced at Alice. She thought about their time apart. Sit long enough, and anything will be over.

"Being good at long-distance travel means turning yourself as much as possible into cargo. The more you can become like a cardboard box, the better you are at withstanding the miles. A cardboard box doesn't need to pee. A cardboard box doesn't need to stretch its legs. A cardboard box merely sits and is transported. And that is how a person becomes good at long road trips. They sit and are transported. They take the world as it comes. A road trip is often seen as an exercise in freedom, but the effect it has on a person is a placating stillness."

Keisha put the mic back, flipped the radio off.

A week later, in a Starbucks in Pasadena. Tamara was cautiously excited by the footage. "I'll tell you," she said, over a cup of coffee she had ordered and then did not touch. "Something like this is easy to stage, and so on its own, not much of anything at all. But everything you've been giving me, it's been checking out."

"It'll all check out," said Keisha.

"Well," said Tamara. "I'll have to be extra careful with all this. A story like this out there, I'll need to be surer than I have been about anything. But stuff like this"—she held up the memory card and a smile pushed its way out through journalistic reserve—"shit, it helps. This helps a lot."

They had stopped bombing. Now they only documented. The goal was no longer to slow down or sabotage, but to blow the whole crooked deal open, and that couldn't happen piece-meal, that had to happen all at once. They filmed Bay and Creek sites, and when they didn't have a site to target, they cruised the abandoned places of the country. Once they knew what to look for in a Bay and Creek location, it was surprisingly easy to find them through educated guesswork. They would set up on an old amusement park based on nothing but a feeling, and sure enough half a day later would spot a dusty sedan, a midlevel model from five or six years ago, and out would come people who definitely were not there to explore an old amusement park. Twice they even got footage of a Thistle Man. They were careful then, feeling that Thistle were much more likely to notice being watched than Bay and Creek operatives. The horror of the Thistle Men didn't quite come through on the video, but still there it was, documented proof of their existence.

"This is good," Tamara would tell them. "This is incredible."

But they didn't need it just to be good. They needed it to change everything.

48

A carpool lot off the parkway in Paramus, New Jersey, a half hour before dawn. Alice and Keisha pulled the truck across several spots. Already there were commuters on their way to Manhattan, yawning from their four a.m. coffees, but the lot was still mostly empty, and the two didn't plan to be there for long.

Word of the place had come through the network of whispers that Sylvia had disappeared into. Safe houses and shelters for runaways. Good people doing good and getting nothing in return. Strangers but at least slightly more trustworthy strangers than most. And besides, the two of them had survived Wisconsin. At least this was in public, near a major highway. The information seemed good anyway. There in the corner of the lot, a figure in a folding chair, wearing a hoodie and watching the predawn horizon; a radio by their side played an old song by Rihanna.

"Thought you might be coming by," the figure called as the two walked toward them.

"Guess you see the future," Alice called back. Keisha whacked her.

"Sorry about her. She's not good on manners. My name's Keisha."

"I know who you are. Your friend was joking. And she's not wrong. Not entirely right either."

"You don't see the future, you just maintain it, we know," said Keisha.

The oracle nodded and waved to a stack of unfolded chairs next to them. "Grab a seat."

"Do I sit down though?" said Alice. "I don't want to disrupt the flow of time if I'm supposed to do anything else."

"Alice, stop being an asshole," said Keisha.

The oracle laughed, a sound like a silverware drawer tossed down a flight of stairs.

"If it helps," they said, "yes, you do sit down."

And Alice did. The chairs were old but comfortable, with a lived-in bow to the bottom of them. There was a history of asses that had passed through this seat, each leaving a few millimeters of depth to it. A harried woman in a business suit pulled in a few spots down, glanced at them as she rushed off to whatever destination she was heading toward, somewhere well outside of this story. Alice gave her a friendly nod. Keisha kept her eyes on the oracle.

"So you aren't the same oracle as we met in Wisconsin?" she said.

"No," said the oracle. "There are many of us. Not as many as we need, however."

"Lot of bad shit in the world," said Alice.

"Indeed."

"That's what we came to you to talk about," said Keisha.

The radio ran through its top-of-the-hour traffic report. Thousands of people using up the hours of their lives doing the stop and start on a highway somewhere. The announcer mentioned a big headline that was stirring up controversy. The music started up again, something aggressive that Keisha figured she was too old to recognize.

"We were told once that we don't even understand the basic shape of this war," she said. "And we want to. We want to learn so that we can help."

"It's an admirable impulse," agreed the oracle. It was difficult to read emotion in their floating voice.

"Thistle," said Alice.

"Yes," said Keisha. "Thistle. We need to understand what they are. Where did monsters like that come from? Are they aliens? Created by the government? I can't find an explanation that doesn't sound like a joke, but I've seen those things, and they aren't human."

The oracle spread their hands wide. They wore baby blue wool gloves that still had Kmart tags on them.

"They are evil and hatred. They are a point of view felt so deeply that it becomes an identity."

"Is there a reason you oracles can't just say what you mean, ever?" said Alice.

"Yes, actually," said the oracle, laughing again. Keisha wished they wouldn't. "Everything about the human language is tied into time. It is a language by and for people experiencing time in linear order, each moment separated from the one before. When time is experienced all at once, it becomes difficult to express oneself the way that one might like." The oracle shrugged. It was an oddly human gesture. "We do our best. There is a reason prophecy must always be interpreted before it can be parsed within linear time."

"So the Thistle Men," said Keisha.

"Not monsters in the way that you mean. Monsters, yes, but not created in laboratories or flown in by flying saucer from the old seabeds of Mars."

The sun broke over the horizon and with it, as though they had waited for their cue, commuter cars started streaming into the lot. What had felt moments before like a rather isolated spot now, in the direct sunlight and with the cars, felt an awkward and silly place to be sitting. The oracle turned their head toward the approaching vehicles. Even in the light, Keisha could not see their face. They gestured toward a man who hopped out of his car, walked a few feet, then swore and turned back for his phone.

"Him, perhaps," said the oracle. "Or him," they said, pointing to another man in construction gear who was rummaging through his trunk. "Any of them could be, at some point. If a point of view becomes one's entire identity, what was monstrous on the inside can become monstrous on the outside."

Keisha took a moment to process this.

"You are saying . . ." she said.

"Yes," said the oracle.

"That the Thistle Men are human."

"Most monsters are."

The construction worker found what he was looking for in his trunk and walked whistling toward a pickup truck across the lot. Alice and Keisha watched him go. They thought of the stooped, boneless fleshmen with their sharp teeth.

Alice's phone pinged. She pulled it out and put her hand over her mouth.

"Keisha," she said, her voice trying to find equilibrium. "The story. Our story. It's out. The whole story is out there."

"I would have mentioned," said the oracle, "but I didn't want to ruin the surprise."

Keisha didn't even remember leaving the lot, what the oracle said as they left, didn't remember weaving the truck out among the morning commuters. She only remembered those words. *The whole story is out there.*

49

It was all there, plus more than they had known. Tamara and her team had found connections, proof of government sponsorship that Keisha and Alice would have had no way of stumbling on themselves. Not only was it there, it was undeniable. There was documentation of every step. They felt a visceral thrill to see their photos and videos, attributed to sources within the organization.

"Holy shit," said Alice.

"Oh my god," Keisha said.

They screamed and held each other. Keisha tried to parse through what she was feeling, like picking out the flavor of individual spices in a meal. She had been shaken by the oracle's claim that the Thistle Men were human. She hadn't had time to let it sink in, hadn't felt any of it yet; it was just a piece of information she had and didn't know what to do with. And then there was this. This story probably made everything else irrelevant. Because now they weren't alone. That was it; she had pinpointed the thought that burned the brightest in her. Before it had only been them who knew how wrong it all was, how things really were, and now everyone would. They wouldn't have to be alone with the knowledge and the struggle. She threw her body against her wife's, forgetting her anger and pain for a moment and feeling the embrace as though it were the first one they had ever had.

"This has got to be everywhere now," she said.

"How do people even process what is being laid out here?" said Alice. She reached for the radio, spun it around until she found a news station. There was talk of a budget showdown in Congress. The nominations for the Tonys had been announced. There was nothing.

"Try another," said Alice. Keisha did. Station after station of news and chat and nothing about the articles.

It felt like an understatement, but all Keisha could manage was a quiet "What is going on?" because a silence this total didn't feel real.

They went to a diner nearby that had several TVs on. Multiple news channels. Nothing.

"Can I get you two a table?" said the woman at the front.

"Tell me," said Keisha. "Did you see an article about this Thistle mess?"

The woman frowned. "Let me know if I can get you a table." She hurried off.

"What about you?" Alice said, accosting a man who was eating pumpkin pie at breakfast.

"Huh?" he said, through a mouthful of à la mode.

"The big story?" Alice said. "Bay and Creek. Members of the government involved?"

"Oh, I don't really go for politics, sorry." He muttered this into his pie, turning away from her.

"What in the fuck is going on here?" Alice inquired at a shout to the restaurant as a whole.

"Children are eating here," a mother shouted back.

"Your children are going to be eaten by government monsters, didn't you read?" Alice yelled, and Keisha pulled her out of the restaurant before they could be kicked out.

Keisha called Tamara from the parking lot.

"I know," Tamara said before Keisha could say anything at all.

"No one is talking about it."

"I'm getting the same reaction," Tamara said. "Even my editors don't want to talk about it, and they worked it."

"This is the biggest story of the century." Keisha felt her skin getting hot. She felt dizzy. She was not going to throw up. "How could no one be talking about it?"

"I've thought a lot about that." Tamara sounded exhausted, her voice was hoarse. "I think people already knew."

"I don't understand. How could they have known?"

"It's not that they knew exactly. They didn't know the details. But they knew, you know? Somewhere inside of them they already knew, and they made a choice not to think about it. So even though we spelled it all out for them, they still are making that same choice."

"So what do we do? We have to make them care somehow."

"Keisha, you're not hearing me. They know. And they have made the choice not to think about it."

"Tamara, that's not—"

"I'm sorry, Keisha." The call ended. Alice paced around, swinging her fists at the air, fuming.

Inside, Keisha had been preparing for this to be the end. After this she would be free, and she could go home. It wasn't that simple, of course, because she didn't know if it was even possible for her to go home with Alice as things were now, but she hadn't needed to think through that. Compared with all the rest of it, the hedge maze of their relationship had seemed relatively simple, a maze that could be hacked through in a straight line once they got tired of the twists and turns of it. But she hadn't reckoned on the article not changing anything. That hadn't entered her consciousness. She felt like she was somewhere quite far from herself. But of course she wasn't that either. She was right there, in this horrible moment.

Alice started to cry, and that slammed Keisha back into her body, because she couldn't remember when she had last seen Alice cry. It made Keisha feel like there was no center to it all, and that what had seemed to be the world was only a temporary arrangement of light. Keisha held Alice. Keisha did not cry.

50

Hank Thompson wasn't taught to hate. He came to it naturally. As a teenager, most of his classmates looked like him, and this seemed right to him. At the time, he wouldn't have been able to explain why it felt right, although later in life he would develop his own logic to explain it, one based on a patchwork of bad science and bad theology. He only knew that the few classmates who weren't like him made him furious. He did everything he could to make their lives miserable. Others in his class weren't as directly cruel, although they tolerated what he did, and this was its own cruelty.

After school, Hank would sometimes follow the classmates home, shouting insults and tossing rocks. He wanted them afraid. Not only in the school or on the streets, but to generally feel that there was nowhere safe. He wanted them to live with a tremble, because he hated them. Once he connected with a thrown rock, aimed at a child, named Theodore, two grades below him.

Theodore crumbled instantly, and an accusatory finger of blood spread out toward Hank. Hank walked away, leaving Theodore in the street. Hank never heard what happened, never cared to ask, but he never saw Theodore in school again. This made him proud.

When Hank was sixteen years old, he was shaving in an old mirror out in the yard, and he noticed something on his cheek. A looseness to one side of the face. As though the skin there had grown bigger than the skeleton. The extra pocket of skin hung down slightly. He poked at it, but there was no pain. Just some extra skin. He ignored it and hoped it would go away on its own.

Hank was two months shy of eighteen when he joined the Klan. It made him feel powerful, the masks, the violence, the threats. When he saw fear in others, it made him feel like he could never be afraid. What he felt, late at night, when it was dark and he worried that he wasn't good at anything and would die unremembered and unloved, none of that fear could be real, because when others saw him in his robes and hood, they trembled. They didn't see a human, but a dangerous and powerful creature. He loved that feeling.

Around two years later, when he was working at a local general store, a woman named Harriet bought some flour and some eggs from his counter, and he found that talking to her was easier than he had expected. Their conversation turned into an agreement to take a walk the next day, and that walk turned into other walks and conversations, turned into discreet kissing in the woods or in quiet parts of the park. They would be married, he decided. But Harriet seemed anxious at the prospect.

"I have something I haven't told you," she told him, on one of their walks, when she was certain there was no one else around.

"Me too," he said. He hadn't told her about his role in the Klan, or the power it made him feel. He wasn't ashamed of it, was in fact proud of it, but he also felt that women had no right to his internal life.

"I'm Jewish," said Harriet. "I don't make it public. As of this moment, you're the only one I've told in town, in fact. Before we went any further, I wanted you to know."

Hank felt sick. She had tricked him. Jews, he knew, weren't even human. They were low creatures. He knew what must be done with low creatures.

She was bending over to look at an interesting beetle, and also so she wouldn't have to see his face when he reacted to the news, and Hank stood behind her holding his hunting knife, which he had taken to always carrying with him because, like the Klan, it made him feel too powerful to worry about his many fears. He knew what had to be done. But he also felt love for her, and this disgusted him. He thought about killing her and then himself, but he couldn't make the move. Instead he walked away. She called after him and he ignored her. He didn't see her again, made no attempt for the rest of his life to find love. He knew what was at the end of that road. It was merely a trick to dilute his pure hatred, and his hatred was what made him powerful. He became isolated, only socializing with fellow Klan members, and then only sometimes.

As the years went on, other strange pockets of skin joined the one on his cheek. The area around his eyes grew dark and baggy, and then started to droop, exposing the pink around the bottom. The whites of his eyes were slowly tinging yellow. He didn't go to a doctor about this. He didn't trust doctors, because he thought that most of them were secretly Jews. He thought a lot of people must secretly be Jewish, and it made him boil. One side of his face started to travel toward the ground, and the other drifted upward. Looking in the mirror, he didn't recognize the creature looking back. He tried to say his name at this strange reflection. "Snarf," he said. "Phlffm." He carefully set his tongue and his teeth and enunciated his own name. "Marm," he said. He didn't look in a mirror again for a long time.

Decades arrived and went. Hank did not age, although his face and his body became stranger and stranger to him. The Klan had been temporarily put down and so he found other groups that had scattered after the humiliating defeat and joined those. He devoted himself to the feeling of hatred, and to the power of being feared. One night, he went one step further and murdered a man out back of a supermarket. The killing felt natural, and it made him hungry. He started tearing into the man with his teeth, and, surprised and horrified at this, he fled home.

He looked again in the mirror, a different mirror from the last time he had looked, in a different home. It was many years later. He wasn't even sure he was human anymore. He looked so different from himself. Blood stained his teeth, but under the scarlet the enamel was a dull, sickly yellow. He howled at his reflection, and his voice didn't sound like the voice he had once had. It sounded powerful and big. He felt feared. "Ha," he said. "Pop." He no longer tried to turn these sounds into words. They meant what they said. Hank walked out of his house, leaving the front door open. He never returned. It took weeks for his disappearance to be noticed.

The creature he had become walked with his now boneless legs along the highways. When he felt his energy fade, he would murder someone, anyone, it didn't matter who, and this would give him the energy for another week or two's walk. He did not question for a moment what he was doing, or what he had become.

Finally, months into his journey, he was drawn by an unrefusable instinct to an air force base in Southern California, and a walled compound within it. A gate opened up in those walls, opened by other creatures like him, and unknown decades after his birth, Hank, who no longer could remember his name enough to try to say it, stumbled cackling into the home that had been waiting for him all along.

51

The Sage Blossom Motel, an hour outside of Dallas. Two people slumped against each other in bed. They hadn't gotten out of bed in days, except to go to the bathroom, and to accept food from the one place that would deliver, a Tex-Mex and Chinese combination that provided a diverse if lousy menu selection. The Do Not Disturb placard had been left on the door for days, and the sheets had a sour smell.

"Maybe we should . . . ," said Keisha, swinging a hand toward the sunlight coming in through the corner of the tightly closed curtain.

"Why? To do what?" muttered Alice into her pillow. "We've lost."

Keisha sat up. "But we're still alive. We have lives now."

"We do?"

"We do."

They contemplated lives together lived outside of this war. Could they live, knowing that all the horror was still out there, undefeated, ever spreading?

"We'll learn to get used to it," said Alice.

"I guess we will. I guess we'll have to."

Keisha let her eyes close as she thought about it. There was a tapping on the window. Keisha's eyes flew open. The margin around the curtain had gone from the bright sunlight to the white reflection of the parking lot lights. It was night. She had no idea how long she had been asleep. Her head felt full of cotton and glue. She couldn't get a focus on anything around her.

Tap, tap, tap. Not like a knuckle. A thinner and sharper body part. A fingernail. Or a part of the body with no human counterpart. She shook Alice, and Alice came awake and upright with a gasp. Both of them were groggy. Had something been put in the air in their room? The two of them flopped out of bed and backed up to the wall opposite the window. *Tap, tap, tap.*

Glass breaking. But the front window was still intact. The sound had come from next to them, in the small bathroom. Keisha nudged the door open with her heel and glanced in. The tiny window above the toilet, at most a foot square, was broken open, and there was a stream of flesh, like an enormous dry slug, oozing in through the opening and tumbling down onto the dirty tile of the floor. The shape resolved itself as it landed, forming back into something like human limbs.

"Hello," said the Thistle Man that was coming in through the window, but his voice was as warped as his body, stretched out and oozing from his long throat. "Hellllo." He giggled, and it sounded like a garbage disposal processing gravel. The part of his body that had formed on the ground started lurching toward them even as the broken window vomited the rest of him.

Alice took Keisha's hand, and they ran for the front door. Likely more monsters waiting there, but better outside than in a small room. Alice flung the door open and they took it at a run. There was no one on the second-floor walkway where they were standing, but every light in the parking lot below clicked off the moment they left the room, and they stared down into the darkness below. There was a chattering from the lot, like a teeming nest of thousands of rats.

"Nowhere to go now," said the man from behind them.

"Nowhere to go," joined a chorus of voices from the lot. The chattering got louder. The malfunctioning lights of the lot flickered, and for a moment Alice could see loose faces, and many sadistic, yellow eyes.

Keisha looked at Alice. Maybe it was ok if this was the end. At least they were together. There were many ways their lives could have gone where they wouldn't have had even that.

"Hey, what are you doing?" said a woman's voice. The woman, whose name was Theresa, although Keisha would never learn this, stuck her head out of the room next door.

Keisha's impulse was to warn her back inside, to get her out of harm's way. This is what she would have done perhaps on any other night but this. But some combination of acceptance of the end and the days of stasis leading up to it had weakened her in some fundamental way and what she said instead was: "Help us." She didn't know why she said it. She said it again. "Help us."

"Back to your room," gurgled the Thistle Man as he advanced into the walkway. Another Thistle Man leaped up from the parking lot and landed on his belly on the railing, where he began to droop forward face-first. "You don't have to have seen anything. Go back to your room."

Theresa's face registered three shades of green and she moved as though to shut the door. But instead she leaned into the frame and shouted.

"Jesús! Get out here!" A man came stumbling out behind Theresa. She had already turned back, was already running forward, putting her hands on the shoulders of the creature crawling over the railing and flipping him back over. The Thistle Man yelped in surprise and there was a sound like wet dough hitting a kitchen floor. Meanwhile Jesús, bleary eyed with sleep but getting the gist of the situation, swung at the Thistle Man and connected. The monster grunted and fell forward into the wall, denting his forehead.

Another room opened, and a woman in business clothes came out.

"What's all the noise?" she said, ready to let them have it.

"Help us!" said Keisha and Theresa. There was no hesitation. The businesswoman, whose name was Angela, although Keisha would never learn this, grabbed the Thistle Man from the back while Theresa, Jesús, and Keisha took turns kicking him. The Thistle Man groaned and shook them off, then leaped forward off the second-floor walkway into the black empty below. There was no sound of him landing. A second later, all the lights in the lot popped on. The lot was empty.

"Thank you," managed Keisha.

"Yeah, sure," said Angela, already heading back inside. "We have to help each other, you know?"

Jesús also went back to his room with a nod, because the game was coming back from halftime. But Theresa stayed for a moment. "If they come back hassling you, you let us know, ok?"

"We will," said Alice. "Thank you so much. I don't . . ."

Theresa hugged her. "Sometimes it's us who wins," she said, and then she followed her husband into the room.

Keisha and Alice hid in the truck while the police ostensibly investigated the disturbance reported by the motel clerk, but of course instead making sure the truth could never be determined. But neither of the women had any desire to return to that room, which had become a spiral they hadn't been able to find a way out of. Both of them had the same thought now, one they could discuss later but were content that evening just to sit with, feeling something other than despair for the first time in two weeks. Because Theresa was right. Sometimes it's us who wins.

52

October. Two months since the motel.

Organizing a country of people into an army capable of fighting the monsters hidden among them seemed an impossible task. But like all impossible tasks, it was made of a lot of small, doable actions. First Alice and Keisha simply held a meeting. They put out word through the people they had met and trusted on their journeys, since public notice would attract the attention of Bay and Creek. A month's lead time, to give people time to travel if they needed to, and a spot at a quiet park in Upstate New York that was uncrowded enough to talk in peace but frequented enough that a small gathering would be unsuspicious.

At twenty miles per hour on the narrow road into the park, Keisha was speeding by ten.

"If it's no one, that's ok," Alice said. "We'll try again. We'll try as many times as we need to."

"Of course. But there will be people there," said Keisha. "You'll see. Maybe even a lot of people."

When they pulled up to the covered picnic tables, there was no one, and Alice nodded, confirming what she had forced herself to suspect so as to avoid disappointment. But Keisha kept a careful watch on the road in and within an hour other cars arrived. A pair of seventeen-year-olds from Texas who had known Sylvia before she had fallen off the map. A quiet woman in her sixties with a knee brace who said hello and not much more. A man in his forties who responded to Alice's friendly hello but couldn't quite make eye contact with Keisha, which she was somewhat offended by until she realized that she recognized him. He had been behind the counter of a convenience store in Swansea, South Carolina, and it was possible that she had spoken fairly forcefully to him. "Dan," he said, introducing himself with a bop of his head and then standing on the other end of the crowd from the two of them. Keisha had the sense that these people had seen things they could not understand and were hoping that coming here might allow them to finally make sense of what they now knew the world to be.

A short man in a baseball hat stepped out of a twenty-year-old Volkswagen.

"Hey, we've never met in person," he said. "I'm Tanya. You once called me looking for Sylvia. I wasn't sure I could trust you then." He looked around at the few others that had come. "Still not sure."

"I welcome healthy suspicion," said Keisha.

"Never anything healthy about suspicion," said Tanya. "But it sometimes will keep you alive."

Then a woman whom Keisha recognized, arriving from what was likely not far at all. It was the woman at the front desk of the

Dutchess County Sheriff's Office in Poughkeepsie, the one who had once given them the video of the murder of Sylvia's mother. As she approached, she bundled her jacket up around her face, as though to hide herself from onlookers, or watchers in the nearby woods.

"Like I said," she murmured, "not all of us are on their side." She wouldn't say any more.

Alice moved through the crowd, greeting people one-on-one, setting them at ease with her easy way. There was no combination of gestures or words Keisha could ever learn to match the instinct of Alice's way with people.

They waited another few minutes to give stragglers some time to show themselves, and then Keisha stood.

"Ok, I guess I'll start by thanking y'all for coming."

"Hold up." A voice shouted from the parking lot. A woman was hurrying toward them. Keisha felt a wave of panic. Alice stepped in front of her, hand in her bag. The teenagers looked ready to bolt. But the woman approaching had both her hands up and seemed to be in a hurry rather than attacking.

"Sorry, sorry," the woman said, and Keisha knew who it was. Lynh, dispatcher with Bay and Creek Shipping who had once given her access to the routing software. "I heard someone was looking into my bosses and I wanted to know exactly what those sneaky fucks have been up to. Lay it on me."

And so they did. The first meeting was a telling of stories. Alice and Keisha told theirs. One by one, each of the attendees, rather than responding directly or indicating any degree of belief or disbelief, recited their own stories back. Things seen, run away from, hidden from, attacked by, encountered. There were things worse than men on these roads, and the people in this park had met them.

That night Keisha and Alice slept, for the first time, in the same cot, pressed close together. The back of Alice's neck was the part that smelled most strongly of her, and Keisha put her nose there. She hadn't forgiven her, but they were doing good now. And doing good together felt a little like forgiveness.

April.

This time Sharon from Poughkeepsie showed up first, even though she had the farthest to come. They were meeting in a suburb of Minneapolis, in the parking lot of a mall. The lot was mostly empty as was, for the last couple years, the mall. A monumental structure hollowed out by internet shopping, and so affording them a good amount of privacy as they slowly rolled in. Lynh soon after Sharon, and Tanya, in sweaty athletic clothes.

"My baseball league," he explained. "Couldn't miss it. Never have. So I had to jump in my car right after and drive eight straight hours here."

"Glad you could make it," said Keisha.

The quiet seventeen-year-olds, two days of driving from Denton. One introduced himself as Jeff. The other one didn't talk, just smoked and watched everyone else talk. Jeff said that he and his friend had been hanging out by the fairgrounds when they had been approached by a person in a hoodie who had told them things that no one else knew, saying that they were needed to help make the world a better place.

"It sounds corny," he said defensively. "But when she said it, I believed her. Or him, I guess. I never saw her face."

"I saw him too," said Sharon from Poughkeepsie. "Only he was standing in the Hudson River. Up to his knees. Except when he lifted out his feet to walk, they were dry as bone. Like he wasn't part of this world."

"What did she say?" said Jeff. Sharon only shook her head.

"I know what they said to me," said Lynh. "They told me that there were monstrous things in this world. And that I could help fix them. And I think I can."

"Amen," said Tanya, wiping his forehead, even though in the cool evening air he was no longer sweating.

Dan from Swansea didn't say anything, just nodded along, following the conversation with nervous flicks of his eyes.

Alice and Keisha ate dinner from take-out boxes, knees pressed together in the seats of the cab. They didn't talk as they ate, but the silence felt light. The heaviness of the months together was temporarily lifted as they ate their turkey sandwiches and Alice looked up and caught Keisha's eyes and they both started giggling and, once they had started, they couldn't stop.

August.

A storefront church in Tallahassee. It was a Monday, and the church wasn't using it, and so was willing to rent it out to what Keisha had described to the owner as a support group. Not quite a lie. The carpet was kept meticulously clean but was threadbare and flat-out missing in a few places. The pulpit was wood laid over milk crates. There was a scattering of foldout chairs in a variety of conditions.

"It's perfect," she had said to the owner, and he had beamed.

"It is, isn't it?" he had said with pride.

The location fit their purpose even better than before. The meetings had quickly taken on a religious aspect. Every soul who gathered had experienced encounters with the oracles, who were, if not messengers from a god, at the very least otherworldly messengers of something. Once Lynh had shown up, thirty minutes late, they gathered in a circle, hands clasped.

"Let's start this the way we always do," said Alice. "Let's thank the oracles for their work."

When this ritual had been introduced, by Dan of all people, one of the first contributions he had made to the discussion, Alice had found the whole business a bit silly, but Keisha had convinced her that it would be useful. It would keep people focused, and believing, and grateful, all states of being that could prove to help protect them in the difficult struggle ahead. Now Alice embraced the ritual completely, taking ownership of its administration, because while she struggled to believe in the concept of faith, she believed completely in anything with a practical utility.

This day there was a muttered babble of thanks from the group, nothing that could be individually picked out but the general tenor was clear. "Now," continued Alice, "has anyone had any experiences with the oracles since we last spoke?"

"Right here," said Tanya. He was looking energized and snapping gum between his teeth. "My backyard has this low wall, and then behind that wall is a field that I think technically belongs to the city but nothing has been done with it in years. I keep showing up at town meetings and I swear that Councilman Gold had headphones on last time I was speaking my bit. Sorry, not directly relevant. The field's home now to a few thousand rabbits and everything that likes to eat rabbits, and so I sometimes sit on the wall and watch the field in the evenings. Nature blood in tooth and cottontail and all that. Well, once a week, every Thursday, at 5:15 p.m. on the dot, one of those figures in a hoodie walks across the field. I've called out to them, but they never answer."

"Thank you for your story, Brother Tanya," the group whispered.

"Yeah, sure thing," he boomed back.

The testimonials continued. Jeff and his friend had spoken to their oracle at the same spot they had seen them before. The oracle had told them that they would be there at the end of this but wouldn't elaborate on whether that was good or bad.

"I hope good," said Keisha.

"Don't we all," Tanya said, laughing.

After, they went over what they knew of Bay and Creek and of Thistle again and discussed strategies for tackling the problem step by step. They hadn't gotten far, but ten months into this process both Keisha and Alice had settled into the long timeline of it. Even if this was the rest of their lives, at least they were living it together.

April again.

The first part of the plan was for each person who came to the meeting to start a group of their own, back where they lived. And to varying degrees of success, related to their ability to motivate both themselves and other people, that's what they did. Tanya, of course, had a group lined up in no time. Jeff and his friend also did quite well, despite their shyness. They knew a lot of other quiet kids, and quiet kids are good at listening. Lynh had the most trouble, since she spent her days at Bay and Creek, which left her with no one she knew who could be trusted.

But gradually the groups spread, among others who had encountered the oracles, and others still who just felt that it was all wrong and wanted to be part of the healing of all that. Soon members of those meetings were given the same assignment, and even more of the groups started. None of them communicated with any of the others except through the occasional encounters with the oracles, who would whisper encouragement or information. All the people drawn to these groups had seen terrible and strange wonders, and they sat in circles and described the shape of the monster that was devouring them. Not for comfort, but for information. They meant to fight that monster and they meant to win. The oracles were treated by the movement as something close to deities, and the further the group was removed from the original circle, the more that the meetings took on the religious aspect, praying to the oracles and asking for their guidance. Almost as revered, though, were the Derelict Bombers, the two prophets who had first borne the message. Among the membership that had never met them, they were considered almost as divine as the oracles themselves, taken as role models in the struggle for a better world. "Thank you to the oracles," they would mutter. "And thank you to Keisha and Alice, who led us to today." All over the country, mouths young and old, of all races and gender identities, speaking the names of two women they believed could offer salvation. The groups called themselves and what they were doing "Praxis." No one could say where that name had come from, or who had decided on it, but there was no question.

Keisha and Alice were lying outside in the grass of a municipal park. It was an unusually warm spring night, and the sky was starlit clear. They held hands and breathed together. There was no need to talk. They had talked enough. For now, they lay together, and breathed together, unaware of all the people just then evoking their names.

53

The radio roared to life, shaking Keisha and Alice out of early morning semisleep, the crackle of the static interacting tactilely with their skin. A voice emerged from the noise. Both of them recognized it, although the memories it called to their minds were entirely different.

"Alice," said Lucy. "I've missed you. I know you probably don't believe that. You'll probably never forgive me. But I want you to know that I did what I did because I believed it was for your best. Everything I'm doing is because I think it's the right thing to do, and you'll never believe me, and I'm ok with that. Listen, I . . ."

Her voice lapsed back into the static and was gone for a full two minutes. Keisha stretched, moved up to the front seat to fiddle with the radio, but the signal seemed to be coming through on every channel. Alice sat on the cot, remembering a time when that voice belonged to a friend. She couldn't explain that melancholy to Keisha without it sounding like treason to the trauma Alice had caused, and maybe it was.

"I want to meet," the voice came again, sounding like a direct continuation of her last sentence. Keisha wondered if the signal had truly lapsed or if Lucy had sat there, holding the radio in silence for those minutes, building tension or truly trying to find her way to what she had to say next. "What you've been doing with Praxis. It's wrong. Of course it's impressive. Alice, you were always an impressive woman. But you're going to hit a point where there won't be a way back down from this. Let me help. There's a construction site near El Paso. Abandoned since the recession. Meet me there. Bring Keisha too. We can all talk about this. Ok?"

Another long pause. Perhaps she honestly was waiting for a reply. Keisha wasn't going to give her one

"Well, think it over, anyway," said Lucy. "To get back to me, send out a message on any frequency. They're listening to all of them. I think you knew that. I hope you were smart enough to know that. Ok, Alice. Until then."

The signal lapsed. Keisha was sure that she had not left the radio on, she never left the radio on. Who had turned it on while they slept? She spent the morning disconnecting it from its power supply, and then they ate lunch at a bench near a gravel lot in Utah that perhaps was once supposed to be something but now would indefinitely be an empty place.

"So they've decided we're too dangerous," said Keisha.

"They want to put an end to all this," agreed Alice.

"They think we're stupid."

"They might not be wrong."

They laughed and didn't say anything else for a bit. This comfortable silence was interrupted by the crunch of gravel. The two of them locked eyes and stood, ready to defend themselves. Keisha thought again of the radio, which she had definitely, for sure, left off before they went to sleep. Alice gestured Keisha around the front of the truck and she headed toward the back. Keisha crept, palms against the sun-warm grille, then popped out the other side with a shout. The teenage girl waiting there screamed with surprise.

"Sorry," said Sylvia. "Shit, sorry. I didn't mean to sneak up on you."

But Keisha had already pulled her into a hug.

"I wouldn't rather be scared by anyone else."

"Anxiety bros." Sylvia laughed.

"Anxiety bros." Keisha hugged her tighter.

Alice decided that this girl was not a threat and emerged from around the back of the truck. "Hi," she said, with a tentative little wave. "You must be Sylvia. I'm—"

"Alice," said Sylvia, crossing her arms high on her chest. "Heard a lot about you. That was real shitty what you did."

"It was," agreed Alice.

"I wouldn't have let you hang around, but Keisha is a better person than me."

"That's definitely not true," said Keisha, happy to let Alice be uncomfortable for a bit. Keisha was allowed to have some friends of her own.

"Well," Sylvia said, turning away from Alice. "Let's talk. It's a long story."

"I love a long story," said Keisha, as she gestured Sylvia up into the cab. "It distracts me from my own long story."

"Speaking of, did you read the newest *Love and Rockets*?"

"Maybe his best."

"Maybe."

Sylvia had gone looking for Praxis and the oracles. Started in that network of safe houses and shelters, gutter punks and activists, and also folks who just had a turn they hadn't seen coming and had ended up on the wrong side of the crushing weight of polite society. A lot of people knew what she was talking about, but no one could point her to any useful information. Everyone knew of Praxis, but no one knew how to get their ear. Failing any specific direction, she settled on all directions, going to any place that seemed likely to attract an oracle of the roads. The bathrooms at gas stations, behind the fading backdrops of roadside attractions, in the farthest room down the hall at motels that had last seen real business in the seventies. She went to those places, and she kept her eyes open.

It had been at one of those half-abandoned motels when she had first seen one of the oracles. The carpet had been damp. There were paintings on the wall by the motel's owner, smears of primary colors. Sylvia had walked slowly to the room with the cracked-open door, feeling at once hope and terror. She wanted to leave, she wanted to run, but she put out her hand and she pushed the door wide. And there was a figure in a hoodie, sitting on the edge of the neatly made bed, waiting for her. The moment Sylvia saw the oracle, she felt neither fear nor excitement. What she felt was recognition. This was where she was supposed to be, and the oracle was welcoming her to it.

They talked all night, and Sylvia could feel the oracle wanted to tell her more but was trapped by the nonlinearity of their thoughts. And so she tried to meet them halfway, tried to think and talk in a way that was untied from time. Even after she left the room, having found herself alone at the instant of daybreak, she continued this practice. If she was going to help them, she would need to think like them. She found that the state she was trying to reach was the kind of thinking done right before falling asleep, when thoughts flatten out and mix with dreams. Each night, she would try to hold on to what that did to her sense of time, and gradually she was able to create that feeling for herself even when wide awake.

Soon Sylvia found more oracles and learned as much as it was possible to learn of what they knew. She, too, found out that the Thistle Men were human. She learned how powerful the oracles were, that physically a Thistle Man was no match for an oracle, although Thistle had a vicious advantage in numbers. She noticed that the oracles smelled of heather, in the same way that Thistle smelled of mildew. Each reacted strongly to the smell of their natural adversaries. Sylvia started to truly love the smell of heather.

"Their timelessness is their power, but it also causes great suffering, because every moment is happening for them, all at once. So if they've done something, they have to keep doing it, all the time. They are always having to maintain what has already happened. They can never rest."

She curled her arms around her knees in the passenger seat, looking out at the sunset through the windshield.

"I never found the oracle that saved my life all those years ago, but I don't need to, I don't think. I found a whole community of them, and they are doing good in the world, and I can help them do that."

"I think I know how you can do that. How we all can do that," said Keisha. "It's time for the Anxiety Bros to face their fears."

54

"Thank you for coming," said Keisha. "Likely this will be our last meeting." The faces looking back at her were confused. Tanya, and Lynh, and Sharon, and Jeff, and all the others from their original meeting. They had met less and less, as everyone had gotten more focused on leading their own groups. But this meeting had been called, and all of them had immediately come from all over the country to be there.

"Bay and Creek has asked to meet with us, and we are going to go." The confusion turned to frowns. "I know," said Keisha. "But we are strong now. We aren't alone like we were before. We are going to meet them, and fight them, and finally make use of this movement we have been building all this time."

"What's the plan?" asked Tanya.

Keisha laughed. "You just heard it."

This wasn't quite true. She had set into motion one aspect that she wasn't going to share with them, because if they were going to walk into this, she needed them to walk into this thinking it was only them against the monsters, and to still come willingly. She couldn't have them depending on anyone else to save them.

"We can't go against Bay and Creek," Lynh said. "Not without some trick."

"We don't need a trick," said Sylvia. She hadn't introduced herself, but she hadn't needed to. Young as she was, there was a confidence to her that was immediately absorbed by the group. She had seen things that they hadn't, and here she still was. So when she spoke, they listened. "We are stronger than we think. They are weaker than they realize."

"I'm a pretty confident guy," said Tanya. "But I'm not that confident. I'm not dangerous confident, you know?"

"This is what we've been preparing for," said Alice. "This is what this group has been about from the start. If we weren't going to confront them, then what was all this organizing for? It's time."

Jeff, quiet as usual, nodded. "I'm tired of waiting." He put his arm around his friend, who nodded. "We're in."

Once Jeff agreed, the others did too. The quiet woman with the knee brace. Sharon, who shook her head and said "this is crazy" over and over, but stayed anyway. "I'm not going to be the least foolhardy in any group," said Tanya. "I'm in, of course."

Finally it was Lynh left. She had her arms crossed.

"It's ok if you want to go," said Keisha. "You've done a lot. It's ok to walk away."

Lynh began to cry. "I'm not going to walk away," she said. "I'm crying because I'm a fool and we're all fools and we're all about to die, but I'm not going to walk away."

"Ok then, it's settled," said Keisha. Then they were quiet. No one knew what else to say. They felt themselves sliding down a steep slope toward a cliff, and they had no idea what lay over its edge. They sat in silence together, waiting for the drop, and for the long fall after.

Keisha had thought a lot about what she was going to say before she started speaking, but still her cheeks went hot and the words felt heavy and clumsy coming out. It's easy enough to map out in your head what should be said, but another thing to find the voice to say it. But it had to be said. Because after that night they were going to be dead or they were going to be free to go on with their lives, and either way she couldn't do it with the weight of Alice's actions slung over them. This had to end.

"Alice," she said, and Alice looked up, worried, hearing the earnest intensity in Keisha's voice.

"Honey, what is it?"

"I need you to hear what I'm going to say clearly," said Keisha. "Because whatever happens next, this is important. You left me. You left me to think you were dead, and to mourn you. You spent all those months hiding from me as I tried to find you. All because of some stupid sense that I needed protecting. I don't need protecting."

"Baby, I believe that now," Alice whispered. She fidgeted her hands in her lap. "I'm so sorry."

"I don't care," said Keisha. "This isn't about you. What you did is not about you, because it wasn't done to you. It was done to me. And so I get to decide what to do next. Here is what I've decided. I'm going to forgive you."

Alice's smile broke like sun through clouds. "Oh, Keisha," she said.

"Not yet," Keisha said, putting a hand up to keep Alice's distance. "I need you to hear all of this, not just the parts that you want to hear. I'm forgiving you. But I'm not doing it for you. I don't know if you deserve forgiveness, and maybe I don't care. Maybe there isn't some great balance sheet of forgiveness where the equation of guilt can be figured until it's all equal on both sides. Maybe it's just what the person who was hurt feels, right or wrong. And if so, then I don't want to think about what you deserve. I want to think about what I deserve."

She breathed. The heaviest part was out of her now, and she could see clear through to the finish. She didn't look in Alice's eyes.

"I deserve to live a happy life. I deserve to have my wife whom I love at my side. I deserve to breathe easy in the morning and to fall asleep easy at night. I deserve to not have what you did intruding into our lives. So I want you to understand this. To have what I deserve, I must forgive you. But I'm not forgiving you for you. I'm forgiving you because it's what I deserve."

Alice was quiet. Quietly she said, "Ok."

Keisha took her face in her hands, met her eyes. "I love you," she said. She leaned her mouth toward Alice and then stopped. "Hey, you never told me. How did you find out that Bay and Creek was working with Thistle? How long had you known?"

For the first time, Keisha met Alice's eyes, only a few inches from her own.

"I didn't know," said Alice. "I had no idea until you told me. I only knew that they were trying to hurt you. And if they were trying to hurt you, then I was against them, no matter what greater good they were working toward. I realized if I had to pick a side, it was always going to be yours."

Keisha kissed her wife, and the feeling of their lips together, the smell of her skin that close, it felt light and true and fine for the first time in years. The kiss was a door to home, and she gladly stepped through it.

This is love, she thought. *This is what it's made of.*

55

Their ludicrous caravan of sedans and minivans pulling into the meeting spot looked more like a church group on a day hike than an army marching into battle. There were still a few pieces of construction equipment left behind by a company that had stopped existing abruptly, gone to the point where it wasn't even worth selling off assets. And stretched out across the mounds of dirt and the leveled-out area seeded by wisps of dry grass were hundreds of Thistle Men, grinning at them as they stepped forward. Beyond that, Bay and Creek commandos, black balaclavas hiding their identities. There would be no attempt, then, to hide the purpose of this day. They intended to finish Praxis.

"Hoo," one of the Thistle Men cried out. "Ha." Others giggled or coughed.

Lucy stood before the monsters.

"I'm glad you decided to meet," she said. "Alice, this isn't how I wanted it to happen. But at least we're doing this in person."

Alice wouldn't even look at her. Stared straight ahead with fixed determination. Keisha spat into the dirt.

"I see you brought some backup."

Lucy looked back at the twitching, loose-skinned men behind her. "I had to go all in," she said. "If I was going to choose to work with them, I had to go all in. I wish you could understand, but I don't expect you to. Besides, it looks like you brought backup of your own. For instance, a couple of teenagers. And one of our employees. Hi, Lynh."

Lynh shrank back behind Sharon from Poughkeepsie, who moved without thinking to step in front of her.

"Now," shouted Keisha. She and all the rest of her Praxis group pulled out bottles of heather oil, started pouring them on themselves.

Lucy nodded. "Smart move. I would have done the same. Won't help, only slow things down, but still smart."

Sylvia was slower opening her bottle. She stumbled a little. Her hands were sweaty.

"I don't feel right," she whispered to Jeff, who looked back at her worried. He had looked worried all morning. His friend hadn't even come. Had decided to stay behind. But Jeff was here anyway. Sylvia started to stumble, and he caught her arm.

"You ok?" he said.

"No, I don't think I am at all. My vision is going all . . . I don't know. Not blurry. There's more of it than usual."

Meanwhile Keisha and Alice stepped forward, dripping with the heather oil.

"I know the boys don't like it," Lucy said, "but honestly that smells pretty nice."

"I don't suppose there's any other way than fighting," said Keisha, not because she actually wanted to know, but to pass the time, because it felt like she should be saying something before the violence started.

"That's up to you, I guess," said Lucy. "You all could give up. I know that seems crazy, but it's actually an option. I'd do my best to protect you. It might not work. I'm being honest on that. But look at you. You don't even have any of the oracles. You don't stand a chance."

"Guess not," said Keisha.

"Lucy, you're a real piece of shit," said Alice.

"That's not fair," said Lucy.

Sylvia fell to the ground gasping, cutting off the conversation. She was shaking. Keisha ran back to her. The Thistle Men chortled and woofed, watching all this with hungry eyes.

"Sylvia, what's wrong?" she whispered.

"It's ok," said Sylvia. "I understand now." She scooted her body back until she was leaning on one of the minivans. "I understand what's happening. And I'm ok with it."

"What are you talking about?" said Keisha, but there was an awful tickle in her stomach because somewhere in there she knew.

"Praxis and Thistle are just people. Thistle Men were people transformed by hate. And the oracles, they're people transformed by a desire to organize a better world. We're all just people fighting for an idea of what living as humans should be like," said Sylvia. "I didn't get to lead too long of a life, huh?" Her voice sounded like she was shouting from hundreds of feet away. Her breath was going cold. "But I'll live it all at once forever." Her eyes closed, and she started to shake violently. Keisha tried to hold her, but she slipped away. Dust flew up into the air as she jittered and kicked. And then she was still again. The dust settled down around them, a fine layer of red on Keisha's hair.

Sitting where Sylvia had been was a person in a hoodie. Inside the hood, Keisha could see Sylvia's face, weak but smiling. When she spoke, her voice sounded layered, like there were many of her talking at once.

"This is what I wanted," she said. "I could have refused this. I want you to know that I chose."

She was standing. There was no in between. She had been sitting. Now she was standing. Her face receded, and even in the bright light of day, Keisha wasn't able to see inside the hood anymore. The oracle that was Sylvia, or had been Sylvia, sprang forward at the Thistle Men, who coughed and hollered back, surging toward her. One of the Thistle Men dropped to all fours, galloping in long, athletic leaps. Another stumbled over his dead legs and fell into the dirt. The others trampled over him, and he whooped into the earth as he was pounded into it. Sylvia roared back at them, and it sounded like a huge window breaking, fragile but explosive.

Sylvia whipped into the mass of Thistle Men and they became a confusion of limbs and violence. A crusted arm with loose skin went flying into the air and another Thistle Man was torn completely in half. The oracle at the old resort in Wisconsin had been strong, but Sylvia, fired by the newness of her transformation, was unbelievable.

When the Thistle Men started to die, the rest of Keisha's group charged, yelling and brandishing knives and bats, whatever items from their homes that seemed the most capable of harm. The Thistle Men that weren't occupied with Sylvia converged on them. One of the men leaped high into the air and landed with a brutal weight on Sharon, who went down instantly. Lynh vaulted over the Thistle Man who was coming at her and started hacking at the one on Sharon. Keisha ignored Thistle, hoping for the best and expecting some serious damage done to their side, and instead locked eyes with Lucy and made right for her.

But Lucy was ready. She met Keisha palm first right in the nose, and Keisha was down. The pain was severe enough to take away her vision, and so she only felt the savage follow-up kick to her stomach.

"You were always foolish, Keisha." Another kick. "You were just always also lucky." A third. Keisha couldn't breathe. "How's that luck holding up?" Lucy growled, furious. "You're a good person, and good people deserve good things."

A little bit of vision came back. Alice was trying to get to her, but there was a line of leering Thistle Men in the way. The small group behind Alice was desperately fighting off attacks from every direction. They all seemed alive for that moment, but that also seemed an entirely changeable proposition, as they were so completely outmatched by the monsters around them. Even Sylvia, who had attacked with such utter ferocity, was disappearing under the crowd of Thistle that kept coming and coming.

Keisha wished that perhaps her vision would go again. Lucy made a kick at her head that would have obliged if she had had better aim. Instead it whiffed along Keisha's scalp, and she felt hot liquid trickle down her forehead.

"It's over, Keisha." Lucy frowned. "I'm not even happy about it. I liked Alice, and you seemed fine. But you made bad choices."

Was it over? It felt pretty over. Keisha winced. The pain of their failure was worse than any of her rapidly blooming bruises. She felt that the world was slipping from her. Because now there seemed to be two of Sylvia. And then three. Keisha knew the world was not slipping from her. The plan had worked. Or, if not solid enough to be called a plan, the gamble. Figures in hoodies, many of them standing on the rise overlooking the abandoned construction site.

And from behind the oracles, a massive crowd of people marching over the rise, all of the people of Praxis, Jeff's friend right at the front.

56

To each of the groups of Praxis, scattered all over the country, an oracle had arrived. The groups had turned, struck speechless by a presence they had whispered stories about for months, savoring the secondhand glory of their encounters, and now here were the divine messengers, in the flesh or whatever they were made of. Each group saw a figure in a hoodie, standing plain and open in the light of living room lamps and hotel conference room overheads and bar neon and sunlight through coffee shop windows. Wherever these groups met, an oracle had come, all bearing the same message.

"You are needed. Now is the time."

And without exception, each member of each group had followed. Some had only a few miles to go. Others drove for days. But all of them had arrived at the same place at the same time. Together, thousands of strangers from all over the country assembled behind the growing line of oracles, and, unsure of what lay before them or what would be asked of them, they marched forward anyway. They had crested the hill and saw the brutal fight before them. None of them turned away. Each had a moment of understanding, and a moment of questioning, but the organizing done in those months had been strong, and their hearts had been prepared, and each of them had picked up their pace into a run and hurled themselves at the seething of monsters.

The Thistle Men were not expecting any further participants in the battle, but they moved in a mindless fit of hunger and anger, and so they lashed and bit at the people as they came. The Bay and Creek soldiers were more easily defeated despite their weapons. A gun can only mean so much to people who are willing to die for a cause. Ten of the newcomers were dead in as many seconds, but still the others ran forward. The oracles who had led them launched into the crowd, churning through the Thistle Men like propellers through water. The ground became thick with sickly yellow fat that spewed from Thistle as they fell. Thistle Men were powerful and they were quick, but there were so many people, and still more were coming over the lip of the site and charging down at them. They yipped and moaned in confusion, sensing the impossible fact that somehow they were losing.

Keisha, seeing this, struggled to her hands and knees, and then up to a kneel. Lucy pulled a vicious little knife from her belt.

"You should never have gone after her," Lucy said as she stabbed. Her aim was good but her arm veered sideways. Alice had knocked the blade out of the way, taking a long slash on her shoulder as she did.

Alice gathered her words, tried to find a way to express all that she felt about Lucy, but all she could find was "fuck you," and so she attacked. Lucy was faster, and far more skilled. She kicked Alice in the head, and Alice went down, stumbled back up. Lucy popped her throat with the side of her hand and Alice was down again. Keisha found the energy inside herself to move to her feet. It was painful but she was upright. She limped between Lucy and Alice and motioned her wife to stay on the ground.

"This time I protect you," she said.

Lucy cocked her head, considering her.

"You're brave, huh?"

Keisha laughed. "I have, never in my life, been so scared."

She threw herself at Lucy. There was no matching Lucy's skill, and so Keisha moved in a fever of anxiety and instinct, lashing out again and again with both hands and both legs. At first Lucy blocked her easily, but then one of Keisha's fists slipped through and cracked across her cheekbone. Each hit was easy enough to see coming, but there were so many, and Keisha was moving so quickly and hitting with such force. Lucy began to tire, and her arms were aching where she was blocking the hits. She tripped slightly and shifted to retain her balance, and in that moment Keisha kicked her square in the chest. She went down, and Keisha was on her.

Keisha felt panic pound through every limb and tried her best to transfer all that energy kinetically into Lucy. She punched and kicked and clawed and Lucy at first struggled to get up, and then Lucy couldn't struggle anymore, and then Lucy would never struggle again, and as Lucy died, she wondered at how completely she had misunderstood her opponent.

Ragged breaths as Keisha tried to find herself again, although she suspected there was no way to separate her identity from her anxiety. Her anxiety was not a monster that haunted her. It was a part of her body, as much her as her blood or her headaches. Around her the lot was quieting down. Those few Thistle Men who were not dead were fleeing, making wet hissing sounds as they ran, pursued by members of Praxis who would not let them escape. All the Bay and Creek commandos were dead or had fled. Alice went to her knees next to Keisha, put both arms around her.

"I killed her," said Keisha. "She was a person and I killed her."

"You saved me," said Alice. "You saved me."

57

The lot was scattered with dead Thistle Men, and dead people. Many who had come had died. Keisha saw immediately that Jeff was one of them. His friend held him in his arms and waved away anyone who approached. He made a keening noise. Jeff's head lolled back and his friend cradled it. There were so many other dead. People she had never seen before, whose names she would never know, who had come from all over the country to finish this fight with her. She knelt next to the body of a woman in her forties whose knuckles were bruised and whose hand was clutched around a long kitchen knife smeared with yellow fat. The woman's face was untouched, as though only taking a nap. Keisha took the knife out of her hand and placed it neatly at her side. She held the woman's hand with both of hers.

"Thank you," she said. She kissed the woman's forehead. "I will never be able to repay you." She placed the woman's hand gently on her stomach and stood.

The oracles, too, had taken heavy losses. Their bodies were flung violently about the field and tended to by the few oracles left alive. The dead ones lay motionless, but their bodies wavered, like digital static.

"They exist outside of time, and so endings don't stick well on them," said an oracle next to her. There was of course no face under their hood, but Keisha knew who they were.

"Somewhere, even now, they are still living, still fighting," the oracle said. "As I, too, am dead, years from now."

"Sylvia, we did it." Keisha grasped the oracle's arm. For some reason, she had expected it to be cold, but the arm was warm and human. "We did it, right? Did we do it?"

"We did it," said the oracle, watching as the other oracles gathered up the ones they had lost. There was a faint whistling sound that could have been weeping and could have been singing. It seemed to come from all the oracles simultaneously.

Alice came up to Keisha and embraced her and Sylvia both. She made a choking laugh that sounded not entirely joyful. And Keisha felt afraid, a fear that was as consuming as it was impossible to trace its source.

"It was worth it, right?" Keisha said. "Sylvia, was it worth it?" She didn't know what she was asking the worth of. This plan, and all the deaths that followed. Or her life, and Alice's life, cast out on the roads for so long. Or Sylvia, who had given up not just her life but her entire being.

"I think so," said the oracle. They bowed their head. "It will never be finished for me. Even now, I am still fighting. I am meeting you, Keisha, on a highway in Georgia. I am sneaking frantic out of a room at an Extended Stay America. I am watching my mother die, killing her murderer, and telling myself to hide. That is all happening now. And I will have to keep doing it forever, maintaining these moments so that time can continue as it has. I will never not be fighting. I will never not be meeting you. I will never arrive in time to save my mother. Was it worth it? In a fractal so complex, how can that calculation be made?"

They stepped away from Keisha and Alice.

"I am glad I met you," they said. "I think I loved you. I don't know if I can feel something as uncomplicated as love anymore. But I know that there are moments I'm still experiencing in which I love you. I don't think you will see me again. But know that I am always seeing you, at every moment we had together, forever."

Keisha felt a sob erupt and reached out her hand, but the oracle that had once been a runaway teenager was gone. All the oracles, even the bodies, were gone. The people of Praxis were left with their dead. Sirens in the distance. The police were coming. The living needed to be gone in minutes. All the dead would have to stay.

She turned to Alice, and Alice turned to her.

"I want to go home," said Alice.

"You are home," said Keisha and leaned toward her. There would be better kisses in their life together, ones that were softer, or more romantic, or swooned deeply down the spine, but there would never be another that felt like the first clear breath after surfacing with burning lungs from a long time underwater.

58

One part tomato paste to one part water, a little basil, oregano, chili flakes, garlic, and a splash of red wine. This wasn't their first pizza night in the year since they had come home. But it was the first one that felt like it had before. Dough from scratch. Sauce from scratch. Cheese from the store.

The dough was the most important part. Keisha loved the making of bread, flour and water in her hands, first separate then merging into a silky whole, the yeast and gluten giving it life and breath. Alice took her turn kneading. Both of their hands covered in flour. A flour handprint on the side of Keisha's shirt where Alice had touched her without thinking. Love is cooking together. It's taking ingredients and transforming them together into a meal. They opened a bottle of wine, ate the pizza, watched whatever on the TV, and fell asleep on each other in a wine-and-bread coma. And it was an hour later, when groggy Keisha coaxed groggy

Alice up the stairs so they could brush their teeth and go to bed that she thought, *Oh my god, we feel normal again.*

A bush off a highway. It doesn't matter what state, or even which region. Most stretches of highway look like most other stretches of highway. Uniformity of transit. The gray blank of the concrete walls. The shrubs that can survive with infrequent care providing wisps of green along a shoulder of tire skids and litter. The bush rattled. There were many people nearby, but all of them were in cars speeding past, and so didn't have the relative stillness needed to see the movement of the bush. It shook harder and harder, like there was a bad storm only it could feel.

Then a hand came out of the bush. It was small, like a child's hand. The hand stayed still for a moment, as though resting after great exertion. Then it hooked its nails into the earth and pulled. Gradually, under the leverage of the hand, a woman emerged from the bush. No one driving by noticed this either. The woman was skinny, and frail. She looked close to death. In a way, she was, although in the reverse of what the term usually means. Her eyes, cold and hungry, watched the passing cars. Her boys were dead, killed by those awful women and their awful organization. But Thistle had been destroyed before, and each time she woke again. There was always a place for her in the human heart. It was simple enough to find the right people and draw them together once more. She found the strength to sit up, then to stand up, then to walk along the highway. Eventually she would need a car, but not yet. There would be plenty of time for that later.

• •

"It's your turn," said Alice.

"You have got to be kidding me, trying to pull that," said Keisha. "You know it's your turn, don't even try to rewrite history on that. Get in there and good luck."

Sylvia Cynthia Taylor, at three years old, was a force to be reckoned with, and never more so than when she needed help getting dressed. Mainly because she hated getting dressed. Didn't see the point of it. Clothes were a stupid adult invention that her parents had come up with to keep her from tearing around outside like she wanted to be. It would be, as always, an unholy fight to get those clothes on her.

"I've fought enough for one lifetime," said Keisha. "You get that girl to see some sense."

When their friend Margaret, who had gradually and with a merciful lack of questions become a part of their lives again, wasn't insisting on babysitting so that the two of them could get a break, Keisha and Alice took turns dealing with their kid. If Keisha wanted to, perhaps she could use the guilt over what Alice had done in order to take far fewer turns than her wife, but she never did. She had forgiven Alice six years ago. And if she was going to mean that forgiveness, that meant never cashing in on the guilt. Even when their daughter made that prospect so goddamn hard.

Alice went toward the room where their daughter was already screaming. "If you don't hear from me again . . ." Alice said.

"I will," said Keisha. "I better."

As her wife engaged in battle, Keisha looked through the attic and found a CB radio that she had bought secondhand. For the first couple years after coming home, she would occasionally listen to it, when she was feeling some perverse nostalgia for her life on the road. She wouldn't talk, only follow along with the lonely chatter of a highway night. This night she took it down-stairs, plugged it in, and turned the volume all the way down, the way she used to. She picked up the mic.

"Love is the way her neck smells. Love is the beat of the heart and the passage of air and it's the circulation of fluids, and it's equilibrium. Love is . . ." She stopped, and let the mic click back into silence. She unplugged the radio, put it back in the attic, never touched it again.

That same day, a woman, slight and frail, leaned on the covered lunch area of a rest stop in eastern Colorado. She was staring up at nothing.

William Hendrick, a youth pastor driving across the state to see family, glanced at her as he headed toward the bathroom. It was a curious glance. She was holding a curious pose.

"Do you like what you see?" she said, loudly.

He was embarrassed. "No, I'm sorry, I didn't. I'm sorry."

"Come here," she said. She still looked up at the sky and not at him. He was flustered, so he walked toward her. There was a strong odor. It wasn't like unshowered human, but something else. An older, deeper scent, the smell of freshly turned earth.

"I need your help, William," she said.

"How did you know my name?" he said. He was nervous. There were only about five feet between them, and he took a slight step backward.

"Don't run away now, William. When a person asks you for help, you should help them."

"What do you need?" he said.

She finally looked down from the sky. Her eyes were wrong. When he looked at them, he felt like he was looking at a place thousands and thousands of miles away. There was a depth to her eyes, and he felt vertigo like he had suddenly realized he was standing on the edge of a tall cliff.

A hand clamped onto his shoulder. The smell was even stronger now. He turned to see a man standing there, with loose skin, yellow teeth, and yellow eyes. The man didn't say anything at all. William screamed through everything that happened next, and the woman watched with a friendly smile.

The house felt too big. Their days felt too big too. Why did they live lives that went on so long?

"They said it would be like this," said Alice. "But think of how much time we spent looking after her. And she'll be home for the holidays soon enough. At least we're free for a little while."

"Freedom can be good or bad," said Keisha.

Alice rolled her eyes. "Sure, there can be terrible freedom. I know. You're very profound."

"This is pathetic. We didn't used to be pathetic."

She grabbed playfully at Alice, who responded playfully back, and then their touches became less playful, became heavy with desire. And they were on the living room couch, going at each other with more energy than they had mustered in decades.

"Wow, where did that come from?" said Alice, afterward.

"We still have it. Or we sometimes still have it. We have some of it, some of the time."

Alice put a hand on the side of Keisha's face. "I'm glad we made it this far," she said.

"We'll make it so much farther than this. This is still the start of something."

It was and it wasn't. Everything is the start of something, but the end of something too. Right then, the two of them felt both at once.

There are always open serial killer cases. Always murders that can't be solved. Disappearances on the highways. Still, there had been a period of relative quiet, and it was apparent to law enforcement all over the country that after twenty-one years, the quiet was ending. Murders at rest stops, at small motels, at all-night diners. Descriptions varied, although many mentioned men with loose faces, and voices that sounded like the wind against a window, and sharp yellow teeth under their sagging lips. And watching over all of it, a slight woman, with a fragile voice gently suggesting new ways that the strange men might hurt their victims.

One last scene from the lives of Keisha and Alice Taylor. Nothing dramatic happens in it. There are no epiphanies. Nothing changes. It is twenty years since their daughter left for college. She lives in Chicago now and works as a graphic designer. She calls regularly, visits sometimes. Sylvia doesn't know anything about what her mothers went through before they had her. She knows that she was named after two women, both of whom sacrificed everything so that her life could contain the happiness it does. But the details are hazy and she prefers them that way. It's a difficult subject and makes her mothers upset. The stories of old women are the quiet, overlooked fabric of history.

But we aren't in Chicago. We are in Northern California, in the home that Keisha and Alice have shared for so long, from before she was dead, and then after she wasn't again. Neither of them have had a nightmare in months, which isn't to say they won't again soon. Some things never die. All people eventually do.

And it's this last fact that has become more present in their lives. Because it won't be too much longer, they suppose. But this isn't met with fear. This is just another turn of life. Because they were born, they would someday die. Because they loved, they would someday die. It's only a tragedy if set into the context of grief.

They are not worrying about death. Which is not to say that Keisha isn't worrying. The anxiety will never leave her. It is not a problem that can be fixed, but a state of being she has learned to exist within. A person is not a problem with a solution. A person is their relationship to the world.

They are reading. It's afternoon. They both had chores to do, but then both separately got caught up in books. And now they are absorbed in their reading. Keisha looks up from her book. Her wife, on the couch across the room, is framed perfectly in a ray of sun. It hits her like a spotlight, and Keisha is reminded all over again of how much she loves her. She watches her for a while. Finally, Alice looks up and sees her watching. They look at each other from across the room. Alice smiles.

A life does not have to be satisfying or triumphant. A life does not have to mean anything or lead anywhere. A life does not need a direction or a goal. But sometimes a person is lucky enough to have a life with all that anyway.

That same sun shines on a woman walking waist deep through the water of a ditch by a highway. The water is opaque, a glossy rainbow of gasoline on the top. Plastic bags, and wrappers for chips, and trash of all other kinds float by her. The woman moves at a steady, easy pace. She sings as she walks. "O, martyrs," she sings. "O, soldiers of a lower cause." Her voice is thin and high. When the uneven surface of the ditch makes her rise a little from the water, it is apparent that her entire body is still dry. Soon she will be back to the level of power and influence she had possessed when those awful women came into her life. And then eventually she will be destroyed again. And then born again. She does not mind the low times, but she grins with a furious excitement at the rush of being back at one of the peaks.

From atop the frame of what had once been a car, deep in the shadows where they would be impossible to spot, a person in a hoodie sits and watches the woman's progress. The person in the hoodie is here, in this moment, keeping an eye on the monster, but they are many other places too. They are fighting alongside other people in hoodies against a vicious army of Thistle Men. They are a scared runaway, trying not to seem scared, being taken in by a scared woman trying not to seem scared, and together driving to Atlanta. They are standing over the body of their mother and telling themself to hide, continually maintaining the moment in which they saved their own life. They are fighting the Thistle Men again, several years from this day, and then several more years beyond that, again and again, a wave that sweeps in and pulls back but is never gone. But if they concentrate, they can go even beyond the bounds of their life. They can see the land as it had once been, before the colonizers stole it, before the indigenous people found their home, before humans at all, when the ditch and the car frame and every-thing else was a dense forest without a name or the possibility of being named. Far in the other direction, they can see a universe that has gone still and dark, long after the struggle is over. Focusing in on smaller time spans, they can stand invisibly in a study room when a college student named Keisha saw a college student named Alice, thought about her plan to be single, and then thought: *Well, shit.*

ACKNOWLEDGMENTS

Thanks first and foremost to Jasika Nicole and Jon Bernstein, who joined with me in telling this story when very little of the story existed to tell.

Thanks to everyone who made this book and show possible: Amy Baker and everyone at Harper Perennial, Adam Cecil, Roberta Colindrez, Jeffrey Cranor, Kassie Evashevski, Christy Gressman, Monica Gasper and Hank Green and the whole Pod-Con team, Mark Flanagan and the Largo, Erica Livingston, Andrew Morgan, and, of course, the indomitable Jodi Reamer.

To my family: Kathy Fink, Jack and Lydia Bashwiner, and all the Barbaras, Bashwiners, Davises, Finks, Pows, Zambaranos, and various other wonderful people with various other wonderful last names.

And to my wife, Meg, whose road trip this also was.

ABOUT THE AUTHOR

Joseph Fink created the *Welcome to Night Vale* and *Alice Isn't Dead* podcasts. He lives with his wife in New York.

Night Vale
presents

Here we both are, at the end of this book. Maybe you read the book. Maybe you just flipped ahead to read the last sentence. I'm ok with that if you are.

If you enjoyed this book, I encourage you to check out the *Alice Isn't Dead* podcast, which provides an entirely different take on the story of Keisha and Alice. All episodes are available right now at NightValePresents.com.

The *Alice Isn't Dead* podcast is a proud member of the *Night Vale Presents* podcast network, which has a number of other great fiction shows, like *Within the Wires*, an immersive mystery series; or the hit *Welcome to Night Vale*, a community radio show from a desert town where every conspiracy theory is true; or *Sleep with Me*, which tells gently rambling stories designed to lull even the most restless insomniac into a blissful sleep. If you've never tried podcasts before, they are free and provide hours of great storytelling, and you are going to be stunned at how easy they are to discover and listen to. Join us at NightValePresents.com and find out for yourself.

ALSO BY JOSEPH FINK
(COAUTHOR WITH JEFFREY CRANOR)

WELCOME TO NIGHT VALE
A NOVEL
AVAILABLE IN HARDCOVER, PAPERBACK, EBOOK, DIGITAL AUDIO, AND CD

"This is a splendid, weird, moving novel." —NPR.org

From the creators of the wildly popular *Welcome to Night Vale* podcast comes an imaginative mystery of appearances and disappearances that is also a poignant look at the ways in which we all struggle to find ourselves . . . no matter where we live.

IT DEVOURS!
A WELCOME TO NIGHT VALE NOVEL
AVAILABLE IN HARDCOVER, EBOOK, DIGITAL AUDIO, AND CD

"A confident supernatural comedy from writers who can turn from laughter to tears on a dime." —*Kirkus Reviews*

A page-turning mystery about science, faith, love and belonging, set in a friendly desert community where ghosts, angels, aliens, and government conspiracies are commonplace parts of everyday life.

MOSTLY VOID, PARTIALLY STARS
WELCOME TO NIGHT VALE EPISODES, VOLUME 1
AVAILABLE IN PAPERBACK AND EBOOK

"This addictive, deeply weird podcast is for anyone who likes his or her quasi-radio listening with a surrealist tilt." —*Los Angeles Times*

Mostly Void, Partially Stars introduces us to Night Vale, a town in the American Southwest where every conspiracy theory is true, and to the strange but friendly people who live there. *Mostly Void, Partially Stars* features an introduction by creator and co-writer Joseph Fink, behind-the-scenes commentary, and guest introductions by performers from the podcast and notable fans.

THE GREAT GLOWING COILS OF THE UNIVERSE
WELCOME TO NIGHT VALE EPISODES, VOLUME 2
AVAILABLE IN PAPERBACK AND EBOOK

"Hypnotic and darkly funny." —*The Guardian*

A collection of episodes from Season Two of the *Welcome to Night Vale* podcast, featuring a foreword by the authors, behind-the-scenes commentary, and original illustrations by Jessica Hayworth . . . an absolute must-have whether you're a fan of the podcast or discovering for the first time the wonderful world of Night Vale.